Linda Clare displays her genuine artistry by weaving color and texture into this poignant Southwestern tale. Authentic characters with realistic challenges pull us right into the Native American world of the 1950s. A memorable story with substance and hope. I highly recommend!
—Melody Carlson, author of *River's Song* and others

A brave and beautiful blending of two worlds, *A Sky Without Stars* brings hope and healing to an often neglected time period and people. Linda Clare is a welcome addition to the Quilts of Love series, sure to win readers' hearts!
—Laura Frantz, Christy Award finalist and author of *Love's Reckoning*

Linda Clare recreates reservation life in 1950s Arizona, capturing both the grinding poverty of rez life and the sweeping grandeur of the rugged yet starkly beautiful Navajo ancestral homeland. In Frankie Chasing Bear, Clare portrays the essence of the Lakota culture and their determination to survive and thrive despite overwhelming odds. If you've ever struggled to find God in the midst of suffering or injustice, don't miss *A Sky Without Stars*.
—Lisa Carter, author of *Aloha Rose* and *Beneath a Navajo Moon*

Discovering who and whose we are no matter where we are is a poignant theme of Linda Clare's inspiring novel. Her words are stitched together with the color of landscapes, the comfort of quilts, and the tension of people trying to make their way in a changing world. We care about Frankie Chasing Bear; her son, Harold; and Frankie's would-be suitor, Nick Parker. Each has grief to weave into hope that they might not be held hostage by their pasts. Linda captures the uniqueness of tribal differences of Lakota, Navajo, and mixed-blood persons, creating for us a realistic 1950s native world that most of us have rarely considered. Linda grants us entry into a journey where hope and faith and the future remind us that we are all connected by the threads of love.
—Jane Kirkpatrick, award-winning author of *Where Lilacs Still Bloom*

What do you get when you combine authentic history, picturesque settings, dynamic characters, and a feels-like-you're-there storyline? You get a Linda Clare novel, and in *A Sky Without Stars*, she delivers all that and more. My advice to readers: Make room for this one on your "keepers shelf." My advice to Linda: save space on your "awards wall" because this tale is sure to earn a bunch!
—Loree Lough, best-selling author of more than 100 books, including *Raising Connor*

Other Books in the Quilts of Love Series

A SKY WITHOUT STARS

STARS

Quilts of Love Series

Linda S. Clare

A Sky Without Stars

ISBN-13: 978-1-4267-5279-7

Published by Abingdon Press, P.O. Box 801, Nashville, TN 37202
www.abingdonpress.com

Published in association with the Steve Laube Literary Agency.

Library of Congress Cataloging-in-Publication Data has been
requested.

Printed in the United States of America

1 2 3 4 5 6 7 8 9 10 / 19 18 17 16 15 14

For my father, Robert L. Fisher, who gave me Cherokee/Choctaw heritage, and for Robert Looks Twice, a present-day Lakota who one day will surely astonish the world.

Acknowledgments

This story was born out of memories of growing up in Arizona, but it could not have grown without a web of editors and writers who so graciously support my efforts. My heartfelt thanks to Ramona Richards for taking a chance on Frankie Chasing Bear and to editor Teri Wilhelms for helping me imagine the past more precisely. Thanks to Cat Hoort for envisioning how far this story might spread. Thanks to Karen Ball for cheering me on. Thanks to my extensive network of mentors and peers: Kristen Johnson Ingram, Melody Carlson, and Heather Kopp; my weekly group, Jodi Henry, Tamsin Morgan, Deb Mohr, Shirley West, and Jennifer Meyer; my online writing buddies Sarah Sundin and Ann Shorey; and my wonderful friend Kay Marshall Strom. Thanks to the Writer's Bloc, especially Rhett Ashley, for help with research and fabulous art work. And most of all, thanks to my family, who puts up with incessant typing, tardy meals, and total zone-outs so that I might stitch together stories.

Prologue

Pine Ridge, South Dakota
Frankie Chasing Bear

I did not come to quilt-making easily. The urge to piece together shapes and colors wasn't my gift.

But when I was twelve, Grandmother said soon the quilt might be all that was left of what we once were. By the time your children wrap quilts around themselves, she told me, the star and all it stands for may be a dim memory, lit only by the fire of ancestors, clouded by ruddy smoke hanging in the sky.

Grandmother's face was crisscrossed with fine lines showing off sharp cheekbones, a strong square jaw, hard work. A silvery gray braid, straight as the truth, hung down her back. I tried to make my stitches as small and even as hers, but my childish hands proved slow and awkward. She said I only needed practice and showed me again: up, pulled through, and down.

Just before she died, Grandmother and I sat together one last time. She stopped to smooth a small wrinkle in the quilt top. "Lakota were favored among tribes," she said. "Our people stood at the top of the hills. The buffalo and the deer bowed to our warriors, and we lived together in peace. The peace

7

pipe showed us how to live, and the stars helped us find good hunting grounds."

Grandmother had told the story a thousand times, but I didn't interrupt. I was fighting the thread again, scribbled into a hopeless knot. She looked up and said, "Keep the thread short." I obeyed.

Her brown fingers reminded me of an old tree branch, but they deftly worked the needle: up, pulled through and down, up, through and down. "One day, the sun rose on white men. They brought their religion, but they often did not listen to their God's teachings." She paused to watch my crooked stitches take shape, nodding when I got them even. "We were brought low and herded like animals."

Again the nod of approval for my efforts. "They had no explanation, except to point to their Book. We were to love their God and love each other."

Grandmother laughed. "Lakota need no instruction on love." Tears glistened in her tired black eyes. She'd seen something terrible in the smoke, she said for the hundredth time. A red rose, unopened. Blood, a river of blood. Another day was coming, she said, when words from the Book would take place: *We were considered as sheep to be slaughtered.*

I dared not remind her she prayed to the God of the Bible. That she stood in two worlds, fully Lakota, fully Christian. I worry it's not possible for me. Indians who go to the church are shunned by their kin and by the whites. Outcasts, their feet in no world at all.

Before we traveled to Arizona, Grandmother made me promise to make this Lakota Star for my son. Sew love into every stitch and remember: a bed without a quilt is like a sky without stars. The quilt will help this child remember who he is, she said. The star will tell him how much he is loved and the light will save him at the last day.

1

Mid-August 1951
Outside Phoenix, Arizona

Frankie Chasing Bear eased the old Chevy pickup to the side of the rutted dirt road. If she hadn't run out of quilting thread, they'd have stayed home on a day this hot. A plume of steam rose from the radiator and disappeared into the pale sun-bleached sky.

She slapped the steering wheel with the heel of her hand. "Not again!" A stab of guilt penetrated deep, an ache she'd carried since Hank's death. At the time, leaving South Dakota for the West seemed to be the only answer. But now, Arizona looked a lot like the moon, dry and far away. And life here wasn't any better.

She squinted out the driver's side window. Dotted with the gray-greens of mesquite and cactus, the desert went on for miles. She swiped at her cheeks—her son shouldn't see her cry. Was getting stranded out here worth a few spools of thread?

Ten-year-old Harold shifted in his seat. Frankie already knew how he felt about the Lakota Star quilt. As far as he was concerned, quilts were for babies. And why, he'd asked, would you need one in a place this hot?

She'd told her son the story again and again. Before her death, Grandmother had made Frankie promise to finish the coverlet depicting stories once told around tribal fires. Grandmother had been adamant—the quilt should also reflect faith in God. Today, Frankie wasn't sure about any of it, but she'd promised. If nothing else, her son should learn to keep his word.

"Rotten luck," she said, smiling at her son.

Harold's smooth face remained impassive. "We should've checked the water back at the store."

Her son had wisdom beyond his years. She patted his hand. "Good thing we wore our walking shoes, eh?" Her eyes closed, she sighed. "I'll get the cans." Harold shook his head and stared at the floorboard.

Frankie got out of the cab and went around to the truck's rusty tailgate. The blue cotton dress she wore was no match for the wind, which kicked up her skirt unless she held it down. She used her free hand for a visor and searched the road, hoping to spot the dust cloud from another vehicle. The heat of summer combined with a light wind to blast every inch of her as she scanned the horizon, but the only movement was from a couple of dust devils twirling in the distance.

She hefted the empty cans out of the bed and tapped on the truck's back window. "C'mon, it's only a mile or so to the gas station."

Getting out of the cab, her son moved like a tortoise, the way he did when he was being stubborn. With the heat bearing down on the crown of her head, she was crankier than usual. "Harold. Come on."

They started toward the gas station Frankie had hoped they could avoid. The fabric store had been bad enough. Elbow to elbow with a bunch of ladies wearing shapeless dresses and face powder the color of dust. All scooting away from her and Harold.

She'd figured the old truck had enough water in it to make it home, but she'd figured wrong. Now Stu, the sassy guy who manned the pumps at the Texaco might taunt her son—call him little Hiawatha, like last time. Stu's kid Orval, a pudgy boy with an ax to grind, had already jumped Harold once after school. Bully. Her mouth was dry. She ran her tongue across her teeth.

She glanced at Harold. He was a good boy and handsome, too, or at least he would be in a couple more years. Tall for his age, he could outrun the kids back home. And he hardly ever complained. Frankie had been thankful for it, all the way here. She smiled as she tried to match his stride. The kid probably weighed as much as the empty gallon can which knocked against his knees.

She pushed her damp bangs off her forehead. "Want me to spot you?"

"Naw. I got it." Harold's face glistened with sweat that dripped onto his brown plaid shirt.

Harold's stick-straight hair was cut short for summer. Even without braids, he looked like his father, Hank Sr. But she was determined he wouldn't turn out like his old man: prone to drink and violence. She shuddered at the memory of Hank's murder only six months before, still ashamed of the small ways she was glad. He could never hurt her or Harold again. If there was a God, her husband's passing was a gift.

Frankie kept a bright look on her face and began singing one of the Lakota songs she'd learned as a child. "C'mon, it'll pass the time," she said, and started again. In Pine Ridge, Harold was always a good sport about these things. But now he stared ahead, as if he didn't want to associate with his own mother. She walked on the road's soft shoulder and hummed to herself. Like it or not, Harold was growing up.

Ahead, the station shimmered, mirage-like—the red Texaco star a gleaming beacon. As they walked across the blacktop, heat radiated through the bottoms of her cheap sneakers. She glanced at Harold, who ran up to the concrete islands in front of the pumps. She walked faster.

The smart-mouth owner was on duty. Stu, dressed in white from head to toe, a cap sitting sideways on his pathetic crew cut. "Hey," he said to Harold. He turned to Frankie. "It'd be nice if you bought something now and then." He wiped his hands on a rag. The place reeked of oil and gas.

She pulled out her charm, the same charm she'd used to get that radiator filled a dozen times. She brushed her bangs aside. "Hey, Stu. You wouldn't mind helping a lady out would you?" Maybe she should've worn the red top with the ruffles again. Gas station attendants seemed to like red. She laughed behind her hand, an old Lakota habit she'd grown up with. When she was nervous, she couldn't stop.

But Stu's jaw muscles worked side to side. "Dry radiator, again?" He scowled at her. "I can't keep giving out free services to you people," he said. Harold stood in back of Stu, narrowing his eyes at Stu, the same way he'd seen his dad do when other men looked at her.

"All's we need is a little water to make it home," she said. Stu was such an ornery cuss—he got maybe three customers on a good day. The wind came up and gusted against her cheeks, then died. Frankie tasted dirt.

They all turned back toward the road. A rumble and dirt-colored cloud trailed a government truck. Stu waved them back. "I got a real customer. You'll have to wait."

Frankie and Harold moved a couple feet and set down the cans. She poked Harold and pointed to a drinking fountain. "Go get a drink," she said.

The white pickup, with "Bureau of Indian Affairs" in raised letters on the door, braked to a stop. She folded her arms. Let Stu attend to Mr. Important.

A light-skinned but dark-haired lanky man stepped out. His eyes were hard to see under his hat's brim. He wore cowboy boots and an agate belt buckle. The buckle gave him away. Most of her male relatives wore the same type of agate buckle. He had to be part Lakota—and who knew what else. The man, in his tan government uniform and all, sparked something in Frankie. His voice was deep, melodic. "Can you fill it up?" The man wasn't sarcastic the way Hank Sr. always was. No, this guy was more than polite and didn't let Stu's attitude chase him up a tree. The man nodded at the most expensive gas pump. "I reckon the government can spring for ethyl," the man said.

Stu nodded, although he seemed a tad disappointed he was serving another Indian. Stu went to work, the gas pump dinging. "Can't say I've seen you 'round here." Stu pulled a squeegee across the bug-encrusted windshield. "You new?"

The stranger smiled; his teeth were white and straight. "Nick Parker," he said, touching his hat's brim. "Just transferred down from Nebraska." He took off the hat and used his forearm to mop his brow. "I'm still getting used to the heat."

Harold snorted. Frankie elbowed her son, but it was too late. The man turned. "You from the Rez?"

Frankie and Harold looked at each other. The local Pima-Maricopa reservation?

Harold shook his head. "Nope." He raised his chin. "Lakota."

Frankie's throat burned, but she couldn't force herself to move away from the stranger. "Go on, son, and get a drink." She pointed again to the fountain.

"Ma! Stop treating me like a kid." He sat on the curb.

Nick seemed interested in the boy. "Where you from, then?" He sat next to Harold, arms resting across his knees.

A guy who likes kids, Frankie thought. She watched out of the corner of her eye as the man spoke with her son. Nick's thick, coppery hair swept back from his forehead. But the handsome ones could be dangerous.

Stu pulled the gas nozzle out and hung it on the pump. He came over. "Want me to check the water and oil?" He shot Frankie and Harold a look. "You can overheat pretty easy on a day like this."

Nick laughed, and his eyes brightened and sent a chill up Frankie's back. "Sure," he said. "Don't want to overheat out here, right?"

Right. Her breath caught, as if she were viewing the Milky Way for the first time. Whoa. She didn't believe in love at first sight anymore, especially when love later grew fists.

An awkward moment passed, as if he'd heard her thoughts. He stood up and turned to the pair. "Are you here to stay or just passing through?"

Frankie drew her shoulders back. The man stood straight, proud; his eyes were a whiskey shade of brown. It would be easy to get sucked in, too easy. She locked her heart. But in the next moment, Frankie let the wind take her caution. "We're hoping to make our home here." She laughed, forcing her hand to stay at her side. "It's the wrong time of year to be snowbirds." She wished again she'd worn red. "As Harold said, Lakota," she said. "We're Lakota."

Nick's eyes lit up. "Not many Lakota this far from South Dakota. What made you want to come live in the desert?"

Frankie shrugged. Why they'd left South Dakota was complicated—too complicated to talk about. "We thought we'd like the nice, cool Arizona summers," she said. "I'm Frankie and this is my son, Harold."

Stu barged into the conversation again. "That'll be three dollars," he said. Nick dug out a bill and handed it to Stu.

"I'll get your change," Stu said.

Nick turned to Frankie. "Huh." He paused. "What a coincidence. Growing up, I spent my summers at Pine Ridge." He used his hat like a fan. "It's got to be a hundred and ten."

Stu corrected him. "Hunert and eleven."

Nick grinned. "Hot enough to fry an egg on the sidewalk."

Slouched beside a gas pump, Harold broke his silence. "Ma overheated the truck 'bout a mile back," he said, pointing to the water cans. "She just had to buy thread. Today." Frankie gave him a look, but this was a good sign. If Harold said more than two words, it meant he liked you.

Nick picked up the cans. "Let's get these filled," he said. He looked deep into Frankie's eyes and held her gaze steady. "Could I give you a lift back to your truck?"

⸻

Nick spooled out the water hose and filled up the cans, studying the young woman and her son. Prettiest girl he'd ever laid eyes on. Her free-falling black hair danced in the wind as she said, "Oh, no, we can make it all right. But thank you." She looked away, giving Nick a moment to appreciate her profile. Water overflowed onto his boot. It's what he got for gawking. He prayed for forgiveness.

She spoke softly. "Harold, get a drink before we go, OK honey?"

Harold dragged himself to the drinking fountain attached to the side of a soda pop cooler outside the repair bay. For five cents, the cooler's top slid open and you could pull out an ice cold drink. Summers in Pine Ridge, Nick and his buddies had pilfered a soda or two from a machine like that. Then, got beat up by a bully named Moose.

He let the water hose reel itself back in and picked up the full cans. He faced the woman named Frankie, the wind pressing her thin blue dress against her body. "These things weigh a ton," he said. Her figure was better than the Rodeo Princess up at Prescott. He said, "You got a bum radiator?"

Frankie shrugged. "Got to get that thing fixed."

Nick hoped he wasn't too pushy, but he didn't try to stop himself from being drawn in, either. "Your old man won't help you?" He set down the water, which sloshed onto his boots again.

She ran her fingers through her hair. "Not exactly." Her hands were plain, capable and strong, not fancied up with polished nails or jewelry or even a wedding ring. Nick liked simplicity. A practical sort, not like his ex, Carolyn. She'd about driven them into the poorhouse with her beauty parlor treatments and whatnot. He preferred her story to Carolyn's version, hers blamed Nick and a friend named alcohol.

The bottle had claimed his dad and half his relatives at Pine Ridge. Nick had nearly ten years sober, and had broken the Parker family tradition—Carolyn hadn't give him enough credit.

He tried to make eye contact, but Frankie stared at the horizon. "You planning on staying out here?"

Her gaze flitted to Harold at the drinking fountain and back again. "The kid's dad died in South Dakota." She paused, as if thinking up a good explanation. "Hank Sr., that's my husband, used to say he had relatives here, so I thought, 'Why not?'" She took a breath, and finally returned his stare.

He took off his hat and got lost in her deep brown eyes. He said, "Sorry. Got to be tough on the boy." He wanted to ask if she was seeing anyone, tell her he liked her simple beauty, offer to cook her dinner sometime. His tongue balked.

Before he could say anything, Stu's voice rang out. "You thievin' injun, pay up!"

Harold raced past Frankie and Nick, with Stu in pursuit. A wet stain down Harold's shirt looked suspicious. Frankie fingered the spools of thread in her pocket, wondering if Stu was in a bartering mood as Harold hid behind his mother.

The attendant wagged a finger. "All right, Frankie Chasing Bear," he said. "That'll be a nickel. And I've got a mind to charge you for the water. That boy of yours is getting to be a real headache."

Nick gave Frankie a puzzled look, but dug into his pocket. "Here," he said, producing a nickel. "Indian head, no less."

Stu took the money.

Frankie pulled Harold around to face her. She spoke in a low, even tone. "You did this?"

Harold looked ready to cry. "No, Ma." He raised his tee shirt to reveal his waistband. "See?"

Frankie nodded. "Look Stu, my kid didn't take anything."

Stu narrowed his eyes. "How do I know he didn't stash it somewhere?"

Nick stepped toward Stu. "The kid says he didn't steal it." He dug out more change. "But we'd like cold ones for the road." Nick strode to the cooler and brought back three bottles.

Stu glared, but nodded and straightened his cap.

Nick handed a cold, sweaty bottle to Frankie. "Thank you." She wouldn't let on, but RC Cola tasted like heaven. She elbowed Harold. "Where are your manners?"

"Thanks." Harold tipped back his soda and began walking back down the road.

"Harold! Wait!"

But Harold waved her off and kept walking. The kid could be as stubborn as his dad.

Nick brought her attention back. "Let me take you back to your rig."

Frankie hoped her son's moodiness wouldn't embarrass the both of them. "Harold's got a mind of his own," she said. "Some days I think one of us won't live to see Christmas." She smoothed her bangs with her palm. "Sure, I'll take a lift."

Nick smiled too. His forehead and cheekbones had a noble hint that tugged at Frankie. She wanted to ask him which Lakota band his mother was from, was he related to any of the famous chiefs. He tilted his head toward the truck. "C'mon, let's get that rascal." He held the driver's side door open.

Frankie climbed into the cab and slid across the bench seat, still gripping the soda bottle. Nick got in after her and started the truck. When he slammed the door, she picked up a whiff of sage.

2

When Nick pulled alongside Frankie's truck, there was her boy, leaning against the fender, squinting mean as if Nick was the devil himself. Had the kid really walked that fast or did he know a shortcut? Even though Nick and Carolyn never had kids, he'd always longed for a son. He guessed it wasn't in the plan, although he'd never stopped hoping. If a son had come along, the kid might've been about Harold's age by now.

Harold was protective of his mother in a way that made Nick smile. He'd been protective too, with the women he'd loved. The boy seemed to be all Frankie had on her side, and Nick wasn't about to egg him on. From out the truck window, Nick gestured to Harold. "You mind popping the hood?"

Harold muttered something Nick didn't catch, but the boy set down his pop bottle and propped up the Chevy's hood. Nick hoped Harold was too smart to try to unscrew a hot radiator cap. Luckily, the kid just crossed his arms again and leaned against the truck's fender. Nick got out of his truck and lugged over the water cans. He stood at arm's length and tried the cap—the pressure had faded, but safety first, his uncle always told him. He waited a few seconds, unscrewed the cap, and set it on the side fender.

Harold never stopped eyeing him as Nick emptied the cans into the thirsty radiator. But he did hand Nick the cans in turn. A good sign and although each time Nick said "thanks," Harold only grunted something unintelligible. Nick shook his head and smiled. Kids.

Frankie hadn't said two words since the gas station, and it rattled him some. Carolyn, blonde, blue-eyed, and gifted with gab, had rarely taken a breath, so Frankie's silence jarred him. Maybe, like a lot of Lakota women he'd known, Frankie was the quiet type. He chuckled to himself. Right. More likely she had no need for another man wrecking her life. He leaned in the BIA truck's window where Frankie still sat. "She's as full as I can get her," he said.

She laughed behind her hand, the same way his Lakota cousin Aggie had always done. Summers at Pine Ridge, he'd spent running around with cousins, nieces, and nephews. His dad's sister always said they did a fine job of teaching a half-breed how to be an Indian. Especially if it included being passed-out drunk. But now, with a real Lakota sitting right in front of him, Nick didn't feel much like a real Indian.

He had to find out what she liked to do and where she lived without Harold jumping on him like a junkyard dog. He rested his forearms on the truck window's ledge. "Say," he began, "how's about I tail you home, just to make sure you get there?"

Harold elbowed his way next to Nick. "We can take care of ourselves. Let's go, Ma."

Nick tried again. "I live over off Priest—those older apart-ments. You live somewhere near there?"

Frankie smiled past her son. "Sorry, it's just been Harold and me so long we forget what it's like to have help." She shot a look at the kid. "Keep forgetting our manners, too."

Harold glowered, then climbed in the Chevy's cab and slammed the door. Nick could practically see smoke coming off the kid's ears. He turned to Frankie. "Hey, I'm not out to cause trouble between you and your boy. Honest, I was only trying to help." He searched for her gaze and held it.

She flushed, but he took it as a good sign. "Harold's a little possessive." She opened the BIA truck's door, stepped one foot out. "I don't mind a bit if you'd see we get this old crate to the house." She glanced at her truck, where Harold's still-crossed arms told Nick she was in for a lecture from her own offspring. Frankie smiled again, this time without her hand in front of her mouth, and her dark eyes took on a sparkle making her whole face light up. "Last time I looked," she said, "it was a public road."

Nick's heartbeat drummed in his ears. "I hope I see you around," he said. Great. He sounded like a seventh grader.

Frankie didn't seem to notice his clumsiness. "Why would I avoid the only other Lakota I've met out here?" She pushed back strands of her hair the wind lifted.

"Part-Lakota," he said. "Half-breed."

Frankie shrugged. "Who cares? It's why I'm making Harold a quilt, to teach him Lakota ways. Maybe you can help."

Nick frowned. "Me? I don't know one end of a needle from the other."

Frankie laughed, open-mouthed, easy, relaxed. "Not with sewing. With the stories." She hopped up into the Chevy's cab and pulled shut its door. "Lakota stories." She pointed at Nick's agate buckle. "Besides, a man only wears one of those if he feels Lakota on the *inside*." She tapped her chest. "Where it counts." She cranked up the engine; ground into first gear.

"Thanks again," she said, and eased the truck off the shoulder and onto the road.

Nick stood outside his own truck, watched the Chevy disappear over the rise leading to a run-down neighborhood outside town. When he drove to catch up with her, he kept his distance. No sense upsetting the kid anymore. Nick nearly sailed past the tiny brown adobe where her truck sat parked, a forlorn-looking place with a broken screen door, a dry patch of grass and a clothesline full of flapping laundry.

He slowed the truck. Her handiwork showed itself in the neat rows of flowers potted next to the two-step porch: zinnias and a couple of morning glory vines made the place look friendlier, along with the bright yellow gingham curtains in the windows. Someone, probably Harold, stood peeking out those curtains.

Nick sped up, peeling out as fast as he could on a gravel road. Fool. He was acting like a peeping tom. He scolded himself, but it was no use. He could hardly remember what he had scheduled to do that day.

The more he tried to think about work, the more a beautiful woman danced through his thoughts: silky black hair, brown eyes, long legs. Lakota, like him. Crowding into those thoughts, the ever-present devil sat on his shoulder, whispering he'd be much smoother if he slammed back a couple. He was glad he had God on his side, to help him keep that monkey off his back. He said an extra prayer for good measure.

He drove around for a while, tried to push the woman and her son out of his every thought. Toward evening, he headed toward the Superstition Mountains, where even the fiery sunset whispered the name of Frankie Chasing Bear.

Frankie left Harold to stand guard at the window. She didn't mention the stranger named Nick. The boy's jealous streak was as wide as his old man's had been, and it was starting to get on her nerves. She didn't know if Harold was protecting her or trying to keep the rest of mankind from taking his daddy's place. She turned to Harold, half-hidden by the checkered curtains she'd sewn. "Give it up, will ya? I told you that guy won't set foot on our place—you scared him off good."

Harold pretended not to hear.

She went straight to work on the quilt, sneaking peeks at Harold who still peered through a gap in the curtains. She was lucky, she told herself. Not only had she managed to get the thread she needed, she'd met a fine-looking guy and got to see firsthand how Harold took his role as man of the house seriously. Maybe a bit too seriously, but he meant well. She tried to sweep Nick from her mind, warned herself once again, when it came to relationships, her record was terrible. Nick didn't appear to be a drinker. But then, neither had Hank at first. She couldn't wind up with another alcoholic, for her son's sake, for her own sake.

Let Harold stand there—she had sewing to do. She hung a tape measure around her neck, and pulled her hair into a high ponytail. She couldn't stand hair in her face as she worked and anyway, it was hot as Hades in here. The one oscillating fan they owned was more of a nuisance than anything.

She cleared the dining table and opened her basket of cotton fabrics, setting out cardboard patterns, stickpins, a yardstick with "Shop at A.J. Bayless" printed on it. She removed the cover from the Singer treadle sewing machine, the best gift Frankie had received from her mother. This machine had chattered throughout her childhood, constructing quilts for naming ceremonies and other special occasions. Frankie smiled at the memory of all the sewing machine needles she'd broken learning to sew.

She glanced up. Harold had finally come away from the window. He read while draped across the sofa, his bare feet slender and longer than she remembered. He was almost taller than she was. "What you reading?"

"It's about aliens. Science fiction."

"What?"

Harold laid down the book. "C.S. Lewis. Got it from the bookmobile." He buried his nose in the pages again.

"There's a bookmobile?" Frankie held several straight pins with her teeth and lined up two shades of blue calico, each folded to a crisp point.

Harold didn't answer.

Maybe the bookmobile had quilting books. Times when she couldn't remember a sewing trick or ran into a problem, it'd be nice to look up the solution. Pine Ridge was a long ways away and asking for quilting help over the phone was like telling a blind man how to tie a good knot.

Frankie got a lot of satisfaction from quilting. Even a little money here and there. She was glad she'd stuck with the sewing lessons, even if some had called her Little Broken Needle until her Naming Ceremony. Besides, quilting helped her and other Lakota escape the suffocating poverty of the Rez.

Ah, but that was all behind them now. Hank Sr. was gone, South Dakota a cold memory. She and Harold were on a new path, a good path. She smiled over at her son, still reading. He was a good boy, and she hoped, not too much like his father.

She lined up the new thread spools by color, matching them to their corresponding yardage, and tried to remember the things Grandmother had told her.

The smoke was the important thing to all Lakota, the old woman had said. The *chanupa* pipe and its smoke carried the prayers and the cries of the people to the Creator. The quilt would show the eight-pointed star, the place where all the sacred songs, dances, and ceremonies came together. At Pine Ridge, had Nick been a dancer? The idea was delicious and Frankie had a little fun imagining him dressed in a Lakota cape and headdress.

She arranged bright yellow, orange, and red fabrics into their arrays and forced herself to think of Grandmother's words. The star, exploding from its center, recalled the circles of eagle feathers, the rays of the sun, the morning star. And, Grandmother had whispered, it was also the star of Bethlehem, the star the three magi followed to Christ's birthplace.

Frankie's eyes had grown wide at those words, and she had long wondered how one could be both Lakota and serve the white man's God. Grandmother had never seemed bothered to have one foot in the Indian world and one in the white, but Frankie wanted—no needed—Harold to be sure of who he was.

She threaded the treadle machine, wishing again her eyesight was still as good as her son's. He looked so comfortable on the sofa; Frankie couldn't ask him to move. The machine's presser foot up, she squinted, and wet the thread's end with her tongue. After a couple of tries, she guided the thread though the needle's eye. Did Nick know who he was? And did he have a quilt of his own?

3

Late that afternoon, Frankie couldn't stop trembling. Harold had said he'd be just outside, and he was never late for supper. Was he out there defending himself from Stu's kid again? This was her fault. She closed her eyes. Leaving Pine Ridge had been a huge mistake

She stood at the window as the shadows overtook the day. The desert sunset, on fire with reds and pinks and oranges, only stoked her worry. Harold never took off without saying where he'd be.

Where was he?

The house smelled like the tall pot of government-issue pinto beans and rice that simmered on the stove. Frankie had even set out corn bread muffins, which Harold loved. Frankie made herself look at the rickety old dinette, at the two place-mats set with bowls and spoons, at the worn, but pressed cloth napkins folded into triangles. Even if this move was a mistake, they had each other. And if things went right—for once—soon she'd have her equivalent diploma, she'd get a great job and they'd never eat pinto beans for supper again. She'd be one of the Indian School success stories if it killed her.

If Harold brought up the fact that before his daddy died Hank Sr. was always coming home from *somewhere*, she'd box his ears. Unless that bully, Stu's kid Orval, had already roughed up her son again. Orval was a red-headed menace.

She sniffed. More likely, Harold was off doing things he shouldn't. Things to embarrass his ma, or at least cost money. She felt like hurling his bowl against the plastered wall. Frankie swiped away a tear, furious and worried and scared to death all at once. Her stomach churned. What would Grandmother do?

She picked up his empty bowl and held it to her chest. He was all she had. Frankie shook off the urge to blubber some more and grabbed the truck keys—she knew what Grandmother would do. She'd go out, find her ungrateful child, and give him what for.

⸙

By the time Nick pulled off his boots in the evening, his feet ached as much as his heart. He hated living alone. Renting a one-bedroom apartment might make sense for the divorce settlement—Carolyn couldn't take what he didn't have—but it also felt cramped and lonely. He plopped onto the sagging secondhand couch and waited for his dinner to heat.

Nick was still learning to cook for himself. He missed watching the evening news on TV. Along with the house and most of its furniture, his ex had taken the nearly-new RCA console for herself. But he wasn't complaining. He hoped she was happy. No hard feelings. Well, mostly anyway.

Nick took his dinner out of the apartment-sized oven and set it on the table in front of the couch. He wished for Cousin Aggie's cooking back in Pine Ridge. She'd fixed up some of the tastiest crappie and hush puppies he'd ever eaten. He stared at his forlorn-looking fried Spam on a shingle.

He glanced at the clock. Every Friday night, the only other Indian friends he had that didn't drink, Monny and the Reverend Honest Abe, showed up to play penny ante gin rummy. They were right on time. Nick swiped a paper napkin across his mouth and yelled, "Come!" The door opened.

Monny and Honest Abe stood there, holding onto a scrawny youngster.

Nick was caught off guard. "What the—?" Frankie's kid, Harold. Same brown plaid cotton shirt, same probing black eyes.

Monny scowled at the boy. "Car thief." Monny was Navajo, small and wiry but the best arm wrestler around. "This here kid was trying to break into your truck," Monny added. Harold squirmed harder.

Honest Abe held Harold by his shoulders. "Whoa, boy. Where you off to in such a hurry?" Abe was a half-breed like Nick—Cherokee and Sioux and Heinz-57—but also one of the tallest men Nick had ever met.

"Lemme go," Harold yelled. He kept one hand on the waistband of his unbelted jeans.

Monny growled, "Not 'til you tell Nick here why you tried to steal his truck."

"I wasn't stealing no truck." Harold kept his chin up, his shoulders back.

Finally, Nick smiled and looked Harold square in the face. The kid's cheekbone was swollen and red. "Ya-hey, kid." He gestured at the wound. "Who gave you the shiner?"

Harold didn't answer. Except for the swelling, the kid's face stayed smooth, impassive. Hard to read.

Nick shook his head. "Leave him be," he told Abe and Monny. They let go of Harold who stared past Nick into the apartment.

Nick backed out of the doorway. "Harold, wasn't it?" All three crowded into Nick's tiny living room. Harold moved slowly, his eyes not missing a single thing.

Abe looked around. "Where's the card table?"

Monny grinned and cracked his knuckles. "Get ready to lose, friend."

Nick wasn't about to play cards until he figured out why this boy was here. "The game can wait." He gestured to Harold. "All right, son. What's your story?"

Harold jammed his hands into his pockets. "I'm not your son."

. "Have a seat," Nick said, and moved the remains of his dinner to one side. Harold's gaze followed the tray. Nick brought out the bowl of unshelled peanuts he'd readied for the card game and poured plastic tumblers full of lemonade. He set them in front of Monny and Abe, who ate and drank like they'd been marooned a week in the desert. Harold kept his hands in his pockets.

Nick let his buddies shell and crunch on the peanuts a spell, then asked, "So Harold, what exactly *were* you doing out by my truck?"

"I'm going back to Pine Ridge."

He took a sip of lemonade. "If you needed it, you could've just come and asked. Isn't that right?"

Before Harold could answer, Monny said, "He's too young to drive, ain't he?"

"'Course he is." Nick paused. "But his mom, her old Chevy's on the fritz. Maybe she needed my truck?" For an instant, the only sound came from Nick's old Kelvinator refrigerator, its motor wheezing in the kitchenette.

The boy didn't so much as twitch, but Nick sensed a rawness about him, like he'd been beat up once too often by the class bully. Nick remembered those days, when he'd had to fight or get creamed by a boy named Moose who didn't cotton to half-breeds. He tried to get the kid to relax. "Harold here is new to the valley," he told Monny and Abe. "He and his mom moved out from Pine Ridge."

Monny said, "Kid's Lakota?"

Nick eyed Monny. "Yep. What a coincidence, eh?"

Monny shook his head and whistled low. "Wait'll his ma finds out he's hotwiring motor vee-hicles."

"Leave my mom out of it." Harold glanced around, his jaw clenched. He let out his breath and spoke only to Nick. "You know Pine Ridge, right?"

Nick nodded and cracked opened a peanut. "Summers. I grew up in Rapid City, but my mom would send me off to the Rez every summer. Said I needed to learn how to be Lakota."

Abe got up and helped himself to more lemonade. On his way back to the sofa, he tousled Harold's hair with one of his oversized hands.

"Get off me!"

Abe turned to Nick. "Well? Did you—learn to be Lakota?"

Nick chuckled and shook his head. "Boy—did I ever." He brushed peanut hulls from his shirt front and stared at Harold. "Got beat to a pulp every day for a week."

Harold looked away.

Nick's hunch was right—somebody was giving this kid a bad time. "I'd never known another Lakota out here until I met you and your mom."

Harold glowered at them all.

Nick stood. "Game's cancelled." This kid needed help.

Monny looked disappointed, but got up. "Aw. Can't we just hang around 'til you get the kid home?"

Nick was firm. "Won't kill ya to wait a few days to lose your shirt. Go on now. Sunday afternoon, we'll get together."

Monny looked glum. "And I was gonna win back my life savings tonight." They turned and left.

Nick closed the door. "Never mind those two clowns." He gestured to the sofa. "Sit. You can tell me where you learned to hotwire an engine." He couldn't let the kid think he was soft.

Harold plopped down, his stick-thin legs poking out of his jeans, soles of his bare feet black with dirt. He stared at the floor for too long. He mumbled, "Sorry."

Nick stood over the boy. He remembered his summers in Pine Ridge. Sure, Aggie's cooking had been good, but that was in summertime. Winters were long and cold and plenty of nights some Lakota he knew got nothing but sleep for dinner. He hoped Harold and his mom never went hungry. "Well?" Nick tried to sound gruff. "What makes you think you can just take my truck?"

The boy still wore an I-hate-the-world look, but his eye was puffier and more purple than before. "Look, I said sorry. Can I go now?"

"Stealing a truck is a serious thing." Nick went to the phone. "Maybe I should get the sheriff. Let him deal with your sorry self." Nick kept his own face as expressionless as Harold's had been.

Harold shot up from the couch. "OK. What do you want?"

Nick reached toward Harold's swollen cheekbone. "Who you mixing it up with?"

Harold jerked away. "Doesn't matter."

"Bet it matters to your mama. How come you're so hell-bent on making her cry?"

"She's too tough to cry."

"Even if she isn't bawling her eyes out right now, she's worried sick."

Harold shrugged.

"Look. Before I take you home, you're going to tell me why you want to go to Pine Ridge."

"I need to be with my dad."

Nick felt bad for the boy and his mother. "Fair enough," he said in a gentle voice. "But I seem to remember your mom telling me that your father was, ah . . ." He closed his eyes.

"Dead?"

Nick's eyes widened. Harold showed no emotion. Nick only nodded. "So he's alive?"

The boy stared and said in an almost-whisper, "His spirit is." Harold's gaze radiated contempt, as if to say, *You're not a real Lakota.*

Nick said, "I see. Can't you be with your dad's spirit without worrying your mom half to death?"

He expected more swagger from the youngster, maybe a string of cuss words or more tough-guy stuff. But Harold just stood there while a tear snaked down his bruised cheek.

Nick wanted to comfort him, tell him everything was going to be OK. But he held back. He wouldn't embarrass the kid. He remembered how the boy had stared at the dinner. "Hungry?"

Harold nodded slowly.

"Tell you what," Nick said, grabbing his keys off a peg. "I know a place not far from here. Got the best burgers around. Let's get ourselves something to eat and then we'll see where we're at. Sound fair?" Again the nod. Nick didn't know how he'd talk this kid into going home, or explain it to Frankie, but a full belly might make things easier. He tossed the dinner into the fridge.

Frankie was trying to get her truck started when gravel crunched in the driveway. She looked up. Another vehicle pulled up alongside the Chevy and its doors opened. It was almost dark, but she could just make out two figures, one tall, one not. She fumbled with the cab's door and slid off the seat.

Nick, the man who'd helped them, stood there with Harold.

Frankie was shocked to tears. "Come in, come in." She didn't care who saw her bawling, and nudged her son from behind until they all stood in Frankie's living room.

Harold looked as defiant as his father had whenever someone asked him to step outside at the bar. Frankie gasped. Her son's left eye was nearly swollen shut. "Your eye!" She reached out to him.

"Ma." Harold leaned away from her. "It's nothing."

Frankie planted her hands on her hips. "You call that nothing?" Her voice was too sharp. She struggled to soften it. "Who did this? Orval?" The bully was going to pay, she'd see to it.

Harold looked flat as a run-over snake. She hugged him hard and even though he squirmed, she held him fast. She focused on Nick. "Thanks for bringing him home," she said, her cheeks warming at Nick's steady gaze. "Did you see the fight?"

Harold managed to wriggle away and dashed down the hall. A door slammed.

"No." Nick took off his hat. "Say, could I have a word with you?"

Frankie stood up straighter and hoped her nose wasn't too red. "Supper's been ready for an hour. I expect it's cold by now." She shoved Harold's books to one side of the sofa. "Excuse the mess." She straightened the stacks of fabrics, patterns, and piles of cotton batt on every surface like lounging cats. "Have a seat. Please."

Nick settled on the sofa. "Nice place you have here."

Frankie laughed at the bare walls, at the threadbare furnishings from the second-hand store. "It will be, once I get things fixed up."

Nick smiled and nodded. The fan's breeze lifted her bangs. She smoothed them off her damp forehead, aware her fingers were shaking, and went to the hallway.

Frankie spoke through the closed bedroom door. "Harold? Supper." No answer. She was puzzled. Even if it was cold, he usually ate like a starved man. For a few more seconds, she stayed with her ear to the door, hoping Harold would change his mind. He didn't.

She felt Nick's stare on the back of her head. She whipped around and caught him gazing at her, but he was unapologetic. She smiled as she made her way back to the little kitchen.

Frankie brought out an extra dish and wiped it out with a towel. "I don't know what's got into the boy," she said, ladling beans and rice into the bowls. "But there's a kid—the gas station guy's kid—who waits for him, lights into him every chance he gets." Frankie uncovered the corn muffins and offered them to Nick. She cast another glance at the closed door. "Harold's never late to supper."

"It's my fault." Nick looked contrite.

Frankie froze. "Your fault?" Panic surged through her. Nick couldn't be anything like her own father, who'd often staggered home drunk and beat her brothers "just to keep them honest." Could he?

Nick held up his hands. "Whoa. I mean it's my fault if he's not hungry." He took a muffin. "We stopped for a burger. Whoever punched him got him pretty good."

Frankie stood in front of Nick. "I'm in school myself—I can't always be here when he gets out of class." She twisted the dishtowel. "Did you have to break them up?" She was never sure if Orval really attacked for no reason or if Harold provoked the fights.

"Actually, Harold came to my place," he said. His smile disappeared. "Couple of my buddies brought your son to my door."

Frankie's insides tightened. She wrung the dishtowel harder.

"They said they caught him trying to hotwire my truck."

She started to cover her mouth, but slowly pulled her hand away.

Nick quickly added, "No harm done. But I'm concerned about some of the things he said." He stepped closer.

Frankie closed her eyes. "I'm sorry," she began. Her knees felt as though they might sink through the quagmire of her life and just keep going. She sank onto the other end of the sofa. "All this has been hard on the kid." She looked away in time to watch Harold disappear from the hallway where he'd been eavesdropping. "These last few months," she said, drying her moist palms on the skirt of her dress, "have been hard on the both of us."

4

Nick's heart ached for them both. "I'm the one who should be sorry." He sat back, rested one arm on the sofa's camel back. "Sorry you lost your husband. Sorry he lost his dad."

"Thanks." Frankie seemed to choke up a little, but quickly composed herself. "I feel bad for my boy. You know, growing up without a father." She took a ragged breath. "But we're here to start over." She seemed to fumble for words. "I mean, originally the plan was to drive on out to LA, take Hank's place in the Indian Relocation program." She sighed. "Old truck had a different plan."

"So you're still planning to go there, LA I mean?" He worried his thumb across the sofa's piping.

She shook her head. "At the rate we're going, Phoenix is home. For a while, anyway. After I get my diploma, I'm thinking I'll be a teacher."

He took a long look at her. He couldn't remember when—if ever—he'd seen a face like Frankie's. The way her hair draped over her bronzed cheek, the quiet simplicity of her voice, those capable hands, all joined in an artful way.

Carolyn's blonde head crowded into his mental picture. That his ex could ruin his life from afar proved he was nothing short of a fool. He reeled in his heart—he couldn't take another chance on any female, blonde or otherwise.

But Frankie had already caught him staring. She ducked her chin. "Life goes on, you know?" She shrugged. "You make lemonade."

Her shy smile reminded him of all the women he'd ever known in Pine Ridge. Somehow it made him feel younger, optimistic. Full of energy.

He'd tread carefully, though. And keep quiet about his alcoholism—ten years sober or not, she might judge him. Without thinking, he returned Frankie's smile. "You said something about school." He turned, so he could see her full face. "You're in school?"

She nodded and exhaled a long sigh. "Harold's daddy wanted to move out here—the Relocation agent promised us a great job in LA, a place to live while we got on our feet, that sort of thing." She waved dismissively. "I can't believe how gullible we were. You'd think we'd have learned not to trust those smooth-talking government types. Even the Native ones, you know?"

Nick had to agree. "So I'm the enemy?" He was glad he'd already changed out of his uniform.

Frankie shrugged. "Don't know you well enough yet."

He hadn't seen that one coming.

Frankie laughed out loud. "Got you good, Mr. BIA agent." Her delicate chuckling was infectious. She stood up and went over to a card table strewn with cotton fabrics.

He was helpless as a smile spread over his own lips. "You did indeed," he said, feeling the heat rise. His eye caught the bright colors of the fabric pieces arranged like the rays of the sun. He fingered the edge of a bright orange calico. "Lemme guess—Lakota Star?"

Frankie nodded. Her hand covered her mouth. "It's for Harold. My grandmother taught me."

"Really?" Nick inspected the quilt pieces, not bothering to hide his interest. "My grandmother made me a quilt a lot like this when I was about Harold's age." He closed his eyes, pictured the now-tattered quilt resting in the footlocker at the end of his bed. Carolyn had tried to machine wash it, one of the last remaining connections he'd had with Pine Ridge. He shook his head. "Mine's falling apart though." He made a face. "My ex stuck it in the washing machine."

Frankie laughed. "I take it your ex isn't Native?"

Nick had to laugh too. "Not hardly. If my grandmother knew what happened to the quilt she made for me, she'd roll in the grave."

Frankie clasped her hands behind her back and stared at the floor for a few moments. When she looked up, her smile made her face glow from within. "Maybe sometime I could take a look at it, see what I can do." She moistened her lips, then looked away.

Nick wanted to gently lift her chin, but he kept his hands to himself. "I'd like that."

Frankie stepped back. "Way things are going, I doubt I'll have time to finish Harold's quilt." She brushed her bangs out of her eyes. "I've been out of school a long time. It's not easy."

Nick thought of his own slog through the civil service exams when he applied to the BIA. "I hear you loud and clear." Those tests had been murder for the Indian guys who lived on firewater, one reason he was glad he'd given up the sauce. He wouldn't raise the subject, though, in case his suspicions about Harold's daddy were right. "What sort of work you looking to do?"

"Harold and I got here thinking maybe I could learn to weld like Hank." She held her hands out in front of her. "I got two hands just like him. How hard could it be? Anyways, Hank was drunk half the time and still got the job done."

He was surprised at how easily she mentioned this guy Hank. "You're a welder?"

Frankie shook her head. "Are you kidding? Those ol' boys wouldn't give me the time of day." She paused, folded the dish-towel into a smaller square. "Naw, welding scares me anyway. Too many sparks involved. Dangerous."

Like you. Nick didn't say what he was thinking.

She turned. "I'm finishing up my high school diploma. Someday I want to teach—but you need a college degree."

"There's a teacher's college over in Tempe."

"Sounds easy, right?" She blew out a breath. "Well I can walk that far if I have to. Even if I end up picking oranges, I'm going to get my diploma." She sank back onto the sofa. "For Harold."

"Speaking of Harold." Nick sat next to her, but lowered his voice. "He says he wants to get back to Pine Ridge." He glanced at the hall to be sure Harold wasn't eavesdropping. "Don't take this the wrong way, but maybe he needs some sort of help."

Frankie sat up straighter. "What makes you say so?"

Nick studied cracks in the coved plaster ceiling. "Well, he says he's going back to be with his dad. I just thought . . ." He let out a breath and briefly closed his eyes.

Frankie appeared about to explain, when Harold appeared at her side. The boy hugged her hard. "Don't blame her. She doesn't know anything about it."

Frankie's eyes grew moist. "You scared the daylights out of me." Her hands trembled slightly, like aspen leaves in the breeze.

Nick shot Harold a look. "What did I tell you? Don't do this to your mom, ever. Understand?"

Harold shrank back, his bravado gone. He nodded.

Nick stood up to his full six feet. "And leave my truck alone." Harold's eyes were glassy marbles until Nick added with a smile, "At least 'til you get a learner's permit. Deal?"

Harold relaxed a bit. "You'd teach me to drive?"

Frankie clucked her tongue. "Now don't go imposing yourself."

Nick shook his head. "No imposition, ma'am."

"Call me Frankie." She stood, her thin dress clinging to her body. "I know you've already eaten, but you're welcome to stay for supper. It's not fancy but . . ."

Harold stepped in front of her. "Ma. We ate hamburgers. And fries. With ketchup. I got a chocolate shake." He licked his lips. "Biggest one they had."

Nick laughed, wide and easy. "He's a growing boy, that's for sure." For a moment, no one said anything, until the whirring fan was the only sound. "Guess I best head back home," he said.

Frankie tucked a strand of loose hair behind her ear. "I'll see you out." She gave Harold a look indicating he should stay put. The boy flopped onto the sofa with one of his library books.

—⁂—

Frankie walked beside Nick, his warmth radiating as they strolled to the truck's cab. She liked a gentleman, although she wasn't sure about being called ma'am. She wasn't old enough to be a ma'am. She shook her head. "Don't know what I'll do with that kid," she said.

"He says he wants to go back to Pine Ridge." Nick faced her. "At least that's what he told me. What does he mean by being with his dad?"

She stared hard, mapping out Nick's features. It was full dark, the Milky Way spilling across the skies, locusts buzzing from cottonwood trees. Hank had been good-looking in a similar way, chiseled features belying his sensitive, artistic personality—when he was sober at least. "I'm not exactly sure myself," she admitted. "Harold never seemed all that happy in Pine Ridge. It makes no sense."

"Maybe he just needs time to adjust." Nick opened the cab door, its interior light illuminating a small circle where they stood.

Time to adjust. She wished she could say *she* had everything squared away: a job, a good school for Harold, enough to live on. But so far, all she had was the dream of a better life and a kid who wanted to run away from home. "I don't know." She let out a long sigh. "When Harold gets a crazy idea, he's a bulldog." Frankie brushed away a moth heading for the light. "He won't let go."

Nick chuckled. "Got a buddy like that. We call him Gila Monster."

"Some friend." Frankie returned his smile. "I saw a photo of one of those lizards in *National Geographic* magazine." She shuddered. "Hope there aren't any around here." Now she was just running off at the mouth. She straightened her shoulders. "Just say the word and I'll be glad to have a look at your Lakota quilt." She smiled. "Your grandmother probably tells my grandmother everything." She meant it as a joke.

But Nick ignored her try at funny and turned serious. "That will be great." His voice was low and smooth, and she thought she could listen to him talk all night.

41

He cleared his throat like something was caught in it. "I'll take a rain check on that dinner offer. Say Tuesday? Maybe afterward, we could take in a movie." He paused, coughed. "The three of us, I mean."

"Maybe. If I'm not too busy." Frankie held her hand in front of her mouth, just as generations of Lakota women had done before her. She had to break herself. "OK. If I can keep Harold from stealing cars, that is."

5

Monday morning, Frankie stood at a long counter, chopping vegetables for the evening meal. Phoenix Indian School was fine for kids like Harold, the headmaster had said at first. But she was a grown woman. Why would she need more education? She brought a heavy chef's knife down on a large onion, splitting it in two.

The headmaster's initial denial had only caused Frankie to dig in her heels. She wasn't leaving until she enrolled in the high school, she'd said. The headmaster shook his wooly white head, but somehow she'd convinced him. She didn't care what head teacher Mrs. Green thought of her, but she had to be careful not to do things to get Harold kicked out.

While she worked in the school kitchen, Harold was downstairs in his classroom learning. At least, she hoped so. At the end of the day, they rode or walked home—depending on her truck's fickle engine. Home was about three miles south of the school, and if they wound up walking, Frankie tried to make it fun for her boy, teaching him Lakota songs, even a few Navajo words she'd learned. Too bad he was more interested in getting back at Orval. Frankie scrubbed the tile counter top with half a lemon. The juice killed the onion smell, but Frankie couldn't help but think of how in Pine Ridge no one would waste a lemon on a counter.

Mrs. Green, a tall beaky woman with steel-colored eyes, patrolled the kitchen with military precision. At first, the headmistress's withering stare made Frankie want to give up. Mrs. Green's disdainful looks proved she thought the Indian girls who boarded at the school were lazy and slow-witted.

But Frankie had kept at Mrs. Green until she gave in and let Frankie study alongside the other girls in exchange for helping out at meals. Helping turned out to be a lot of peeling potatoes and washing dishes but Frankie didn't mind. She and her new friend Jeanette made jokes or sang the hours away. Frankie wiped her damp forehead with her arm.

Jeanette, a Navajo teenager about as wide as she was tall, wiped her hands on her apron. "All these onions—they stink."

Frankie rinsed her hands in a bowl of water. "It's Indian perfume!"

She held her nose. "Gives you fresh breath, too!" Jeanette's close-cropped hair poked out of her hair net.

She reminded Frankie of a fat little deer mouse. "You're so funny!"

Jeanette stuck her hands on her hips and frowned the same way Mrs. Green always did. "Where's your hairnet? We don't have all day! Let's move!"

Frankie stifled laughter. Holding the knife in midair, she whispered. "Careful—she's got spies, you know."

Jeanette made a hissing sound, and then dumped peeled carrots into an industrial-sized pot. "They cut my hair." Her eyes narrowed to slits. "They can't do nothing worse." She turned away.

Frankie's smile faded. She kept her own hair in braids, carefully wound around her head, partly because the school demanded it, partly out of respect for girls who'd been torn away from family and then forced to forfeit their beautiful long hair. Her heart became a stone, weighed down by such injustice. But she forced herself to hope. Another reason to keep studying, keep walking toward her teaching dream. Someday, she'd help kids like Jeanette get an education, but without stripping away all what made them Indians.

Frankie kept her fingertips tucked under as she plied the knife. Poor Jeanette. And just last week a homesick Klamath girl nearly chopped off two of her fingers—was it an accident? No one was sure.

Frankie stopped long enough to wipe the tears from her stinging eyes. The Klamath girl from Oregon hadn't stopped crying since she had been taken from her family in Oregon. She'd seen plenty of the same kind of desperation in Pine Ridge. She finished off the onions and scooped the pieces into a large stainless bowl.

The noon whistle shrieked. Frankie jumped. No matter how many times she heard it, the steam whistle managed to startle her every time. Jeanette leaned in. "Don't look now but here comes the old witch."

Mrs. Green walked like she had a broomstick holding her up. Rumor had it that her own grandmother had seen half her family massacred by Apaches during the Indian wars. Whatever the true story, the headmistress believed in precision, diligence, and cleanliness. Idleness was of the devil, and woe to the girl caught standing around or working too slowly.

Mrs. Green's voice rasped like coarse grit sandpaper. "All right, girls. Noon meal in ten minutes. Let's move!" She approached Jeanette, who had the misfortune to be humming a Navajo tune to herself. Mrs. Green leaned in so close even Frankie smelled stale cigarettes on the woman's breath. "Didn't you hear?"

Jeanette took her time before she looked up. Frankie detected a slight mischievous smile on her friend's lips, but was helpless to stop her. "Noon meal in ten minutes." Jeanette took a deep breath and bellowed. "Now move!"

Frankie closed her eyes. She hated to think of the punishment awaiting Jeanette. Frankie rinsed her hands and walked briskly toward the dining hall.

Tuesday, Nick tried to tell Frankie he couldn't come for dinner. But she had no phone and Nick was forced to leave a message with Stu at the gas station. Nick would be surprised if Stu bothered to pass along the info if he saw either Frankie or Harold. It was the best he could do, though. Window Rock was a long drive from Phoenix, and he had to set out before dawn.

Last minute, his boss had assigned him to calm down the Navajos. It'd take all day and maybe more to get the sheep problem fixed and hot tempers cooled. All the way up the highway, he saw Frankie Chasing Bear in the watery mirages shimmering on the road. Around every curve, as he climbed the truck through the mountains, there she was, standing in that blue dress, her son at her side. He reminded himself he was through with members of the opposite sex, even Lakota ones. It didn't do any good.

He pulled up in front of the Navajo BIA office in the late afternoon, hoped the situation would resolve without too much trouble. Nick was always leery—most on the Rez thought he was a sell-out, a half-breed. Well, the agency had sent him, and he was all they were going to get.

He parked the truck on a dusty side street. Wind roared between the buildings; he put his head down as he walked.

He'd already been briefed: the tribal council was up in arms over the sheep population again, and demanded the government back off its position the Indians' flocks were growing too large. He was here to help everybody simmer down, if possible.

Mama Brown stood outside. She was one of the few Navajo who liked him. Her dark velvet blouse glinted with Mercury dimes sewn down its front. The lines on the woman's face were etched deep as the canyons where the "Diné" or "people" lived. She looked up. "Glad you could make it."

Nick tipped his hat. "Came as soon as I could." He smiled. Lakota and Navajo weren't traditional enemies, but if they had been, Mama Brown would still have greeted him as a friend.

The tribal elders inside weren't as cordial. He greeted them in the Navajo way, yet they sat like stones, watching his every move as he took his seat in the spare room. He tried to get comfortable in the ugly office chair. It was impossible.

Martin Brown was one of the young Navajo hotshots who stirred up trouble every chance he got. He scraped his chair loudly as he stood up. "I asked Nick to come and see if he can talk some sense into the agents who've been telling folks to thin down their herds." He seemed tipsy and steadied himself against the table as he turned to face Nick. "I don't know how you expect us to survive."

The old men seemed to agree, nodding at Martin's statement. The old men generally didn't trust Nick, even though he'd told them he wanted to help. But he never should have admitted he'd been baptized. Christian Indians were suspect. If Mama Brown wasn't so fond of him, he'd be afraid to show his face.

Nick acknowledged the council. "I've put in an official request to Agent McCollum. I'm sympathetic, but there's pressure from Forestry. It seems the sheep love the plants the feds want protected."

Another elder spoke. "Maybe we just need sheep that don't eat."

Martin Brown's lips hinted at a smile. "Or maybe we need to have kids who don't eat."

From the back of the room. "Or rise from the dead." A wave of hard-edged laughter.

Nick's insides roiled. "Look." He held up his hands. "I'll try to convince them to ease off the restrictions—but I'll need your cooperation."

The council fell quiet, and Nick thought he'd finally gotten through to them. But he turned around and saw what had hushed the men. Mama Brown, Martin's sister, leaned in the doorway, her arms crossed, an impatient scowl on her face. Next to her stood Wanda Brown, the spinster daughter Mama Brown paraded in front of Nick every time he visited the Rez.

Nick faced the council. "I'll have the decision for you by next meeting. Thanks." He put on his hat and squeezed past Wanda and her mother.

But Mama Brown wasn't finished with him. "So good to see you, Nick. I heard your divorce was final." The dimes on her velvet shirt winked in the light.

Nick's goose was cooked. He stopped, painfully aware he would have to make small talk with Mama's daughter. Her eligible daughter. He nodded. "You heard right. It was tough, but for the best."

Mama's hair had more gray than he remembered. "That's what happens when Indians marry white girls."

Nick looked her in the eye. "Carolyn's got some Cherokee in her, you know."

Mama sniffed. "Like everybody else." She motioned to Wanda to say something.

Wanda, a tall, girl with a pretty face and a lisp, had taken pains to dress for the occasion. Her dark blue skirt flowed over her curves. "Hi, Nick." She looked away.

"Nice to see you again, Wanda. You look nice."

"Thanks." She refused to say or do more.

Mama stepped in front of her daughter. "No matter what those old buzzards say, you're our guest. Will you stay with us tonight?"

"Sorry, Mama. I got to be back in the valley tomorrow. Appreciate the invite though."

Both women seemed disappointed. Mama shook her head. "What a shame—you're always welcome here." Wanda stole glances at him whenever her mother spoke.

"I'll take a rain check, then." He cringed inside, thinking of Frankie. "OK?" How many rain checks could a person take?

"Mighty fine, Nick. Mighty fine." Mama nodded while behind her, Wanda smiled shyly.

He walked briskly to the safety of his truck. He could feel the women watching him.

Before he left the area, he parked on the top of a ridge overlooking the valley. He got out of the truck and turned against the wind. Below him, sheep grazed in clusters, their wool shaggy and grayed. Hogans with stacked poles and sod roofs dotted the high desert, and clumps of ragged mesquite fought for a place in the sun.

It was a wonder anyone made a living up here. Sure, the land itself was a miracle—strange rock formations like ribbons of water or melting ice cream. With hot, dry summers and winters to rival the bitter cold of South Dakota, Navajo land was nobody's idea of paradise for sheep or man.

One hand shielding his eyes, he squinted into the sky and listened. Sheep bawled, their bells tinkling. A hawk circled.

The wind had a voice, too. The voice was a mighty God whose son had been sacrificed long ago.

The voice rushed on the wind and told him there was only one God, one Creator. The Creator wove his ancestors into a single whole cloth. He thought of the Lakota star. He thought of the woman named Frankie. He jumped across a sandstone formation and imagined Frankie mending his quilt his grandmother had made for him. All night down the highway to Phoenix, he thought of little else.

6

Tuesday evening, Frankie sat on the sofa, staring at her hands. Behind her, the table was laid. She'd even picked zinnias and displayed them in a glass jelly jar. She'd spent far too much on the chops, which were by now stone cold.

Harold, who lay on his stomach reading, looked up from his spot on the cool linoleum. "Told ya he wouldn't show." He went back to his book, legs bent at the knee, his feet softly kicking the air.

Frankie set her jaw. "It doesn't matter." She stood and dragged the card table in front of her seat on the sofa.

Harold glanced up again. "'Course not."

"My grandmother used to say you can kill your enemies with kindness."

Harold snorted and tossed down his book.

Truth was, she wanted to throw something herself. It had been a rotten day all the way around, and Harold wasn't help-ing. But she wouldn't cry. She slung her tape measure about her shoulders and pulled the pincushion closer. If nothing else, working on Harold's quilt would make her feel like she was still home.

She let her fingers ride over the smooth cotton fabric, avoided the pins and matched the edges of two triangular pieces. Grandmother had always frowned on machine-sewn piecing of quilts but maybe it was just common sense. Frankie sat on a chair and threaded the treadle Singer with golden-rod-colored thread. She lined up the fabric edges under the presser foot. Sorry, Grandmother. It would have to be enough to do the quilting by hand.

The Singer's sound was balm for her wounded pride. At first, it repeated Nick's name with each needle stroke, mocking her the way Hank used to do. But as the quilt pieces became one piece, she relaxed. Her soul sang with the machine's rhythm, her fingers guiding the fabric, her feet working the foot pedals, the needle chattering a thin straight line. At the end of a seam, she used her teeth to break the thread, then was startled by a knock at the door. The pincushion fell off the table. Harold got up.

She held her breath. Should she be angry with Nick for standing her up? Or should she act as if she didn't care one way or another? Her heart jumped around in her chest. She scooted back her chair and went to see.

Harold stood glaring out at Orval, the bully son of Stu's. Harold started to shut the door, but Orval held up a folded piece of paper.

The pudgy redhead wore a smirk. "My dad says your injun lover boy left you a message." He squinted past Harold. "Here." He held out the paper with the tips of his fingers, as if it was infected.

Frankie took the note. "Thank you." She hoped the note was from Nick, but she didn't open it. She wouldn't give the little brat the satisfaction.

Orval sniffed. "My dad says don't start thinking he's your personal mailman."

She tried to smile through clenched teeth. "'Course not."

Harold stepped forward. She took his shoulders, held on.

What had Grandmother said? To entertain strangers, angels unaware? Orval was no stranger. But dinner was going to waste. "Say." Frankie put on a smile. "We were just about to sit down to supper. Care to join us?"

Harold shot his mom a pleading look. She stroked the top of his head and he ducked out of the way. "You and Orval shouldn't be enemies." She caught Orval's smoldering gaze. "You like chops?"

The boy cast a lingering glance at the table, but then backed up. "I gotta go. My dad's expecting me." Orval walked backward down the path, turned and rushed through the gate. The kid beat it down the road. Frankie didn't think such a husky boy could run so fast.

"And don't come back!" Harold yelled after him.

"What'd I tell you?" Frankie grinned at her boy, who stared at her as if she'd just grown a second head. "Kill 'em with kindness."

⸻

A couple hours before dawn, Nick was only a few miles out of Phoenix. Passing through Verde Valley, he couldn't help appreciating the metro area below. All lit up, Phoenix seemed almost inviting. At least it did until he considered how artificial the whole place was. Take away the Colorado River water—as California was busy doing—and in a few years Phoenix would revert back to parched desert. He guided his truck down the hill, windows down, cool desert air rushing past him. By modern standards, no water equaled certain death.

Certain death. Just like his most recent attempt at reentering the dating scene. Frankie Chasing Bear had no doubt written

53

him off by now. If Stu had delivered his message to her, he'd be surprised. Carolyn was right. When it came to women, he was nothing short of an idiot. Best leave it that way.

Besides, her son was disturbed. If Harold wasn't a car thief, he'd probably turn out alcoholic, like too many Pine Ridge men. Nick pulled into his driveway and made sure to lock the truck.

His porch light was out again, but he could just make out two familiar people slouching near his door. Monny and Abe. "What's going on?"

Abe straightened up. "Monny here, got us thrown out."

Nick took out his keys. "Thrown out of where? A bar?" He squinted against the dark, looking for the right key. Neither man drank and he knew it, but it was fun to give them what for.

Monny shook his head. "Not exactly."

"Thrown out of our apartment." Abe stuffed his hands into his pants pockets. "Mind if we stay here? Just for tonight?"

Nick unlocked his door and waved in his friends. "Can't wait to hear what you've done this time."

Abe ducked inside, followed by Monny, who kept his head down.

Nick hung up his hat and keys, rubbed at his eyes to ease his fatigue. "OK. What's your story?"

Monny raised his chin. "Aren't you going to offer us a snack?"

Abe threw his friend a sidelong glance. "It's after midnight, Gila."

Monny eyed the sofa. "You and Nick can share. I'll take the couch."

Nick was too tired to argue. "I'll find you a blanket." He headed to the bedroom, and knelt as he pulled the scuffed footlocker out from under the bed.

Monny stood behind Nick. "Don't go to no trouble." He reached in front of Nick and released the footlocker's clasps. "I'll just grab something." Throwing open the box, he grabbed for Nick's tattered quilt.

Nick clamped a hand over Monny's wrist. "Not that one." Nick dug under his old quilt and found an army surplus blanket. "Here, this'll do." He handed the olive green wool blanket to his friend.

Monny screwed up his face. "Wool gives me hives." He ran his hand across the quilt. "What's so special about it anyway?"

Nick grabbed an extra pillow from his bed and shoved it into Monny's arms. "Hit the sack. We'll talk in the morning."

Monny looked wounded. "You don't have to bite my head off. Can I help it if we get asked to leave in the middle of my preaching?"

Abe stood in the doorway. "If you're not on that sofa inside a minute, you're sleeping on the floor."

Still kneeling, Nick rested his forehead on his arm. It was going to be a long night.

Wednesday morning, Frankie had trouble rousing Harold. They were going to be late. "Come on. Wake up." She practically dressed the boy herself as he stood like a totem, eyes half-closed and crusty with sleep. She licked her fingers and ran them across Harold's cowlick. He jerked away. "Ok, mister. Let's go." She grabbed his hand and led him outside.

She climbed into the truck, settled her books on the bench seat's middle. Harold leaned his face against the passenger window and dozed.

The truck wouldn't start. She tried again. Nothing.

"Battery's dead." Frankie thought of the three-mile walk ahead of them, picked up her textbooks, elbowed her son. "We're walking today, kiddo."

Harold groaned.

"What kind of warrior are you anyway?" Maybe pride would get the kid moving.

"A tired one." He grimaced.

Frankie opened the cab's door and slid out. "An Indian who won't go to school is a dumb Indian. Probably spend the rest of his life getting beat up by bullies named Orval." She slammed the door, started walking north.

Harold caught up. He took the books from his mother and carried them.

"You're a good boy." She smiled. First thing to go right today. "Hey. When does the bookmobile come by? I want to look up some quilting stuff."

Harold seemed surprised, but pleased at her interest. "Every other Saturday. Don't know if they have any books like that—about quilts I mean—but just ask the librarian." He squinted into the sunlight. "Mr. Ashley."

Frankie pulled a hairpin out of her braids and stuck it in again. "A man librarian? Never heard of such a thing."

Harold walked faster. "He knows a lot about a lot of stuff. He says books are—"

"Are what?"

Harold ducked his head. "Don't look now, but Nick's truck is right behind us." He narrowed his eyes.

Frankie turned. Sure enough, the BIA truck was pulling up, with Nick driving and two passengers shoulder to shoulder in the cab. He slowed to a crawl and rolled down his window. "Care for a lift?"

Harold refused to talk. Frankie peered inside the truck. "Looks like you got a full load."

Nick stopped the truck and the passengers piled out. "These are my buddies, Monny and Reverend Honest Abe." The two men smiled and nodded at Frankie, then climbed into the truck bed. "Where you headed?" Nick kept his smile bright.

Frankie bit her lip. "Indian School." Should she act hurt about the dinner he missed? Act like she didn't care? She shook her head—it was too early to play games.

Nick gestured with his head. "I'll drop you off. Hop in."

Harold growled something under his breath.

Frankie ignored her son and opened the truck's door. "Get in." They were late, after all.

———

Nick ground the gears as he pulled away from the curb. Harold kept his eyes closed. Nick figured he could do a little explaining in the time it took to reach the school. "Did you get my note?"

"Did I ever." She rolled her eyes. "Orval came face-to-face with Harold." Frankie's smile was the best thing he'd seen so far today.

Harold's eyes popped open. "I was going to pound him good, but Ma said no."

Nick tried to look sincere. "Whole thing's my fault—the council up in Window Rock called an emergency meeting. It's about a twelve-hour drive round-trip." He pulled over at the Phoenix Indian School's red brick building, three stories high. The place looked more like a prison than anything. "Give me another chance?"

Without a word, Harold got out and trudged up the main building's steps.

Frankie scooped up her books and cast a glance through the back window. "What about your friends? They need a decent meal, too?"

Nick chuckled. "I warn you—Monny eats like a locust."

"Is he the one you call Gila Monster?"

"The one and only."

"He's kinda cute." She scooted toward the passenger door. "OK. Friday night. Seven o'clock." She got out and leaned back into the open window. "And no excuses."

He nodded.

———

Nick watched her climb the steps and disappear inside the school's massive coved doors. No doubt about it. Frankie Chasing Bear was getting under his skin. He took off his hat, mopped his sweaty forehead. Careful, he told himself. A man on the rebound is hungry. But he sensed something special about this woman and her son. And if God delivered something special to him, he'd best respect it.

A pounding on the rear window. Monny yelled, "Let's go, man."

Honest Abe flung his long legs over the bed's side and jumped to the ground. He came to Nick's window. "The church is only a few more blocks." He stared back at Monny. "Besides, Gila Monster needs the exercise." The church was the tiny Temple of First Americans, Abe's start-up congregation housed in the back room of a Pentecostal church.

Monny, aka Gila Monster, made a face, but climbed out of the truck's back. He joined Abe at the window. "Coming down to the meeting tonight?"

Nick glanced once more at the school, hoping to catch a glimpse of Frankie going up the staircase. A sea of Indian teens swarmed, but Frankie wasn't anywhere to be seen. He let out his breath, put his hat back on. "Don't I see enough of you clowns?"

Abe frowned. "I'm working on getting us another place." He smiled as he shoved Monny's shoulder. "And keeping a certain big mouth preacher quiet."

Monny looked wounded. "I was only sharing the good news."

"At eleven-thirty at night?" Abe was always the more reasonable one.

"Hey. I couldn't sleep."

"Look." Nick downshifted. "I gotta go."

Monny leaned in and whispered. "That Frankie's a real looker. Maybe she's sweet on you?" His eyes twinkled.

Abe pulled his friend's arm. "C'mon Gila. Stop torturing the man." He raised his eyebrows at Nick. "You can tell us all about your new girlfriend tonight. Seven sharp."

Nick eased off the clutch and pulled out into traffic. Girlfriend? What did Abe mean by that?

7

Frankie was right. Mrs. Green made sure Jeanette got latrine duty. Frankie missed the Navajo teen's antics, although Frankie was careful to keep her head down now. Didn't talk much to anybody, even the Klamath girl, whose bandaged fingers gave Frankie the willies. She guided the girl to duties not involving a knife.

Frankie was afraid to hum like Jeanette had, in case Mrs. Green saw fit to end her studies; get her and Harold both tossed out. She hated how someone had so much say over her life—especially someone as mean as she was. But what could Frankie do? Harold's education was more important than anything.

Frankie punched down a batch of rising bread dough. She didn't belong in a kitchen. What would Grandmother say? Frankie closed her eyes, her floury hands kneading, turning, kneading.

The quilting needle goes up, down, and pull it through, Grandmother always said. Up, down, and through. Let the star guide you, she said. Frankie kneaded the dough with as much force as she could muster. A bed without a quilt, Grandmother said. Frankie had to get that quilt finished. But when? Sunday was her only day off, and attendance at the Phoenix Indian School's Sunday services was mandatory. You went whether you wanted to or not. From the looks on the students' faces, most would rather be doing anything else.

All around her, white folks were trying to shove their God down Indians' throats. Their God, who they said was loving, peaceful, compassionate. Frankie socked the yeasty mass. Just before they tried to beat your heritage out of you. She rolled dough and laid it in a bread pan for the second rise.

The swinging kitchen doors opened. A hush fell over the room. Frankie kept her eyes on the oilcloth table in front of her, pulled another loaf-sized ball of dough from a stack. She sprinkled flour over her work surface and let the heels of her hands do the work.

Mrs. Green's cigarette smell arrived before she did. Frankie whipped around. Standing ramrod straight, Mrs. Green's lips pinched together, as if she was disappointed not to find fault with Frankie's efforts. The headmistress's eyes narrowed. "Hmmph." She started to walk away.

Frankie took a chance. "Mrs. Green?"

The teacher stopped, slued around on her heel. "Yes? What is it?"

Frankie kept her eyes averted, but her voice firm. "Is all singing against the rules, then?"

Heads of the other Indian girls jerked up in unison. Before her outburst, Jeanette had also been punished for humming a Navajo song. The room got quieter still, the only sound was an industrial-sized mixer.

Mrs. Green frowned. "I don't know what you're talking about."

Frankie overrode the urge to speak behind her hand. "If we sang *hymns*, it would make the time go faster." She stressed the word hymns, but didn't add perhaps Jeanette singing Navajo songs had set Mrs. Green's teeth on edge. "No doubt we'd be more efficient, too."

Mrs. Green looked as if she'd swallowed a cactus. She glanced around at the pairs of student eyes fixed upon her. "Well, I suppose." She cleared her throat. "If it doesn't distract anyone, I mean." She fidgeted with a lock of hair curling around one ear, the lobe stretched long by a gaudy clip-on earring. "But remember." She wagged her finger in Frankie's face. "Only hymns glorifying God are permissible." Her gaze travelled around the room. "I will not tolerate any heathen worship in my kitchen." Her soles squeaked as she stalked out.

The whole room breathed in unison. Nobody cared if the songs were hymns—singing helped pass the time. Several gathered around Frankie's oilcloth table.

Even the Klamath girl wore a shy smile. Someone said Frankie was their new leader. A Pima teen with a clear, high voice started singing "Amazing Grace," and the whole kitchen rang with harmony. Frankie smiled to herself.

Her smile was short-lived. Halfway through the hymn's last verse, Mrs. Green returned, holding a struggling Harold by the arm. "Lemme go!" He wriggled out of the woman's grip and stood rubbing his arm. "I didn't do nothing!"

Mrs. Green crossed her arms and said, "We'll see about that." She turned to Frankie. "Your son was caught trying to steal a sewing machine from Home Economics."

Frankie blinked. "Sewing machine?" A few kitchen helpers scurried back to their stations, but the rest stood listening. Frankie frowned at her son. "This makes no sense. We don't need a machine."

Mrs. Green sniffed. "Fact is, we've bent over backward to accommodate you and this . . ." She shot Harold a look. ". . . this boy. We can't abide a thief."

"I'm not a thief. Ma!" Harold's eyes pleaded. "It wasn't me. I swear!"

Mrs. Green ignored the boy. "You're dismissed, Miss Chasing Bear, and Harold is suspended."

Frankie's insides boiled. "Can't we get to the bottom of this first?" The mother grizzly in her rose up. "My son's no thief. Do a little investigating. I'm sure he's innocent."

Mrs. Green's words were icy. "The decision has been made." She turned to the others, still gawking at the scene. "Dinner won't prepare itself, girls! We haven't got all day!"

Frankie's feet weighed tons as she dragged herself out of the kitchen and down the main steps of the school's front entrance. When she finally found her way out into the sunshine, Harold was waiting.

⨀

Just before noon, Nick pulled into an empty slot at the Burger Shack Drive-in and cranked down the driver's window. On a post next to the car, a metal speaker crackled to life and he put in his order. The long and boring morning BIA meeting had helped him work up an appetite. He could eat a buffalo. Two burgers, fries and a shake. He sat back and waited, drummed his fingers against the steering wheel.

Minutes later, a waitress in white shorts and a sailor top, skated outside. She propped the tray with his lunch on the edge of his truck's open window. Nick got a good look at her, and she smiled before gliding back inside the restaurant. He was glad Monny wasn't there to tease him.

He imagined Frankie skating around, delivering trays. She'd make business go through the roof. He slowly unwrapped one of the burgers, inspecting it for sufficient pickles, onion, and ketchup. He'd just taken his first bite when he looked up at the street. He stopped chewing.

Walking against the wind and the traffic, Frankie and Harold trudged along the dusty shoulder where a sidewalk should've been. He managed to open his cab's door without knocking off his food's tray, and slid out. Had school let out early? He waved.

Neither seemed to notice. He whistled through his fingers. This time, Harold stopped, nudged his mom. Even at this distance, Nick could tell something was wrong. He left his truck and crossed the street in a few easy strides.

"Hey, you two." Nick thought Frankie had been crying. He'd tread gently. "Is everything OK?"

Harold stuffed his hands in his pockets.

Frankie's voice was low, almost inaudible. "The Indian school was holding us back, you know? Who needs it?" She glanced at Harold and shrugged. "We're going home."

Nick rubbed at his chin. "Let me drive you." He gestured at the drive-in. "I was about to have some lunch." He turned to Harold. "Hungry?" On the road behind them, passing cars created a dull roar.

Harold shook his head, stared at his feet. Something was definitely wrong.

Nick searched out Frankie's eyes, held her gaze. She seemed defeated, but her expression remained a blank wall. "What is it? What's wrong?"

Frankie stared straight ahead. "We're going home." The wind was picking up again. A ways down the street, a dust devil swirled loose wrappers and trash into its vortex.

Nick held onto his hat. "At least, have some lunch. I'll drive you home after."

"Thanks." She shook her head. "But you don't understand. We're going home to Pine Ridge." Her eyes glistened as dust blew across her face. She blinked. "They accused Harold of stealing a sewing machine."

If it hadn't sounded so sad, he would've laughed. "A sewing machine? Did they check under your shirt for it, too?"

Frankie's eyes sparked. "I have a perfectly good machine. Why on earth would I need Harold to steal me one?"

Harold looked defiant. "They just needed some excuse." He scoffed. "I wouldn't go back there if they paid me."

Frankie's voice rose against the wind. "I don't know how we'll get back to South Dakota, but we'll find a way. Won't we, Harold?"

Nick's appetite vanished. "At least, let me get you back to your place." His insides roiled.

Frankie looked up. "Seems like we're always begging rides from you."

Harold scuffed his sneaker's toe in the dust.

Nick smiled. Maybe he could make their day a little better. "My truck's across the street."

Nick's heart ached for both of them. He asked if they'd mind stopping by First Americans church and pick up Monny and Abe. Frankie said of course she didn't mind, but Nick could tell she wished the day was over with. He swung into the church lot and led them around back.

A folding chair propped open the church door. Nick poked his head in. "Abe?"

Monny, holding a worn Bible, looked up from where he sat across from a beat-up old wooden desk. "Abe's out front. He'll be back in a few."

Nick took off his hat and ducked into the tiny office. He waved in Frankie and Harold, who stood shifting from foot to foot as if they didn't know what to do. "You remember Monny, right?" He pulled out two more folding chairs. "Have a seat."

Monny grinned ear to ear, leaned toward Harold. "You ever hear the story of the battle of Jericho?"

Harold's mouth drew into a thin line. "Nope." His expression said he didn't care to hear it, either. The boy jiggled one foot. Frankie sat like a frightened mule deer ready to bolt.

Nick shot Monny a look. "I didn't finish my lunch." He held up a paper bag full of his burger and fries. "Help me polish it off?" Nick raised an eyebrow, gesturing to the outside.

Monny sat still for a few seconds. "I get it. You want to talk to Abe alone. Right?" He took the bag and stood.

Nick smiled. "Just for a few minutes, OK?"

Monny started for the door. "I'll be back."

Frankie fidgeted with her fingers. "I don't want to be rude, but Harold and me . . ." She glanced at her son. "We had all the religion we could stand at the School. No offense." She removed a pin holding her braids in a circle around her crown and they fell about her shoulders. She craned her neck, and peered out a dirty window.

Nick couldn't hide his surprise. "Oh! You think." He blew out a breath and sank into Monny's vacated chair. "No, no. I'm not trying to proselytize anybody."

Harold elbowed Frankie and smirked. "Heap big word."

Nick rolled his eyes. "I didn't bring you here to convert you. My buddy, Abe, has some connections though. If you need help to get to Pine Ridge, Reverend Honest Abe's your man."

Honest Abe appeared from a dim hallway. "Your man? For what?" He folded himself into the chair behind the desk.

Nick gestured to the pair. "Remember Frankie and her son? They've run into a little trouble." He glanced sideways, smiled. "I'll let them tell you their story."

Abe stood, extended a hand to each in turn. He sat down and nodded at Frankie. "I'm listening. Shoot."

8

Frankie hadn't appreciated how tall this Honest Abe guy was before he stood in front of her. Her insides shook, or was she just hungry? Nick and Abe stood in the doorway, speaking in low voices. Nick was trying to help them, sure, but she got annoyed when people whispered like that.

"Be right back." Nick put on his hat and Frankie's irritation melted away. Boy, he was easy on the eyes. He turned to Frankie. "I'll track down Monny. Maybe he'll share some of my lunch." He went outside, and Frankie gazed after him until she felt Harold's disapproving stare. She twisted back around to face Abe.

Was he trustworthy? After all, he went by Honest Abe. But he was a reverend, which put him in the same category as the white folk at the Indian School. Ah, well. Any help was better than none at all. She started to open her mouth to explain, but Harold jumped in.

"Look." He eyed Reverend Abe. "We gotta get to Pine Ridge." Harold crossed his arms. "But we're not asking for no handouts."

Frankie smiled at how her son had taken charge, but couldn't stop herself from correcting his grammar. "Any handouts."

Harold frowned. "That's what I said."

Abe looked thoughtful. "Why'd you come out here in the first place? Arizona's not exactly known for giving Indians a leg up."

Harold stiffened. "Wasn't my idea." He shot a sassy look at her, one that Grandmother never would've tolerated. "My dad was in the Indian Relocation Program, to start a job in LA." He shifted in his seat. "But before we even left . . ." The boy's voice faded away.

Frankie put a hand over Harold's and he didn't pull away. She straightened her back. "My husband, Hank Sr., got killed. Stabbed. Bar fight." Her stomach knotted at the memory.

Harold spoke. "You said the bar parking lot."

Frankie shrugged. "Anyway, Harold and I were on our way to LA—thought I'd take Hank's place, become a lady welder." She paused at the thought, and a smile crept into her voice. "Imagine that—a lady welder. A Lakota lady welder."

Abe leaned forward. "Lakota, huh? Nick's part Lakota, too."

Harold looked impatient. "All's we want is to get back home."

Frankie nodded. "I got an old Chevy truck with a mind of its own. Broke down outside Phoenix. Hank knew some people here with a place we could stay." A small bookcase in the church lined one wall; she scanned it for no good reason. A whole row of Bibles stared back at her. "Otherwise, we'd have been out of luck."

Harold chimed in. "Looks like we got no luck at all."

"Any luck." When was her son going to start sounding as smart as he was?

Abe stood, his frame filling up the room. He addressed Harold. "You say you don't want a handout? Fine. Nick tells me the Indian School thinks you swiped a sewing machine from their workshop. What do you say about it?"

Harold glared but kept quiet.

Abe walked back and forth across the room. "I happen to know a couple of Navajos—they're starting up a little business."

Frankie was intrigued. "What sort of business?"

Abe took a book from one of the shelves and thumbed through its pages. "Sewing business. Making quilts for folks on the Rez." He rested his gaze on Frankie. "Nick tells me you're an expert at quilting."

Frankie couldn't stop Grandmother from whispering into her thoughts. The star. Look to the star.

◦◦◦

Nick leaned against his truck's side. He nodded and listened as Monny prattled on, talking with his hands, chewing, and gulping in-between words.

"So there's this old Medicine Woman." Monny stopped to stuff a wad of fries into his mouth. "I tell her she's already got an in with the Creator—now alls she's got to do is believe on His Son and she's in like flint." He wiped greasy fingers on his dungarees, chewed and swallowed.

Nick's gaze kept drifting back toward the office where Abe was counseling Frankie and her son. He hoped Abe wasn't laying it on thick, too.

Monny shook his head. "Man, you ain't even listening." He polished off the last of the fries.

Nick snapped to. "Sorry, Gila."

A sly smile edged the corners of Monny's mouth. "She's one good-looking squaw, I'll say that."

He bristled. "Don't call her a squaw."

Monny looked offended. "Why not? You know what I mean."

Nick straightened. "That's the problem, Gila." He headed for the office. "I *do* know what you mean." Monny wasn't educated,

69

but he wasn't abusive toward women either. The old ways were fading fast, but with words like squaw, it might be a good thing. He grabbed the church's doorknob and flashed a grin back at Monny.

The man shrugged and balled the paper sack, tossed it into a trash can. Nick went inside.

Reading glasses perched on the end of his nose, Abe looked up from a small desk file. "Nick. Remember those two gals who were sewing quilts?"

Nick glanced at Frankie and Harold, still sitting, looking like captives. He took off his hat and let his thumb glide along the felted brim's edge. "How could I forget? Mama Brown sent her cousin Lucie to keep an eye on Navajo girls at the school. If they ran into trouble, they'd have some people here in town was her thinking. Their names?" He used the moment to appreciate Frankie's smooth bronze skin. "Lucie. Lucie and Netty." He wanted to grin at Frankie, but stopped short of an all-out smile.

Frankie rolled her eyes, started unweaving one of her braids. Netty? Could it be a nickname for Jeanette?

Nick frowned and acted wounded. "What? Navajo can't sew?" Maybe these quilters could convince her and Harold to stick around a little longer. Maybe the idea was pie-in-the-sky.

Frankie's hand shielded her mouth before she could stop herself. "Don't know any Navajo—except one."

"Who's that?"

Harold narrowed his eyes at Nick.

Frankie began to unbraid the other side of her hair. "Used to know." She used her fingers like a comb. "Till we got suspended."

Abe leaned across the desk, a slip of paper in his hand. "Found it. Here." He handed the scrap to Frankie. "Lucie and Jeanette. Nick tells me your quilts are something special. I'll bet they can use a gal who's good with a needle and thread." He smiled.

Frankie's hard glare told Nick that the word "gal" wasn't any better than "squaw." Heat crept up his neck.

Frankie chafed at Nick's friend Abe's slight. She was no more a "gal" than she was a "squaw," the term Stu liked to throw in her face. But like his nickname, Abe seemed honest and truly trying to help. She let her hair alone and laced her fingers together in her lap. "Not sure I'm any good with a needle and thread, but I'm not shy when it comes to work."

Abe smiled, his long face growing a bit wider. "Nick, you mind introducing Frankie?"

Frankie smiled. "Jeanette? If it's the same one, we've already met."

Nick never took his eyes off Frankie. "You'll give it a try?"

"Well, maybe." She tried to control her stomach's fluttering, but sweat dampened the nape of her neck. "Until we scrape up the cash to get back."

Harold stared at her. "How long'll it take?" His expression said probably a million years.

"Don't know." She tried to find a safe place to rest her gaze.

Nick seemed fixated on her. The small room was too hot to leave her hair hanging. She gathered it into a bunch, let it fall over one shoulder.

Nick ducked his chin when she caught him staring.

Monny burst into the room, his eyes wide. "Say I ain't here, Abe." He darted into the darkened church hallway and peeked around the corner. "You don't even know me."

Abe removed his glasses, pinched the bridge of his nose. "What's going on, Gila?"

Monny hissed. "Shh! She's coming." He crouched behind a stack of folding chairs.

Abe and Nick exchanged looks. Harold jumped up from his seat and ran to one of the room's high windows. He climbed onto a wobbly-legged worktable and peered outside.

Frankie scolded her son. "Harold!" She shook her head. "You'll hurt yourself."

He made a face. "Ma. I'm fine." He held his arms like airplane wings. "See?" He balanced on the table while he watched the window.

"C'mon. Get down." No doubt about it. He was growing up too fast.

Before Harold could move, the door swung open again. Backlit by the afternoon sun, the headmistress didn't wait for an invitation. Mrs. Green marched up to Abe's desk. "The police are on their way."

Frankie froze.

Abe glanced at Nick with a sharp nod. Nick stood tall and faced Mrs. Green. "Help you with something, ma'am?"

Abe stood too, and the room shrank even more. The reverend smiled and extended his hand. "Welcome to the Temple of First Americans." Frankie was relieved when Harold jumped off the table and scooted next to her.

Mrs. Green kept her arms at the sides of her brown pencil skirt, and if she noticed Frankie and Harold at all, she didn't acknowledge them. Frankie squeezed Harold's arm. They had to get back to Pine Ridge.

Mrs. Green addressed only Nick and Abe. "The police won't take kindly to anyone who harbors a fugitive." She jabbed a finger as she spoke. "Especially thieving Indians."

9

Frankie's throat tightened. The words *thieving Indians* stomped through her head. She forbid herself to glance at her son, now slumped low in his chair, his gaze fixed on the floor. He couldn't be responsible for this one. A small comfort.

Nick stepped forward. "What's this about? And who are you?" He stood his ground, arms crossed.

Mrs. Green's eyes widened, then narrowed. "I demand to speak to someone in charge."

"That would be me." Abe sidled around the desk and stood toe to toe with the woman. "There must be some mistake, madam." Abe's voice was low and cold. "If you'll take a seat, I'm sure we can get this straightened out." He unfolded a metal chair and set it down with a thunk. "Now. What makes you think your thief is an Indian?"

"It's a school for Indian students. *Poor* Indians." Mrs. Green sank into the chair. "Naturally I just assumed . . ."

Nick broke in. "The thief's Indian?"

Frankie had never seen the woman look flummoxed. But she savored the moment.

"Of course not." Mrs. Green blanched. "Now see here. I teach girls useful skills to help them get along in society." She trained her gaze on Frankie and Harold. "If they're willing to learn, that is."

Harold squirmed in his seat. "I didn't take your stupid sewing machine!" Frankie pressed her foot hard against Harold's leg. He glared at his mom. "I didn't. I swear it!"

"Hmmph." The headmistress fidgeted for a moment, then regained her composure. "We'll see about that."

Frankie folded her arms and sat back in her chair, stealing glimpses at Harold. He seemed to know he should become invisible.

Nick examined his nails and leaned against the very corner where Monny hid while Abe interrogated Mrs. Green. Gradually, the reverend got her to tell her story. Things were coming up missing at the Phoenix Indian School.

Frankie felt as sorry for the woman as she could, considering. When she mentioned the theft of the sewing machine again, Mrs. Green fastened her gaze on Harold, who stared balefully back at her.

But when Mrs. Green got to the matter at hand, she shook her head. "I don't understand it at all. What would anybody want with calico cloth and a side of pork?" She swiveled her head at Frankie.

Frankie stared back. Obviously, the woman hadn't been raised on mutton and government cheese.

Nick and Abe raised their eyebrows at each other. Nick said, "Why indeed?"

Abe was more direct. "So you saw the person who did this? And you followed that person here?"

Mrs. Green shifted her weight. "No, not literally. But the kitchen girls saw someone running out of the cold locker." She tugged her pencil skirt's hem over her knobby knees. "And they know an Indian when they see one."

The last bit of breathable air evaporated. Frankie stood and pulled Harold with her toward the door. "Excuse us." Fury and tears threatened to erupt as she brushed past Nick and out of the cramped office. "We'll let you know if we see any more thievin' Indians."

Nick's chest went hollow. He hadn't been ready for Frankie's exit. He should've chased her down, told her not to mind the old biddy. But he stood there while Frankie got away, nearly running down the street, Harold loping along next to her.

Nick set his jaw, faced Mrs. Green. "I'm one of the local agents and I get the skinny on most everything." He wanted to throttle her. "You call off the cops." He put on his hat. "And I'll find out who's stealing from the school. Deal?"

Mrs. Green puckered her lips into a tight smirk. "Hmmph." She turned to Abe. "Are you willing to guarantee justice is served?"

Abe shrugged. "I'm a pastor, not a judge."

Mrs. Green glanced at her watch. "I thought you people had your own legal system."

Nick held out a hand. "I'll walk you to your car."

Mrs. Green shrank back. "That won't be necessary." She stood straight as a totem and stalked out.

Nick waited until the door clicked shut. "All right, Gila."

Monny eased out from behind the chairs.

Abe massaged his temples. "Brother Monny, what sort of trouble are you in this time?"

Frankie could hardly see through her blurry tears. She walked so fast her shins began to ache, but not as much as her heart. It had taken less than twenty-four hours for her life to unravel even more.

"Ma." Harold had no trouble keeping up, but he tugged on her arm. "Ma. What we gonna do now?"

She didn't slow down. She swallowed hard, but the lump in her throat was stubborn. "Doesn't matter." The strong breeze kidnapped her words. The house was another mile and a half away.

Harold ran ahead, then stopped at the next intersection. Red light. He caught her arm again. "Come on. You always say we got to have a plan. What's the plan?"

Frankie pulled up, leaned her hands on her thighs. She couldn't lie. But she had no plan beyond giving up on Arizona and seeing how far her miserable truck would take them. "Don't know." She took in gulps of air, coughed, pushed her loose hair off her face. "We'll think of something." The light turned green. Frankie and Harold surged toward home.

That evening, Frankie slouched onto the sofa. Her instinct was to cover her face, wail, and then hightail it for Pine Ridge. But Grandmother wouldn't approve. It would be the coward's way out.

Harold touched her shoulder. She grasped his hand, squeezed it. Her boy seemed taller today, as if he'd grown a foot, just by protecting his mother. "I'm proud of you." She meant it.

"Ma." Harold yanked his hand away and grabbed the book he was reading. He tucked a pillow under his head and lay with his bare feet across Frankie's lap. She could've stayed this way a long time, just clinging to her dreams.

But her stomach rumbled and Harold was a growing boy. She'd made soup from the pork chop bones, added carrots and an onion to the pot. Tossed in some dry spaghetti. "Let's eat." She ladled out two bowls, picked green specks off the rest of the corn muffins. She imagined the soup was the same venison stew that kept them going through South Dakota winters.

She didn't have to tell Harold to chew slowly to trick his stomach into thinking it was full. "When are we leaving?" His eyes were round, and he glanced at her with quick bird stares.

She leaned back in her chair. "Truck will need a lot of gas to get to Pine Ridge, you know."

Outside, the air buzzed with evening cicadas. Harold shrugged. "Maybe Nick will chip in?" He finished off the last muffin.

Frankie let out a long breath. "We aren't beggars. We're not going to start now."

"Stu sure won't be handing out free gas." He took his bowl to the sink, rinsed it. He needed a haircut.

Frankie had to laugh. "You're right." She tidied the kitchen, thinking about what Harold said. She wasn't about to ask Nick for charity, but maybe she'd ask him if she could fix the old quilt he talked about. Wouldn't be much, but it would be a start.

Harold thought it was a great idea. "Maybe I can mow his lawn—who knows, white folks see a hard-working Indian and next thing you know, I got a business." Frankie smiled, nudged his bangs out of his eyes. He leaned wide of her hand. "Ma! I'm not a kid."

"You're my kid." She sat at the sewing machine, planted her feet on the treadle. Yep. First thing tomorrow, she'd be at Nick's door, offering to fix that quilt and anything else that needed mending. Tonight, though, she finally had time to work on Harold's Lakota Star. His bed seemed so empty without one. The quilt top was quickly coming together. Her feet worked the treadles in a rhythmic song, and just as she hoped, Grandmother seemed to smile.

—∞∞∞—

Six a.m. Nick dragged himself out of bed. All night, Monny's snoring had shaken the walls. Nick rubbed at his haggard face, peered into the shaving mirror in his tiny bathroom. "Gotta get these guys out," he told himself. "Today."

He buckled his belt, ready for another day on the Rez, listening to problems he couldn't solve, sorting out arguments between drunken brothers, handing out lollipops to undernourished children. The local tribes were so different from Navajo—and Lakota.

A knock? He jabbed Monny's backside, where he still lay sleeping on the sofa. "Somebody's here," Nick said. Monny wrapped himself in the army blanket and trudged off to the head, slamming the door. Nick shook his head, chuckling. That was so much fun, he'd do it again. He opened the front door.

Frankie and Harold stood on the stoop.

Nick couldn't mask his pleasure. "Morning." He grinned. "What brings you over so early?" He hoped nothing else had gone wrong.

Frankie nodded. "We're OK." She stepped forward. "The quilt you were telling me about? The Lakota Star you said your grandmother made?" She moistened her lips. "I was thinking—Harold and I need to get to Pine Ridge. You need your quilt mended." She hesitated. "Maybe you have clothes might need fixing, too?"

"Ma says she'll sew for free. I'll mow your yard here for a dollar." Harold jerked his thumb at the overgrown Bermuda lawn, its star-like tops gone to seed. "Needs cutting. Bad."

Behind Nick, Abe crossed the room. The tall man waved. "Hey."

"A dollar, eh?" Nick scratched at his chin. "I'll think on it." He addressed Frankie. "I'd ask you in, but I've got houseguests." He winced inside, wished Monny and Abe were anywhere but here. She must think he was running a YMCA.

"We're fine." Frankie glanced away. "It's early. I'll come back later." She touched Harold's upper arm.

"Wait." His heart sped up. "That quilt really does need fixing. Wait here." He darted toward the bedroom, nearly colliding with Monny, now fully dressed, peering into the open refrigerator.

Monny straightened, a leftover chicken drumstick in his hand. "Whoa, partner. Where's the fire?"

Nick ignored his friend. He went into the bedroom and dropped to his knees in front of the old footlocker. He threw back the top and dug through its contents. He never thought he'd be so excited about a blanket.

But the moment his fingertips brushed the quilt's surface, there was that same quiet connection he always felt. He couldn't deny it: even if he was only half-Lakota, he had a connection with a people who had once covered their loved ones with hides and buffalo robes, a people who later adapted quilts like the one his grandmother had made especially for him.

He held up the crumpled, ragged quilt. There. Even in its sorry state, the star blazed from its center. Star of warriors, Star of Bethlehem. He hastily rolled it up and gathered a couple of shirts with missing buttons and a pair of jeans with a hole in the knee. He made for where he hoped she still waited, alongside her son.

She'd almost decided to go on home. Her fingers shook a little as she took the quilt and clothes from Nick. "Thanks."

"You're welcome." His teeth showed when he smiled. She liked his easy humor, the way he didn't seem to get mad about small things. Anger at small things had been what killed Hank as much as the knife that cut him open. Well, that and hooch.

"Let's get one thing clear." She gave herself the luxury of gazing deep into his eyes. "I'm not charging you—just need to practice some before I go over to see the Navajos."

Harold piped up. "I can't mow lawns for free, Ma."

Nick eyed him. "You got a mower?"

Harold raised his chin. "I can get one."

"A dollar you say?"

Harold deadpanned. "For fifty cents I'd mow half."

Nick's eyes crinkled at the corners and he chuckled. "You drive a hard bargain, Harold Chasing Bear. Tell you what. I just happen to have a push mower out back. Trim the lawn's edges, too, and you got yourself a job." He extended his hand. "Deal?"

Harold paused, then shook Nick's hand. "Deal." He walked around the corner, his head high.

Nick called after him. "Mower's parked next to the clothesline."

Frankie gestured at her son, the clothing and battered quilt cradled in her arms. "You didn't have to do that."

"He's a hard worker. Besides." His gaze was like fine dark chocolate. "My lawn needs cutting. Bad."

10

At home, Frankie hung the old, cracked tape measure about her shoulders. She'd watched Grandmother perform this ritual hundreds of times. Now as always, this small gesture felt sacred, as if Frankie was putting on a mantle of honor, one earned only from years of experience.

She unfolded Nick's old quilt and gently spread it out on the floor. He was right about one thing. The pieced-together quilt top was not only frayed, some pieces had shredded edges, causing them to tear away from the backing. The cotton batt had bunched in spots, and the star's brilliant goldenrod had faded. But it was still there. The star was there.

She closed her eyes, listened. Grandmother always cautioned Frankie to use the strongest thread to mend a quilt— silk if you could get it, thick cotton lisle if you couldn't, twisted for extra strength. Make every stitch count.

Grandmother said that a damaged quilt was like a broken heart. You could patch it, stitch it back together, but it would never be the same. There would always be a weak spot, Grandmother said, the very spot where one could always find real love.

Well, hadn't Frankie found enough love to last a lifetime? Real or not, Hank had stolen her heart and then scrambled her brains—what was she thinking when she drove out to Nowhere, Arizona? Now she and her son were more than halfway to Hades. Why hadn't they used needle-punched batting? She massaged the cotton batt, coaxing it to lie flat. It was no use.

Frankie's life was as lumpy as the cotton between the quilt layers. With the flat of her hand, she smoothed out wrinkles as best she could and admired the straight small stitches that bordered each piece of fabric. Someone had put a lot of effort into this thing. Someone had sewn it with love.

Frankie thought of Nick cocooned in the quilt on winter nights, his body's heat trapped under its layers. She tried to conjure his scent—a kind of earthy, pine smell. Was he what he seemed to be—honest and caring and generous? Or like Hank, did Nick have his own secrets?

The door slammed. Harold came in, his arms loaded with a stack of books.

Frankie stood up, spread her arms wide. "Don't walk on the quilt, OK?"

"Quilts!" He picked his way around the edges and set his books on the table. "Ma." He was grinning. "I got you books about quilts."

Frankie came around and stood next to her son. He fingered the top book. "See?" He looked up through his bangs. "Mr. Ashley let me borrow twice the limit—I told him you needed these books. Bad."

Frankie set her hands on her hips. "You did, did you? You think I don't know what I'm doing?"

Harold looked serious. "It was the only way he'd let me check out this many."

Frankie glowed inside whenever Harold got going about reading. She wouldn't embarrass him though. She flipped through the quilting books. Nothing she didn't already know, but the thought was what counted.

He pulled a thick book from the bottom of the pile. "It's called *The Robe*—about ancient Rome or something. It'll be the last time I can use the bookmobile before we go." He flopped down on the sofa. "Wish they had one in Pine Ridge."

"Maybe we'll start one." She knelt beside Nick's quilt, finger-pressed the edges and then pinned together the torn places the best she could. She was careful to keep the pins at right angles to the seam—the old treadle Singer was finicky about running over crooked pins. She glanced up. "I'll drive the truck. You can be the librarian." Boy, did he ever need a haircut.

Harold tented his knees. "Ma. You gotta go to college to be a librarian."

Frankie smiled. "So? We're both going to need to go to college."

Harold let out an exaggerated sigh. "Right. Where do we get that kind of dough?"

She shrugged. "Who knows? You keep mowing lawns. I'll keep on mending quilts and such."

"That's a laugh."

"Careful or I'll take the pinking shears to your hair."

Harold rolled his eyes.

"And turn on the lamp so you can see." She was sure reading in bad light was hard on the eyes and any day now, the electric company was probably going to shut off the juice.

He groaned but switched on the little lamp sitting on the end table.

Frankie sat back down at the sewing machine, paused to pull her hair into a high ponytail. She tucked a frayed bit of

Nick's quilt beneath the presser foot, got the stitches going. For once, the needle didn't hit any pins. But Frankie's mind hit plenty of snags as she pieced together frayed edges and reinforced the torn stitching.

Harold seemed to think getting back to Pine Ridge would be easy. He hadn't yet learned nothing in this life was easy. Frankie reversed the machine's needle for a few stitches, tacked the end of the seam and cut the thread.

He was right about one thing, though. Stu and every other gas station owner in town wouldn't be giving away gas for free. Her stomach rumbled; only a while past supper and already hunger gnawed at her. Harold must be starving.

After basting a few more seams, she stood and stretched. She didn't bother to turn and look at her son. "Still hungry?" Maybe they'd take a stroll down to Baseline Road. It was early for oranges, but they'd see what kind of fruit was on sale at the roadside stands.

No answer.

Frankie's heart plummeted as she swung around. Oh no. Where'd he run off to now? She held a hand to her chest, willed herself to calm down.

She heaved a sigh of relief. Harold had fallen asleep on the sofa, his open book lying across his chest. He deserved better than this, so much better. She gently nudged his feet to one side and sat with Nick's quilt in her lap.

She threaded her needle, put on her quilting thimble and stitched in the ditch around the star's points. Was Nick the real thing, a man who honored the Lakota ways? Or was he just another drunken Indian, full of promises he couldn't keep? She was careful to keep the thread short, careful to keep Nick at the edges of her mind.

Nick hoped he wasn't being nosy. But hadn't Netty and her older cousin Lucie Brown asked him to stop by? Anyway, he'd promised to introduce Frankie to the two Navajos. He peered out the dust-covered window at the low-roof adobe where they'd set up shop.

Netty's chopped-off hair still only reached the nape of her short thick neck, but she wore a broad smile. "Nick. Good to see you again."

"You, too." He grinned, took off his hat. Boy, was it warm in here. "Was up in Window Rock just a few days ago. Your aunt seemed healthy."

Lucie, taller and thinner than Netty, looked up from the quilt frame where she sat. "How's cousin Wanda?" Lucie's dark eyes sparkled. "She still chasing you?"

"Don't know Wanda's doing the chasing." Nick shook his head. "Mama Brown keeps on pushing the poor girl."

Netty cleared piles of fabric squares from a chair. "Sit, Nick. Don't mind Wanda—or Mama B." Nick marveled at Netty's maturity—how she managed to attend school and start a business was admirable, to say the least.

Lucie sniffed. "Wanda's not the brightest, you know."

Netty's eyes widened and she clucked her tongue. "Lucie, I can't believe you'd say that about one of ours. A Hopi girl, maybe but not another *Diné*." Netty leaned over, inspecting something on the quilt the pair was working on. "My dear, your row of stitches is as crooked as a rattlesnake's back."

Lucie seemed offended. "This coming from a Navajo who gets in trouble at school."

Netty stuck her hands on her ample hips. "Now you're sounding like Mrs. Green!"

Nick shook his head. "Hoo boy."

Lucie cocked her head to one side. "You hear about the Wicked Witch of the Indian School?" She puckered her lips as

85

if she'd bit down on a lemon and mimicked Mrs. Green. "We
don't have all day."

Netty set her jaw. "That's not what got me riled and you
know it." She stared down her sister.

But Lucie wasn't put off. "Who was the first Navajo ever
to get put on latrine duty?" She clipped at a stray thread with
such ferocity, Nick blinked.

Netty turned her back, was silent a few moments. Lucie
glanced at Nick as if to say, *oh now I've gone and hurt her feelings.*
Musty air hung heavy in the crowded shop.

Netty twisted around. "This is about pride. Our pride,
Navajo pride." She heaved a breath. "The Green woman said we
couldn't sing our own songs to pass the time in that miserable
hot kitchen." Her words grew thick as she ran her hand across
the framed quilt top. "I had to speak up." She drilled Lucie
with a stare. "And so should you."

Nick saw his opportunity. "Took a mighty big risk there.
But I'm glad you did." He ignored the drop of sweat inching
down his forehead. "I dropped by to tell you about someone I
met who needs a little help."

Lucie spoke through a mouth lined with straight pins. "Abe
already filled us in." Her fingers were a blur as she whipped
her needle in and out of the fabric stretched taut in the frame.
"Netty here says she got all the students singing hymns." She
shook her head. "Hymns!"

"Now Lucie. Frankie was only trying to get Mrs. Green off
my back." Netty went around to the opposite side of the frame
and pulled up a chair. She fitted a thimble on her finger and
picked up her needle and thread. "But what we need to know
is, is she any good at quilting?"

Nick was amazed at how quickly Netty's stitches traced a
line around the shapes on the quilt face. Frankie was at least
this good, he told himself. Had to be. "I haven't seen much of

her work yet." He paused, picturing her gentle fingers bringing his Lakota star quilt back to life. "But she's mending one for me."

"I don't know." Lucie clipped off a thread. "If her corners don't match . . ."

Netty chimed in. ". . . or her stitches go cockeyed . . ."

Lucie removed the last of the straight pins from her lips and smiled closed-mouthed at her friend. "Or she's Hopi!"

They both laughed.

Nick shook his head. "You two are merciless. She's Lakota. Like me, except I'm a half-breed."

Lucie rolled her eyes, spooled out a new length of thread. "Now Nick." She licked the thread's end and squinted as she aimed the thread at the eye of her needle. "Lover boy."

"Cut it out." Nick ducked his chin. "She's coming by first thing tomorrow."

Netty stopped sewing. "You been spending a lot of time getting to know Miss Frankie? After all, you're barely divorced." She shook her head but a smile tugged at the corners of her mouth. "I heard she's pretty as any Navajo Queen."

Nick had to get outside. These two were getting personal. Too personal. "We've met, yes."

Lucie stared him down. "You sweet on her?" Mercy. She was downright nosy.

His neck burned as heat crept up to his cheeks. He swallowed, took his leave. Until that moment, he hadn't known the answer.

"Do I look OK?" Frankie stood facing Harold. There wasn't a mirror in the house. If there had been, it probably would've cracked and given them seven years of bad luck.

Harold lay reading on his back on the sofa, his long legs dangling over the arm. He just grunted, and Frankie took it to mean she was presentable. But he wasn't happy.

"Ma." He put down his book. "I'm old enough to stay home. Honest. I won't go off. Promise."

Frankie closed her eyes. "We already went over this." She held half her ponytail in each hand, pulled to tighten it.

"But Ma . . ."

"Look." She wheeled around, searching for her sewing basket. "You can read anywhere. You're coming with me."

Harold struggled to his feet. "I'm almost eleven! Besides, sitting around with a bunch of old ladies—I'd rather be at school!" He stomped around the living room, gathering his books.

"Watch who you call old, my son. Didn't you keep some of those English workbooks? Bring them too."

"You expect me to sit there and diagram sentences? I'd rather die."

Frankie narrowed her eyes. "If you don't cut out the lip, you just might." She scooped up Nick's quilt along with the covered sewing basket filled with her prize scissors, the tape measure and a few quilting sharps. "Now get your stuff and let's go."

Frankie wouldn't mention walking to the shop had taken the better part of an hour. Or how Harold walked at least ten paces behind her the whole way.

"Morning, Frankie."

"Jeanette!" Frankie dipped her chin in greeting. As she'd suspected, it was her friend from the school.

"Call me Netty." Netty gestured at the other Navajo woman—an attractive woman in her twenties. "This is my cousin Lucie." Lucie nodded.

"How do." Frankie's hopes soared. Maybe working here wouldn't be so bad after all.

Lucie sniffed. "Netty says you can sing. But can you sew?"

Netty clucked. "She's not even got both her feet in the door and you start in."

Frankie stood straighter. "I'm here to work. Whether I can sew or not, well, I'll leave it to you to decide." She gestured. "This is my son, Harold. He's going to do some homework, if it's OK."

Netty nodded, circling her needle around a length of thread. She tugged on the knotted thread and clipped it short. "Heard your boy had a run-in with Mrs. Green, too, and walked out before she tossed you both out." She waved her scissors at Harold. "Smart kid. I like you."

Harold pushed his straight black bangs out of his eyes and said nothing, but Frankie noted his shy smile. Maybe Netty knew how to cut hair. Frankie would remember to ask.

As she and Harold stood in the tiny shop, Frankie let herself appreciate the work fixed to the frame—a small but beautiful quilt top decked with appliqués of lambs. Frankie brimmed with questions, but she already had at least one answer: she'd bring in the fan from home. It was like an oven in the cramped work space.

The walls were a gallery of their handiwork: small quilts in every color, pattern, and theme. Her heart sank—not one Lakota Star among them. Maybe she could change that. The two didn't say much more.

Netty and her cousin didn't tell Frankie what to do, either. They simply went back to their tasks, one on each side of the frame. Frankie glanced around, spotted a long table underneath the single dust-covered window. Fabrics, templates and a portable sewing machine—one of those fancy Singers with a motor added on—covered the work space.

She lifted off the boxy cover. Embossed gold curlicues decked out the shiny black metal body. Made her treadle model at home seem ordinary. She wasn't sure how to thread the machine correctly, but the Navajos looked intent on their work. She'd figure it out.

Frankie scooted two chairs over to the long table. She sat, opened her basket, got out her scissors, and draped her tape measure around her neck. Harold hung back. She motioned for him to sit, too. He plunked down and looked as if he were going to his own funeral. Maybe he *was* getting old enough to stay home alone.

After an hour of piecing straight seams, the thread had only broken once. The fancy motorized Singer ran like a dream. Arm resting on the chair back, she turned to where the two women sat hunched over their stitching. "I gotta ask." Frankie smiled at Netty. "How long do you have latrine duty?"

Lucie shot her a fierce look, but Netty waved her off. "Are you kidding?" Netty looked triumphant. "The old cluck doesn't scare me. Soon as the business takes off, I'll be too busy for school." She mopped her forehead with her sleeve. "I'm thinking of quitting."

Harold's head popped up. "Me, too! See Ma? School don't do Indians no good."

Frankie made a face. "*Doesn't* do *any* good. And any education is better than nothing."

Lucie chimed in. "Pffft. I wouldn't set foot in any school run by Mrs. Green—especially if latrine duty's involved."

Netty glared.

Lucie pointed with her scissors. "Hey. I'm not the one who's thinking of dropping out."

Netty smiled as she held a yardstick to the quilt and muttered the measurement under her breath. She looked at Frankie. "You kept the girls singing after I got out of there?"

Lucie said, "Hymns! You got them to sing hymns!"

Frankie's cheeks grew warm. "Had to. Kept our spirits up. Didn't matter if it was a hymn or a nursery rhyme." She stood, stretched.

"White man songs!" Lucie clucked her tongue. "Gila's always trying to convert us, too."

Netty nodded. "At least Reverend Abe's got class. He's the one who helped setup our business. We quilt blankets and he helps us sell them."

"Five." Lucie pursed her lips and held up the fingers of one hand. "So far we've sold five. If it weren't for donations, we'd be in the hole right about now."

Frankie's stomach grumbled loudly. "What sort of donations?" She slapped her hand over her middle—they'd eaten exactly nothing for breakfast.

Netty smiled. "Oh stuff. Like that calico you've been working on."

Frankie longed to haul out Nick's Lakota Star, but she wouldn't mention it. Not yet.

Netty went on. "Abe's church has been generous—even if we aren't 'believers,' as Gila likes to say. Ha!"

Lucie glanced at a finished quilt. "Hope we do better at the Fair."

Suddenly dizzy, Frankie held on to the edge of the quilt frame. "Fair? I thought it was over." Her mouth was dry.

Lucie chuckled. "Not the state fair, the Navajo Fair. At Window Rock. Next week."

Netty said, "It's a big deal—tribes come from all over. Rodeo, livestock. A beauty pageant too." She smiled.

"Like a powwow?" Frankie's memory swelled as she recalled the *Inipi*, or Song of Isolation, the ceremony in which Lakota girls became women. "Do Lakota ever travel to the Navajo Fair?"

Netty's black eyes danced. "Don't tell me Nick hasn't invited you?"

"Netty!" Lucie stood up and adjusted the quilt's top, pulling it taut again. "Isn't that a little personal?"

Netty ignored her cousin and turned to Frankie. "Stick with us. We'll show you and your boy a good time, Navajo-style."

Harold grinned. He'd begged to go to the Arizona State Fair. Before he died, Hank would've spent his last dime to see his son get sick on cotton candy, but Frankie'd said no. Maybe she shouldn't be so practical. "I'll think about it."

"Well, think fast—we're leaving next Thursday."

Harold tugged on her sleeve. "Can we, Ma?"

Frankie couldn't look like a pushover—even if she was. "Maybe." Her stomach gurgled again, louder this time. Beads of sweat blossomed on her forehead.

Netty stood. "Getting on to lunchtime." She addressed Harold. "Hungry?"

"Starving!"

Frankie held her breath. If only it weren't true.

11

A headache was forming behind Nick's eyes. After his trip to Window Rock, the federal man, Mr. McCollum, called him in. Typical bureaucrat.

McCollum scratched his balding head. "I've tried to set up a tour three times. To show them the benefits of our plan." He scowled. "I'll never understand those Navajos." He puffed on a cigarette almost nonstop. The smell made Nick sick.

Blood thumped in his ears—he was so tired of explaining. "The Navajo—*Diné*—don't think of time the way whites do." He didn't add McCollum ought to know this by now. "With the Navajo Fair coming up, they're pretty busy." And they surely didn't want some starched shirt parading around, taking all the credit for making sheep profitable. Nick stood there nearly choking in the smoky blue haze.

But McCollum led Nick to where a large map of Arizona hung on the wall. McCollum stabbed at the Navajo reservation with his forefinger. "What's not to like? The government will allot forty acres to each family for farming, in exchange for smaller sheep herds." He paused, took stock of Nick's raised eyebrow and frown. "What?"

The tribal elders would flat-out reject it. Irritation swelled in Nick's chest. "Sheep are vital to their culture. Spinning, weaving, mutton—Navajo don't waste much." He shook his head. "Sure, they grow some vegetables and peaches. But giving up sheep is going to be a tough sell."

McCollum crossed back to his desk and leaned back in his creaking office chair. "That's *your* problem." He lit up a fresh cigarette and set it beside the last one in an ashtray filled with butts. "I'll expect you to have good news about this as soon as the fair is over."

By the time he escaped out the smoke-filled room, Nick was sorry he worked for the government at all.

He'd had it. He'd rather dig ditches. Men like McCollum were intent on *termination*—the ending of Indians' reliance on the U.S. Government. Those who didn't want to farm their forty acres would be forced to leave the Rez and join a relocation program, like the one Frankie's husband joined.

Nick stood outside the office and drew in a breath. Frankie. The woman crept into his thoughts more and more. Had she made the connection with Netty and her cousin? He hoped they wouldn't make it easy for Frankie to leave town.

He squinted into the high September sun. In the valley, it would be October before the days cooled. Was going back to Pine Ridge the answer for her and her young son? Was reservation life good for any Indian? Working for the BIA certainly wasn't doing him any favors. He strode across the parking lot, kicking at dirt clods in his way.

McCollum was blind. Did the feds really believe Indians would drop their entire lifestyle for the government's convenience? It was as pathetic as history: the forced marches, land grabs, and schools to assimilate Native peoples. Nick gritted his teeth. He had to find a better way to make a living than selling Indians down the river. He walked faster.

He climbed into the truck. He'd drive some back road as fast as he could, just blow off steam. But when he crammed the key into the ignition, his hands shook. They'd been shaking all morning. Why?

A vast empty spot opened inside him, a void he recognized. Without warning, he craved a drink in the worst way. Maybe he'd swing by a liquor store, get just one to calm his nerves. Just one.

Frankie couldn't believe how hot Phoenix was. Mornings still had a blast furnace feel to them, especially walking into the wind. She and Harold trekked to the shop every day, and every day Harold pleaded to stay home alone. His last effort included a threat to hitchhike to Pine Ridge. Frankie retorted he'd make a great lawyer—if he ever got back into school. Harold's hair hung past the tip of his nose now, but if she'd seen some of his dirty looks under that fringe, she might've stood him in a corner.

Truth was, she had no idea what she was doing at the Navajo workshop. After days of sewing, Frankie still wasn't sure Netty and Lucie could pay her, and they hadn't even brought up the subject. They each claimed the Fair would jump-start the business, but so far, quilt orders weren't flooding in.

Getting back to Pine Ridge depended on scraping up gas money. And even so, half the time the pickup refused to start. But Netty and Lucie fed them lunch every day and it kept them coming back. Fatback and beans, mostly, but one day they served thick sliced bacon with fry bread. She didn't ask how they came into such bounty, just kept her head down and her presser foot running.

Harold had already finished his last crop of library books and begged Frankie to spare him from the grammar workbook. After noon meal, their bellies all full, Harold peered through his bangs. "Ma." Harold's fingers traced the raised lettering on *The Robe*, the thickest book he'd ever finished. "The bookmobile comes today."

"So?"

Harold shifted in his chair. "So I'm dying of boredom. And my books are due."

Netty and Lucie kept their eyes on the quilt they were stitching, but Frankie was sure they were listening. "I've got another hour or two of work here."

"The bookmobile comes now."

"You can turn in your books next time."

Harold scraped back his chair. "Ma. I'm old enough to be home by myself."

Frankie's heart bumped. She wanted to say he was her baby, her only baby. "I'll let you know when you're old enough."

"It's only two hours. You said so." Harold's chin jutted out. He hugged his book but stood firm. "Mr. Ashley won't like it if my books are late."

She sighed, got up. She brushed away his bangs, gazed into his eyes. "Go straight home, OK? The only time you leave the house is to return those library books. You got it?" She made her voice sound stern, even as her heart split.

Harold beamed. "Thanks, Ma." He raced out of the shop, the door slamming behind him.

Frankie couldn't watch him go, but she listened, hard, and hoped she'd done right. The Singer's thread broke for a second time.

Nick sat in front of the liquor store, staring at the steering wheel. His hands still shook; his belly was a cauldron of anger and regret. He closed his eyes. The Navajo elders hadn't exactly warmed up to him and as soon as they rejected this farming scheme, McCollum would probably have him transferred to some other godforsaken place. He'd failed at marriage. Even Frankie and her son puzzled him now as much as the day he met them. Nick's throat burned, dry as his lips. Just one. He opened the cab's door and put one boot on the ground.

He drew in a breath. Was he really going to throw away almost ten years sober? Since arriving in Arizona, he hadn't even been to church much, unless Reverend Abe roped him into it. He gripped the door handle; thought he heard a whisper. *Pray.*

He whipped around. Only brilliant sunshine streamed into his eyes. More than mere brightness, the light seemed to reach down inside him. The One who had bought him now called to him, bearing a comfort he couldn't describe. A tear slipped from his eye as he begged for help. When he opened his eyes, the craving had ebbed. He was ravenous.

He'd hit a taco stand; buy a whole sack full of the greasiest, tastiest taquitos he could get. Then he'd stop by Netty's shop. As he pulled out into traffic, the truck's steering wheel was almost too hot to touch.

Nick eased the pickup around a corner near the Indian School. He slammed on the brakes. Just ahead, a kid lay sprawled on the ground, with several books strewn nearby. A pudgy boy stood over him, and a crowd of onlookers laughed and pointed. The boy on the ground looked a lot like Harold.

Nick threw the truck into park and cut the engine. He charged out and strode to where Harold still lay. "Break it up! Break it up!" The crowd shrank back, but the pudgy boy didn't move. Nick gave Harold a hand up. "What's going on here?"

"Nothing."

Nick wanted to shake Frankie's son. The boy's lip was bleeding, and a nasty scrape blazed across his forehead. Nick gestured at Harold's cuts. "Doesn't look like nothing. C'mon." He grabbed Harold's arm. "I'll take you home."

"Ow! Let go!" Harold's knees buckled but he didn't fall. He winced and held his forearm against his side.

Nick released Harold and took a step back. "You hurt bad, then?" He could see the Lakota in the boy taking over, eyes set hard and gray as a Pine Ridge winter. Was he faking it or really hurt? Nick wasn't sure.

Harold stuck out his chin. "Told you. It's nothing." He narrowed his eyes, raised his voice. "He's gonna get the snot kicked out of him, though. Wait and see."

Nick followed Harold's gaze and whipped around. The pudgy kid was edging away—and wasn't he the gas station owner's boy? Orval?

Nick started to say he'd take Frankie's boy to a doctor, get that arm checked out. But Harold flew past him, and tackled Orval from behind. Using his uninjured hand, Harold pummeled Orval's face until blood spattered. The crowd of mostly Indian students chanted, "Get him!" They cheered Harold on while the redheaded Orval begged him to let up.

Briefly, Nick got caught up in the moment, rooting for the Harold—until the school headmaster and the insufferable Mrs. Green split the school doors and marched toward the melee. Nick raced to get between the two boys and managed to hold them by their shirt collars.

Mrs. Green's shrill voice rose above the clamor. "Stop it! Stop it this instant!" She squeezed through the crowd. "This is unacceptable!" She stood a few feet from where Nick gripped the two boys. Her eyes widened. "Harold Chasing Bear." A sigh escaped her as she shook her head. "I might have known."

Harold glowered, cradling his right arm.

Orval felt around in his mouth. "My teeth! He knocked my tooth loose!" He spit into his palm. A thread of drool hung from his lip.

Mrs. Green conferred with the doddering old headmaster, who turned and went back into the school. She addressed Nick. "Let them go." She wagged a finger at the boys. "If you can't behave, I'll get the truant officer down here."

Nick gripped their shirts harder. Just in case.

Orval twisted as he mewled. "He started it!" The boy wiped his nose with his shirttail and stared at the spot of blood. "I'm bleeding. My nose is probably broke too." Dirt and tears stained his puffy cheeks, but he recovered enough to shoot nasty looks Harold's way. "You wait. My pop'll sue your mama."

Nick clamped down hard on the back of Orval's plump neck. "Don't get ahead of yourself, son."

Mrs. Green waved her arms at the loitering students. "Get going, now. We haven't got all day." When she seemed satisfied she'd dispersed the crowd, she set her hands on her hips.

In a barely audible voice, the woman spoke through clenched teeth. "Orval, I'm surprised at you." Orval hung his head. "Get on home and don't let me catch you fighting again. Hear?"

The instant Nick released his grip on the boy, Orval trotted away.

Mrs. Green used the same hissing whisper on Harold. "Now see here, you little thief." She narrowed her eyes to slits. "If I catch you on school property before your suspension's up, I'll see to it you're expelled. For good."

Still favoring his arm, Harold returned her stare.

Mrs. Green wasn't finished. "Mark my words." She turned to Nick. "You a friend of his mother?"

Nick's annoyance with the woman swelled toward irritation and flat-out disdain. He folded his arms. "Maybe."

Mrs. Green exhaled cigarette-tinged breath. "Perhaps you won't mind seeing the boy home safely?"

Nick smiled tight-lipped. "Of course." He kept a firm hand on Harold's nape and steered him toward the truck. "Get in." Today, Nick had managed to beat back his demons, but he wasn't as confident he could help Harold with his.

Harold leaned against the passenger side door as if he were a prisoner of war. Nick started the engine, shifted into gear. "All right, hotshot. What's the scoop?" Nick pulled into traffic. St. Joe's might not take a poor Indian kid. Nick steered the truck toward the county hospital. He glanced at Harold's arm. "You think it's broke?"

Harold shot him a look, but shrugged. "Doesn't matter." The boy faced the open window, as hot air whistled through it.

Nick downshifted, coasted to the road's shoulder, braked to a stop. What would he do if Harold were his own son? "Look." Nick rested his wrists on the top of the steering wheel and stared straight ahead. "Your mom's going to hit the ceiling."

Harold whipped around. "Don't tell her, OK?" His eyes widened. "C'mon."

Nick couldn't believe how stubborn the boy could be. "You want to tell me how you plan to keep a broken wing a secret?"

"It ain't broke."

"Really? Let me have a look." Nick reached for the injured forearm.

Harold pulled away.

Nick sat for a moment. Ten-year-old boys were harder to manage than Navajo sheep. "I won't hurt you. Just need to see how bad you're hurt."

"Like you care." Harold's gaze hardened. "Leave me alone." He gripped the truck's door handle. "Leave us both alone." He opened the door, but aided by the wind, it swung back and thudded against him. He doubled over, his face creased in pain.

"Shut the door, son," Nick ordered, and ground into gear.

Harold glanced up, salty tears tracking down his proud cheeks. For once, he didn't argue, just clicked the door shut and stared out the windshield.

Nick eased out into traffic. He'd heard Abe talk about an old country doc who'd still take a case in exchange for barter, somewhere out near Apache Junction. Nick headed to the Temple of First Americans, hoping Abe knew if the doctor was still alive, praying Harold's arm wasn't as bad as it looked.

After tidying up her work area at the shop, Frankie walked home double-time. He'd better be right where she told him to be. Harold was ten, but if he wanted to see eleven, he'd better not disobey. Besides, he was her only child. The only thing she had.

Frankie shook her head. Many Lakota boys of his age had already gone through their first steps to manhood. When they got back to Pine Ridge, Frankie would see to it that Harold went through the ceremonies. But for now, he was living in the white man's world. A dangerous place.

Frankie stopped at the house's rickety gate. It moaned on its creaky hinges as she swung it open. Shadows engulfed the house, and no light was on inside. Had they cut off the power? She hurried to the door and burst inside. "Harold?"

She held her middle, peered into the darkness. A faint odor of cooked beans hung in the air. Where was he? "Harold!" She jerked the table lamp's string. A yellow glare threw her shadow onto the wall. Come straight home, she'd told him. Her stomach caved in on itself as panic jumped into her throat. She should've heeded the warning, the odd feeling she'd had. *Straight home, you hear?* A million awful thoughts swirled in her mind. Frankie sank onto the sofa and put her head in her hands.

12

Frankie knew it was late. She sat on the sofa with her feet curled under her, peering into the dark—she could see outside better then—and tried to think of what to do. Should she wait here, hoping he was out goofing around? Or should she go for help? She rocked gently, her arms hugging her sides.

She called on Grandmother for wisdom, murmuring Lakota songs in a shaky voice. She held the Lakota Star quilt she was making for her boy, pressed its cool softness against her cheeks. *A bed without a quilt*, she remembered. In the black sky, the moon hung orange and nearly full.

She had to stay calm. Harold was smart and brave. He was blessed among their people. He'd tiptoe through the door any minute now, armed with a bunch of flimsy excuses and a guilty look.

In her thoughts, Grandmother hovered, a tender expression on the old Lakota's aged and weathered face. Thinking of Grandmother comforted her, but tonight Frankie needed more than comfort. She clamped a hand over her mouth to trap the sobs that gathered in her throat.

She willed herself to stand. Sorry, Grandmother. Old women sat and waited. She had to act.

She grabbed her coin purse and a sweater—it was hot during the day, but the desert air could get chilly at night. Where to start? She hustled out to the road, wrapping her sweater around her, taking long strides. She begged Grandmother to guide her steps.

The gas station was closed, of course. The harsh blue haze of fluorescent lights above the pumps felt cold, unwelcoming. Still, she was grateful for the pay phone that stood at the end of the asphalt near the road.

It wasn't really a phone booth. More of a platform with a coin-operated telephone and a phone book hung from a thick cord. She stared at the black telephone. Should she call the police? Netty? Nick? Her fingers refused to stop shaking as she dug in her coin purse.

Only pennies winked back at her from the zippered pouch. She closed her eyes and dialed "O" for Operator.

Words stuck in Frankie's throat as she requested the sheriff's office. "I need to report a missing child." She managed to tell the dispatcher. "Harold Chasing Bear. He's ten."

The female voice on the line asked for a description. When Frankie obliged, she could've sworn that the voice tsked. "What tribe, ma'am? Maricopa? Pima?"

Did she sound like a ma'am? "Lakota," Frankie said, lifting her chin in the dim light. "My son is Oglala Lakota Sioux."

Nick's neck ached, his eyes were tired, and if they hadn't grabbed taquitos on the way here, he'd be starving too. Tracking down Abe and then getting out to Apache Junction had taken the better part of the evening. The doctor pronounced Harold's arm sprained but not broken, and fitted him with an ace bandage and a cloth sling. Nick relaxed. He had to promise the doc some choice lamb chops, but that was easy. He'd pick them up at the Navajo Fair next week.

Now it was late and Harold hadn't said thank you—in fact, he hadn't said two words. The kid just held onto the sling as if it were made of glass and stared out at the night desert. Nick's eyes stung as he drove the narrow two-lane road back to Phoenix.

Nick tried again to get the boy to open up. "You've taken a lot of grief from that kid, haven't you?"

Harold stared at the floor mats through his overgrown bangs.

"When I was about your age, there was this bully kid—we all called him Moose. He hated everybody." Nick glanced sideways, smiled. Harold had raised his head. Nick continued. "Moose hated me most of all. He was bigger than any fifthgrader you ever saw, and every day he'd wait for me." Nick whistled softly. "And every day I'd get beat up."

Harold's mouth opened slightly. "He jumped you for no reason? What did you do?"

Nick was glad the cab was dark—Harold couldn't see the mischief in his eyes. "There was this girl, Yolanda—tallest Indian girl you ever did see." Well, almost true.

"Like Ma's friend Lucie?"

"Taller. See Yolanda kind of liked me. One day after school, old Moose was giving it to me good and here comes Yolanda. She's got her two best friends with her and they all pile on Moose. I got away and Moose never bothered me again."

"Orval's not giving up." Harold made a face. "Besides, I don't got a girlfriend."

"How come you let Orval get to you?"

A shrug. After several moments, Harold said, "He calls me names. Calls Ma names, too. Guess I just go crazy."

105

"You're a good kid—your mom knows it. But listen." Nick turned onto the road leading to Frankie's house. "If you're going to fight, you gotta learn to fight smarter."

"What's that supposed to mean?" Harold sounded like he didn't trust anything.

"I could've saved myself a whole lotta grief if I'd learned what's worth fighting for."

Harold made a fist. "Yeah. And I know just who I'd like to learn on."

"You going to go through life pulverizing everybody who gets in your way?" Nick blew out his breath. "Great plan."

"Can I help it if people hate Indians?"

Nick had lived that life, too, he wanted to say. He'd nursed more than one busted lip defending his heritage, and it had never changed a thing. He nodded. How could he tell this boy he'd had to rein in his temper? And finding God made all the difference? "Sounds nuts, I know. But somehow you gotta be the better man."

Harold shrugged. "My daddy never backed down."

"And did it help?"

Harold's chin trembled.

Nick felt bad. "Sorry, I didn't mean . . ."

"Forget it."

The gas station sign came into view as Nick turned off the main road. Had he ever been this rebellious? If Harold was his son, he'd share his faith—and maybe teach him to throw a decent right hook.

Harold groaned and slid down on the truck's seat. "Great."

"What?"

"Look." He pointed.

Nick hit the brakes, swerved into the gas station lot. Next to the pay phone stood a slender woman with long dark hair.

When the truck's doors opened, Frankie ran to her son and hugged him hard. He yowled. Her voice got higher as she examined the scrape on his forehead, the sling. "Your arm! What happened to your arm?" Tears cascaded down her face, but she didn't care. "What happened?" She glanced back and forth between Harold and Nick. Both looked like they'd been caught playing with matches.

Nick cleared his throat. "You want to explain?"

Harold shook his head.

Frankie raised his chin so that he had to make eye contact. "You scared me to death, baby. Is your arm broken? Who did this?"

"It's not broken." Harold scuffed at the gravel. "Can't we talk about it later?"

"No." She shot a look at Nick. "All right, you two. You've kept me up half the night, worried sick. Spill the beans. Now."

Nick scratched at his chin and exchanged glances with Harold. She braced herself.

Tires squealed into the gas station. A sheriff's patrol car, followed by a second car, braked to a stop next to Nick's truck. As the deputy got out of the patrol car and ambled over, Frankie's heart thumped. Stu strode up.

Stu looked like a bull that's seen red. "What's this all about?" His crew cut, waxed shiny and stiff, glinted under the sheriff's flashlight. Stu stopped in his tracks. "I mighta knowed." He shook his head. "You're some kind of troublemaker."

Harold stood tall. "Your fat kid started it!"

"That right? I heard different." He addressed the sheriff but made sure Frankie heard every word. "This injun kid beat the tar outta my boy. Nearly knocked out Orval's teeth. I'll be sending his mama the dentist bill." He paused, scowled. "Or I'll be seeing her in court."

Harold lunged toward Stu. "You let my ma alone!"

Nick stepped between them. "Calm down, son." He edged Harold away from Stu. Frankie held onto her son's good arm. Tight.

Pausing every few moments to glance sideways at Frankie, Nick defended her boy. "Now Deputy. It was a just a little dust-up. Boys will be boys, right?"

Even she could see Nick's smile was too broad to be sincere. *Boys will be boys?* How could he sell out his people? Frankie's mouth got a stale taste.

The deputy considered Nick's story, nodding at the "boys will be boys" line. Frankie wanted to get up in Nick's face and scream, "No!" This was about their heritage. This was about who they were.

The deputy chuckled. "Now you boys keep it clean, OK? No blows below the belt."

Stu pounced on the deputy's remark. "Are you kidding? Indians fight dirty!" He gestured with his arms. "They'll scalp you for every cent you got!" Stu jabbed his forefinger in Frankie's direction. "Your heathen kid started the whole thing." Stu stared at her like a riled-up rattlesnake. "My Orval swears it's the truth." He licked his lips.

Frankie suddenly understood the saying, *if looks could kill.* She'd never really hated anyone before, but with Stu, she came mighty close. Still trembling from cool air and fears subsiding, she faced him. "You don't care about the truth." Her voice took on a strength she didn't recognize. "You've already made up your mind."

"I'm just telling it like I see it." Stu spit out his words, a sneer on his lips. "Why don't you ask your BIA friend here for help? He's on your side." Stu crossed his arms.

Frankie was too upset to even look at Nick. A little dust-up? She blew out a breath and turned away. He'd just proven he was Lakota in name only.

The sheriff's deputy snapped his pocket notebook shut. "Folks, it's too late to stand out here jawing. Stu, if you're set on it, you can go down and put in a complaint." He shined his flashlight on his watch. "In the morning." He seemed to stifle a yawn. "Things make more sense in the light of day."

Frankie turned to Nick. "I'll pay you back for the doctoring. It was kind of you to tend to him."

Nick opened his mouth as if to speak, but Frankie was in no mood for conversation.

"C'mon." She touched Harold's shoulder. "Let's go." She started toward home, long angry strides matching her mood. *Boys will be boys?* Maybe she had no use for a man, either.

They walked so fast her eyes watered in the chill night air. Or was she just too tired to staunch her tears? If she had to make an assessment, she'd have to say she was embarrassed, relieved, and yes, furious. Every time Harold slowed down, she prodded the small of his back.

Harold kicked up dust along the dirt shoulder. Any other time, Frankie would've reminded him to pick up his feet, but she worried if she once said a word, there would be no stopping the flood of scolding inside her. All the way to their place, the only sounds were the slapping of their shoes and the heavy breaths of exertion.

They came to the sagging little gate. As Frankie fumbled with the latch, Harold touched her arm. "I didn't start it, Ma. I swear."

Frankie pushed open the creaking gate and looked back. "But you didn't stop it either. And that's what worries me."

———∞———

After Stu and the sheriff left, Nick sat in his truck under a carpet of stars. He'd done everything he could for the boy. Yet discomfort gnawed at him. She was upset all right, but why? He peered into the rearview mirror, hoping to spot Harold and his mother. Should he follow them? He prayed for direction.

When he opened his eyes, all he saw was empty road stretched over the horizon and the red star sign holding up the sky. He and Carolyn had split in large part over Indian traditions. He wanted to embrace his heritage; she'd had little use for anything except modern conveniences. He wanted to live as a proud Lakota man—minus the booze, and with God at his side. She'd laughed as if it was the funniest thing she'd ever heard.

All right, so it was unusual. He may have lost Carolyn, but he also managed to get off the bottle and find God. The hard part was ignoring the deep chasm of loneliness—his earlier cravings had been a wake-up call. He needed someone besides Monny and Honest Abe. He needed someone to share his life.

He stared up into the sky, looking for a sign.

Frankie Chasing Bear lifted Nick in a way no one ever had. Should he tell her how he felt? How could she decide on what she didn't know? He started the truck and gunned it down the road.

———∞———

He caught up to them as they were going into the house. He left the cab's door standing open and sprinted to Frankie's front stoop. He wasn't sure why he was in such a hurry—only that he had to hurry. "Frankie." He stopped to catch his breath.

"Nick. It's late." She wouldn't look at him. From the living room, Harold peeked around her from the sofa.

"I know, I know. Back at the gas station you seemed upset." He held out his palms. "Whatever I did, I'm sorry."

She heaved a sigh. "Listen, whatever I owe the doctor, just have him send the bill."

Nick took a step closer. "You don't owe anything."

Her hand hovered in front of her mouth. "Doctors aren't cheap. I'll pay—I just need a little time."

"I took care of it. The doc accepts lamb chops as payment."

Frankie briefly closed her eyes. "Kind of you, but I can't be beholden. To you. To anybody."

Her answer couldn't be the sign he'd asked for. Nick refused to believe that. But something was wrong. "I can explain."

"No." Frankie stood like a fencepost, arms at her sides. She glanced back at Harold, then turned to Nick and spoke in a low, hard voice. "We should talk about this later."

Nick stuffed his hurt deeper. "Tell me what's wrong. I want to know." He didn't care if it was four in the morning. He wasn't giving up.

"All right then, Mr. Boys Will Be Boys." She drew a breath and pointed to his belt buckle. "You wear that agate buckle like a proud Lakota. But when everything you are, everything you claim to be is on the line, suddenly you're best pals with white men who'd just as soon see all of us go away."

He took his opportunity. "Stu can be a real scorpion when it comes to people who cross him. Likes to make us miserable whenever he gets a chance. I was trying to protect you and Harold—that's all."

"By laughing it off? You're a half-breed. You can be white whenever you need to be."

"Not fair." He'd only meant to cajole Stu and the law into leaving Frankie alone.

"Life's not fair, in case you haven't noticed." Frankie wasn't backing down, either. "Especially to Indians."

"I'm sorry. I didn't mean to come off as the enemy." *I really like you*, he wanted to say. Needed her around. His hands suddenly felt too large. He stuffed them into his pockets.

Frankie's eyes glassed over with tears. She dabbed at them with the back of her hand. "My son gets hurt and you act like it's no big deal." She shooed Harold. "Go to bed." When he hesitated, she barked. "Now!" When the boy had scampered out of sight, Frankie turned back to Nick. "To me it's a big deal. Stu's kid knows he can beat the snot out of an Indian kid and all people will say is, 'Boys will be boys.'"

Her eyes sparked in such a way it made Nick determined to smooth things over. "You're sore at me, and I guess I'm as dense as petrified wood. But I didn't mean to make you mad. Honest." He took a shaky breath. "In fact, I've been meaning to ask you something."

"OK, but make it quick, would you?" She put her hand over her mouth, this time as if she needed to yawn. "I could sleep standing up."

In the doorway, Frankie stood backlit by the yellow glow of lamplight. He was shaking, but more attracted than ever. "The Navajo Fair's next week, up in Window Rock." He swallowed. "Will you and Harold come with me?"

Frankie stared at him like he really didn't get it.

"Please?"

She closed her eyes for a moment, shook her head. "Thanks for the invitation. Really. But I've already made plans. Night, now." She closed the door softly.

He stood there, running a trembling hand through his hair. So much for signs.

13

Frankie overslept, and who could blame her? She quickly dressed and roused Harold, still asleep on the sofa where he'd spent the night. "We're late," she said, careful not to shake his injured arm. "Come on."

Harold's eyelids fluttered. He groaned softly and turned over.

"If you don't hurry, Netty and Lucie will leave without us." Frankie brushed tangles out of her hair and pulled it into a ponytail. "They promised to feed us breakfast."

Harold's eyes popped open. He sat up, blinked. "Breakfast?"

Frankie smiled. "You heard me. Ten minutes. Then we're out the door." She watched her son trudge off down the hall. His shoulders were broader this morning, she was sure of it.

She sat down to wait for him. Harold's Lakota Star quilt top called to her from the card table, and she idly picked up two of the last remaining pieces of the center star. She and the star were supposed to keep Harold safe. So far, she hadn't been able to keep the boy out of trouble. She matched the sides of the star pieces, pinned them together, straight and true. The kind of life she wished for her son.

And what about Nick? Was he Lakota or white? She was still miffed at the casual way he seemed to float in and out of both worlds. Why wouldn't he stand up for his people? Or at least the other two Lakota he happened to know? She couldn't abide a hypocrite.

She sighed, long and loud, releasing all expectations. Would Grandmother remind her to be more understanding? A little less critical, a lot more forgiving?

She didn't feel forgiving. She tossed down the quilt pieces, and her fingertip brushed the business end of a straight pin. A dot of bright blood sprang up. When Harold came back down the hall, she was sucking on her finger, mentally grinding her axe.

Frankie hadn't counted on traveling from Holbrook to Window Rock by horse and wagon. Netty hadn't mentioned it. There was talk of building a government road, she said, but for now, it was a rough ride. And a long one.

When they finally arrived at the fairgrounds, Frankie was tired and her backside ached. She climbed down gingerly from the wagon, but the vista spread out before her eyes energized her. Wind swept the clouds along in a washed-out sky, but the sun shone steady against distant mesas and rock spires.

She gazed out at the fairgrounds. She couldn't prevent herself from imagining Nick showing her and Harold around the exhibits. No. Somehow she had to get beyond her habit of picking messed-up men. She arched her back to stretch out the kinks and addressed Netty and Lucie. "Hope we sell a lot of quilts."

"Don't worry. We will." Netty, in a traditional Navajo tiered skirt paired with a scarlet sateen blouse, helped Lucie down from the wagon. "Tourists and Indians come from all over. Thousands show up for our fair."

Lucie pulled a stack of quilts from the wagon bed. "Netty's only sixteen, but she's a genius—the tribal symbols will get the Indians to buy. With any luck, the tourists will go nuts too."

Colorful displays showcased traditional Navajo rug weaving, the upright looms tended by women whose hands deftly worked shuttles across the vertical weft. Smells of barbecue and fry bread boosted Frankie's mood. Indians having a good time was exactly what her son needed to see. Harold had eaten nonstop on the way here, gorging on the peaches and baloney sandwiches Netty provided. With more energy than usual, he was excited and ready to explore.

"Ma!" Harold pointed toward a gaggle of Indian boys playing a ball game. "Think they'd let me play?"

"What about your arm?"

"It's only sprained—the doc said." Harold moved his arm around to prove it had healed. "C'mon. Please?"

Frankie handed him a grocery sack filled with quilts. "First, you help us get our stuff to the right building. Then you play."

He stood up straighter, eyeing the game. "I can catch a pass."

"If they say no," Netty said, "just tell them you're one of our cousins." She chuckled and gestured wide. "Welcome to Navajo country."

Lucie smiled at Harold. "And make sure they know you're *not* Hopi."

After three trips from the wagon to the exhibit building, Harold tugged on Frankie's arm. "Can I go play now?"

Lucie's eyes sparkled as she turned to Frankie. "He'll be all right out there. We'll see to it."

Frankie had to believe this place would be safe. "Think you can stay out of trouble today?" Harold nodded solemnly.

"You check in, mister Tough Guy." She didn't want to smother him, but put her hands on his shoulders. "I mean it." Harold trotted off.

For several minutes, Frankie tried to keep tabs on Harold while helping Netty set up their booth. He seemed to be having a great time—although she worried he'd bust an arm for real this time.

As the game progressed, it became harder to spot Harold, as he ran amongst the boys. She tried though, not taking her eyes off him. When she managed to spill a basket of threads, Netty stooped to help her pick them up.

"Relax, Momma," Netty said as they scooped multicolored spools back into the basket. "He'll be fine. Go take a look around—if you stop by the fry bread booth, get yourself an elephant ear—tell 'em I sent you." Netty set the thread spools on the booth table and began hanging sample quilts on a makeshift clothesline. "Go on now." She grinned, her short black hair sneaking out from under her scarf. "Have a little fun."

At first, she was reluctant to leave, but soon all the bustle lightened Frankie's mood. Window Rock hummed with activity: sheep and livestock judging, a rodeo, blanket, silver exhibits, and the Navajo Queen pageant. Frankie learned the women also held competitions for fry bread, spinning, weaving, and all manner of vegetable growing. At night, there'd be more pageantry and ceremonial dancing. Frankie had never seen so many tribes in one place. It was every bit as exciting as when all the different Sioux clans got together.

A stiff breeze, much cooler than the Valley's hot wind, pelted her face with dust. She turned her back to the blowing sand and grit and shielded her eyes. The spare, yet majestic land spread out before her.

On the horizon, strange rock formations gave the land an eerie quality, as if giants had played here. Netty had told her about how wind and water had carved the sandstone into mesas and canyons. Frankie couldn't ignore the connection she felt with the land.

As she'd done many times in Pine Ridge, she closed her eyes and listened. In the wind's mournful song, her ancestors urged her to be at peace with all things. Grandmother wept over those who had lost their lands and their lives.

Frankie bowed her head. There was, if she were honest, a void inside her, too, an empty place as big as the sky. She listened as Grandmother spoke through a passing gust: *It is not good for you to be alone.* Frankie's cheeks burned with the wind's chafing.

She opened her eyes and turned back to the fairgrounds. Seeing so many Native peoples in one place flooded her with pride. Here were many tribes, many traditions. Yet peace rippled across this place, echoed in hugs and laughter and claps on backs. She smiled and walked toward the crowds, scouting for Harold. He was here all right. She felt it.

She kept walking until she came to a traditional Navajo hogan, constructed especially for the fair and the tourists. Logs and adobe formed the low roofed living space of the round home. She ran her fingers along the rough exterior surface— the thick walls would keep the cold out far better than the mobile home she'd grown up in on the Pine Ridge reservation.

She followed the hogan around to its entrance and stopped. Not twenty feet away, Nick stood talking with a young woman Frankie didn't know. The Navajo woman was tall, thin, and traditionally dressed. More than nice-looking, too. She wore a bright yellow tiered skirt, dark velvet blouse and an ornate squash blossom necklace. Frankie's breath caught. The woman stood there and stroked Nick's cheek, smiled into his eyes—

and he didn't even try to back away. A wave of jealousy washed over Frankie. Then, the woman threw her arms around his neck and planted a long kiss on Nick's lips. Frankie could hardly believe it. Her heart turned to ice.

Nick walked with his head down. The day was blustery as northeastern Arizona nearly always was, and the air felt crisp—winter often came early to the high country. The first snow wouldn't be long.

His truck was a workhorse and had managed to get over the rutted wagon track up to the fairgrounds, but instead of Frankie and Harold, Nick had to settle for Monny and Abe accompanying him to Window Rock. Thankfully, his buddies had found another place to live, but he'd hoped to show Frankie and her son around the Navajo Fair. While Monny and Abe were hooting and hollering over at the Men's Fry Bread contest, Nick got trapped by Mama Brown.

"Nick." In her trademark velvet shirt, her black hair set in a low knot, Mama was her usual cordial and matchmaking self. "Good to see you again."

"Mama." Nick touched his hat's brim. He'd pay his respects and move along.

Too late. Mama's maiden daughter, Wanda, stepped out of the shadows. "Hey Nick."

He swallowed. It wasn't that Wanda was bad looking—far from it. In fact, a heavy silver squash blossom necklace set off her bronze complexion and her silver concho belt defined her slender hips. But she was as timid as a mouse and somehow, maybe because Mama pushed her, Wanda just wasn't his type. But it didn't stop her mother from trying to pair them off.

Mama seemed to nudge her daughter from the rear. "Wanda's dying to give you the royal tour." Mama smiled at her daughter. "Aren't you, honey?"

Wanda looked embarrassed. "I guess *tho*." Poor girl's lisp was worse than ever.

Mama smiled wide. "We've been working hard since you were here the last time—wait until you see what we've accomplished."

Nick demurred. "I'd love to accompany you beautiful ladies, but I've got to go check in with my boss. Maybe later?"

Mama crossed her arms. "Nonsense. Agent McCollum can wait." She beckoned. "Come this way."

"Well. If you insist."

Mama stood pat. "I do."

Nick glanced around but there was no one to rescue him. He glanced at his wristwatch. "Maybe we can take the short tour?" He'd rather clean out a sheep pen than get stuck with Mama and her matchmaking ways. "Technically I'm here on business."

Wanda gave him a coy look. "Nick, you work too much. You should have a little fun now and then."

Mama tugged Nick's arm. "Wanda's right. You need to loosen up."

Nick put on a brave smile as Mama Brown dragged him around to the different exhibits, but he felt like a sheep being led to slaughter.

In her deerskin moccasins, Wanda walked delicately across the grounds. "*Thay*," she said, her lisp more noticeable than ever. "I like your belt buckle. Agate?" She smiled shyly. "I like agate."

He looked up. "Yeah. Agate—Lakota." Couldn't he just step into a sinkhole and disappear? Nick's every step felt as if his boots were too small. He couldn't think of a single thing to say.

He jammed his hands in his pockets and put his head down against the wind.

After twenty minutes of traipsing the fairgrounds, Nick gathered his courage. He turned to Mama and asked, "Where we headed?" For all he knew, Wanda and her mother could be leading him to some kind of shotgun wedding. Was there something about him screaming *available*?

Mama stopped in front of the Big Hogan, the fair's central focal point, where a banner stretched, proclaiming both Traditional and Modern Navajo Queen competitions. She made a sweeping gesture. "See? Wanda's running for traditional queen." Mama waggled her fingers at them. "Have fun, you two." The older woman floated away, leaving Nick standing alone with Wanda.

She ducked her chin. "I want to show you something."

He tried not to look bored when they walked into the building. Photos of past queens lined the walls. In the looks department, Lakota girls could keep up with Navajo young women. Or any women. But Navajo queens had to be more, and excel at spinning, weaving and other traditional skills. Wanda was gorgeous, but wasn't known for any of these things. Why would she run for Queen?

Nick said he'd like to see the livestock exhibit, but Wanda linked her arm in his and pulled him over to a framed photo of herself. "Like my picture?"

Nick raised his eyebrows. "Real nice. I mean yes." He smiled. She really was pretty.

"There's something else." She pulled him toward the exit. Nick waved to several Navajo elders standing in a knot. Their knowing looks made his ears burn. Where were Monny and Abe when he needed them?

"Wanda? I've gotta get back to work." Nick couldn't think of a better excuse. But Wanda wouldn't let go of his arm as they threaded their way through the carnival-like atmosphere. He shoved down his hat so the wind couldn't snatch it. And, so folks wouldn't recognize him.

Wanda stopped next to an upright loom sitting beside an exhibition traditional hogan. A few yards away, an Indian man in a tall chef's hat poked a long pitchfork into a large metal pit, as mouth-watering smells of slow-cooked barbecued beef wafted by. Nick's stomach rumbled—come to think of it, he hoped lunch was soon, too.

He was about to say so, when Wanda stepped so close, her heavy squash blossom necklace bumped against his shirt front. She stared into his eyes and stroked his cheek with the back of her hand. He put his hand over hers, gently pulled it away. "Maybe we should get in line for lunch."

She laughed. "Silly." Wanda Brown pulled him in so quick he didn't have time to protest. She held the back of his neck and kissed his lips, hard and long.

Nick wrested out of Wanda's grip. He didn't want to anger Wanda's mother, but he wouldn't lead a girl on, either. His cheeks were hot and some of Wanda's red lipstick was probably on his face. "Wanda?" He used his sleeve for a handkerchief. "What was that for?"

"Mama says a ki*th* before the pageant brings good luck." Wanda suddenly turned shy. "It wasn't that bad was it?"

Nick swallowed, shook his head. "I just wasn't expecting you to . . ."

"Ki*th* you?" She stepped back and gazed at him as if he were the last man on earth.

He glanced around, desperate to distract her. Not three feet away, a partially woven Navajo rug stood on its upright loom. He pointed. "Say, what a handsome rug. You weave it?"

She went to the loom, ran her palm over the nubby woven surface. "I'm making it for you."

Nick examined the rug, adorned with patterns in yellow, deep brown and rose. "It's beautiful." He smiled at Wanda as thoughts of *why me?* rang through him. "I don't know what to say."

"How 'bout thank you?" Wanda grinned. "I should have it done pretty soon. Now let's go watch the sand paintings."

Sand paintings? Nick drew in a breath. "Listen. I appreciate everything—really—but I need to get to work."

Wanda stepped back, stared at the ground. Great. Now he'd hurt her feelings, and Mama Brown wouldn't be happy. But Wanda looked up, hope still in her eyes. "Just be sure I can see you in the crowd when they crown me Queen."

"It's a deal." He tipped his hat. "Good luck."

"Thanks. See you, Nick."

He made his strides long, ignoring the loneliness mocking him.

14

When Nick finally spotted her, Frankie and Harold stood holding plates in one of the lines for the barbecued beef. What had started as a single queue now tentacled out in several directions, and there had to be a hundred people between Frankie and where he stood. It was a hungry, yet cheerful crowd, and any other time Nick might've stopped to admire all the different ages, styles of dress, and tribal affiliations. Should he call out? He strained to keep Frankie in his sight.

He still hadn't located Monny or Abe, but then again the fair sprawled for acres. Nick had heard that the chefs cooked seven whole cows. Judging from the mob, they would need all of the meat in order to feed so many.

The line crept forward, but Nick was getting no closer. He waved, but when he tried to muscle his way to where Frankie was, Nick received too many cold stares to jump the line. It simply wasn't the Navajo way.

Two branches of the food line parted. Finally, Nick could still see Frankie ahead of him, but she didn't turn around. He briefly considered whistling or shouting to get her attention, and edged up next to one of the enormous metal pits where beef had simmered all day. A voice behind him sounded upset.

Nick turned. Martin Brown stood with his arms folded across his western-style shirt. Next to him was Agent McCollum, dressed in the kind of fancy Western suit coat tourists favored. Martin Brown stared at Nick, but tilted his head at the agent. "He claims you got something important to tell me."

Nick moistened his lips. "Mr. McCollum. I didn't know you were . . ."

"You didn't know what?" McCollum looked like he'd eaten something sour. "If I was going to show up at this shindig? I told you, we're moving ahead with this program." He brushed a shock of his thinning hair out of his eyes. "With or without your help."

Martin Brown shot Nick a hard look. "So whose side you on? Our side or the white man's way?"

"That's not important, Martin." Nick's stomach roiled, but he tried to look calm. "What's good for Navajos is good for all of us."

Martin stared off into the distance. McCollum's jaw worked side to side but he said nothing.

Nick glanced at a covered area filled with tables and chairs. "Why don't we sit over there and discuss this?" He hoped Frankie stayed long enough for him to find her.

Martin gave them both a *drop dead* look, but grunted.

Nick led the Navajo and McCollum to a table and bought the pair bottled beers and a soda pop for himself. If he wanted to keep his job, he'd better sound cheerful. "Martin. You interested in owning a farm? Say, forty acres?" McCollum took a drink as he eyed Nick.

Martin stared off into space. Finally, he looked up and focused on the federal agent. "You ever been up here before?"

"It's been a few years." McCollum shifted in his seat. "But yes. I've been here. I'm a soil expert, after all." He said this as if he were the King of Dirt.

Martin glanced sideways at Nick. "In winter? You ever come in winter? When snow's so deep it hides the wagon ruts? When it's so cold your breath freezes in midair?"

McCollum fidgeted with his jacket's lapel, then picked at a loose thread. "I don't see what this has to do with . . ."

"It has to do with truth. The land's truth." Martin leaned toward the agent. "The land will not do what it can't do. No man—white or Native—can change that."

Nick jumped in. "See? The Navajo know they aren't farmers. This land won't support farms. Some years the sheep barely make it." He swallowed, clenched his fists under the table, summoned his courage. "Farming won't work here, sir. Not the way you've outlined it." He hoped he'd convinced Martin he wasn't the enemy.

McCollum lit up a smoke. "I thought we were clear on this, Parker." He paused. "Your job isn't to sell the project. Your job is to inform these folks of what's going to happen." He stood and fastened the button on his jacket. "It's a done deal. Now if you'll excuse me, I have a tour to finish." He walked off, the blue haze of smoke following him.

Nick shook his head. As far as he was concerned, McCollum could go jump off a mesa.

Martin Brown twisted his bottle between his fingers. Finally he stood. "Forty acres, huh? Pssh. Where's he going to get the water to irrigate all this *farm*land?"

Nick held out his hands. "Beats me." Maybe he'd finally won the guy over.

But Martin snorted. "And they're sending a half-breed like you to teach us all to be farmers?" He laughed, and began to walk away.

Nick called after him. "I'm trying to help you, can't you see that?" Martin Brown was as stubborn a man as he'd ever met.

Martin stopped, turned, pointed. "When you figure out who you are, let me know." He disappeared into the crowd.

Nick stared through the brown glass of the bottles. He was thankful that so far, he had no urge to drain the last of the beer. But if he had, he'd be justified. McCollum could get him transferred or even fired. But Martin could make sure the elders wouldn't cooperate with this cockeyed farming plan. That much was clear.

He flicked a bottle cap across the table. What difference did it make? Indians had always been on the losing end of things—the government made sure of it. He gathered up the bottles to throw them away. Maybe he'd lose his job. He set his jaw. Maybe he didn't care.

───

Frankie wished she hadn't run into Nick at all. But Harold, carrying his plate of food, ran right up to the table where Nick sat. Alone.

"Hey!" Harold pulled out an empty chair and sat on it backward. "I got to play ball." Harold's bangs were wet with sweat. Frankie hung back, avoided Nick's inquiring gaze.

Nick scrutinized Harold's arm. "Thought you had a sprained wing." Was he avoiding her eyes as much as she was avoiding his?

Once again, her boy twisted and flexed his muscles.

. "OK, I get it." Nick laughed. "But you healed awful fast. You sure it's OK?"

Harold nodded, then dug into his plate of barbecued beef.

Nick looked as great as ever, the wind blowing his coppery hair across his dark eyes. "Can I get you something?" His smile was the same smile he'd given the Navajo woman she'd seen him with. Frankie's insides sparked, but she stifled the anger. Nick Parker wasn't worth getting all het up over. No man was.

Frankie stiffened her spine. Harold's father had never admitted as much, but she suspected he was a womanizer, too. She noted the bottles Nick clutched. The insides of her mouth turned sour. Hank had been a mean drunk. "No, thanks." She made her expression blank. Let him try to explain.

Nick didn't seem to grasp the fact that he was holding beer bottles, or what that meant to her. "I wasn't expecting to see you here." He stood, his agate belt buckle catching glints of sun.

Frankie fumbled for words. "I wasn't expecting to see you here, either." *With someone else.* She wrestled with jealousy; tried to quell it with nonchalance. But it shoved its way to the front of the line, green-eyed, making her care.

Nick raised the bottles briefly. "I was about to go throw these away. You sure I can't buy you a cold one?"

"Excuse me?" She took a breath, held it. "I don't drink." She gave him a look that said he should know that much.

"OK. Be right back." He started to walk away. "Oh!" He spun around, held up the beer bottles and grinned like the guy who finally got the joke. "I had to buy a round for this Navajo hothead and Agent McCollum. I'm only drinking soda pop. Cross my heart."

"I see." Frankie was stingy with her smile. The voice of reason poked up its head: He was no doubt just doing his job—he was a BIA agent after all. She tried to relax.

Harold gestured with his fork at Nick. "Can I have something to wash this down?"

"Sure thing," Nick said. "Wait here, partner." He went in the direction of a nearby stand.

Frankie sank down onto a folding chair. The day had taken a strange turn. Why couldn't she get past the image of Nick flirting with the Navajo girl? She had no claim on him. Plus, she'd turned down his invitation. She picked at her sandwich, wishing she knew what she wanted.

Harold forked a big bite of his meal and asked, "Ma? You sick? You look bad."

Frankie forced a smile. "Bad? If you tell a woman she looks bad, you're in trouble."

Harold's cheeks bulged with food. "Kinda like you don't feel so good. Or something." He turned, looked behind him. "I wish Nick would hurry up with those sodas."

Frankie tried to wipe the barbecue sauce from her son's face. "Don't talk with your mouth full."

Harold ducked. "Ma! I'm not a baby!"

She wouldn't say it. *Yes, you are my baby. Yes.* She rested against the chair back, marveling at her son. He was the one thing she knew for sure. A gust of wind whipped her hair into her eyes and made them water.

The back of Frankie's neck prickled. She felt eyes on her, and whipped around. Standing a ways off in the crowd, a Navajo man stared at her. She wasn't sure what to think, but his gaze made her feel awkward. Dirty in a crazy sort of way. She scooted her chair closer to Harold. When she looked again, the man was gone.

Moments later, Nick brought back three cold sodas. "RC, too. Your favorite, right?" He straddled a chair like Harold had done and rested his forearms across the top of the seat back.

Frankie's heart was still jumping around from the leering man's gaze. She cut sideways glances to be sure he hadn't come back.

Nick leaned forward in the chair. "You sure you're OK?"

She couldn't tell if Nick was talking to her or to Harold. But she accepted the cold sweaty bottle of pop. "Thanks."

Harold chattered enough for both of them. His plate cleaned, he stood. "Ma? The guys from the ball game asked me if I'd come back—OK?" He turned to Nick. "I'm the quarterback."

She forced a smile. "When they get on the loudspeaker about the Queen contest, come find me." It seemed pointless to keep Harold on such a short leash—she had to let him grow up a little.

Harold raced off. She arranged her hands in her lap and swallowed the last of her fear. Maybe she'd reminded the man of someone he knew. Nothing more. "So." She'd be polite to Nick—no sense getting worked up. "Having a good time?"

Nick blew out his breath. "Man, what a mess. The feds have put me between the Navajos and a hard spot. The government thinks it can solve all the problems by turning them into farmers. Farmers." He shook his head. "I tell you, I'm about ready to walk."

"It's hard to do what you love and still pay the bills." She mentally separated herself from Nick Parker. He wasn't hers to be jealous over in the first place.

"Amen to that." Nick flashed his million-dollar smile.

"What *would* you love to do?" Efforts to keep her distance collided with true interest.

He glanced away. "Build a school for Indian kids." Another grin, this time shy, boyish.

"That's pretty ambitious." Her insides pinged. He did have a great smile. She tried to stay cool, but her resolve leaked away like the tide pulling sand from under her feet. "Would you start a school out here or back in Pine Ridge?"

Nick shrugged. "Don't know. It's only a dream."

Frankie leaned in. "Does it have to be? I mean, Harold and I are going to get an education if it kills us." She pictured Lakota children during long hard Pine Ridge winters, children who had little to eat and less to look forward to. "You'd be doing your people a favor if you went back. Or are you afraid?"

"Afraid? Maybe." Nick tilted his head so the afternoon shadows crossed his face. "What about you? You got the guts to go back to Pine Ridge?"

Guts? Frankie hadn't seen that one coming. She took a breath. "Harold's bound and determined. After the flap about stolen goods and the Indian school, I went along with it." She looked away. "For Harold's sake."

Nick's voice was soft and low. "What about you? What does Frankie want?" His gaze probed.

She swallowed. She wished she could tell Nick a lot of things. "Oh, you know." She manufactured a weak smile. "You have kids, you put your dreams on hold."

Nick's mouth pressed into a thin line. "You don't know how lucky you are—to have a son I mean." He clasped his hands.

"Parenthood's not easy, here or on the Rez." She thought of the hard work of raising a son alone, the loneliness of an empty bed. Her mother had cried alone at night while Frankie's father drank his life away. Tears stabbed at the corners of her eyes.

Nick said, "Even worse when your old man's a boozer."

Had he read her mind? She pretended to be interested in the scenery, crossing and uncrossing her ankles.

"Frankie." Nick cleared his throat. "Did I say something wrong?" He held up his palms. "I went dry nearly ten years ago—honest."

"It's OK, really." Except it wasn't. She gathered her hair into a low ponytail, twisted it into a chignon. She fastened it with a couple of bobby pins.

Nick's eyebrows bunched together. "If I've done something . . ." Her will softened, while little chinks of forgiveness chipped away at her resolve.

"Frankie!"

They turned in unison. Waving a sheaf of papers, Netty wore an ear-to-ear grin as she marched up to the table. "Look! More quilt orders than you can shake a stick at!"

Lucie followed, with Monny, their arms linked. "What did I tell you?" Lucie said. "Who says Navajo women only weave rugs?" Even Reverend Abe was smiling.

They pulled over more chairs. Monny scooted himself close to the table and barely caught Harold's soda before it tipped. "I got three Navajos and one Paiute coming to church next time they come to Phoenix." He crossed his arms and beamed at Lucie beside him.

Frankie groaned inside. Not another sermon by Nick's nutty friend.

Abe shot a look at Monny, who proceeded to look wounded.

Netty took charge. "With all this business, we'll need at least one more sewing machine." She slapped down the papers like a winning hand of cards.

The news buoyed Frankie's spirits. "Are more of the orders coming from the tribes or the tourists?"

"Tourists!" Lucie pointed to the orders. "Plus, they'll pay top dollar."

Netty's cropped black hair poked out of the scarf she'd tied under her chin. She nodded at Nick. "Just like we talked about. The tourists will bring in enough to where we can start sewing blankets for the Indian School." She shuddered. "Those dorms get plenty cold at night."

Frankie remembered Pine Ridge winters, many spent in thin-walled trailers without electricity.

Nick pushed his hat back. "I knew you'd make a great team. Can you get another machine?"

Frankie's insides pinged. "Isn't the one in the shop the same model the school uses?" She remembered Mrs. Green's accusations. Was the Singer in Netty's shop stolen? Who would pinch a machine from a school and then let Harold stand accused? Her throat tightened.

Netty's eyebrows bunched. "Frankie? You all right?"

She stared away. "Just that we're using the same model Mrs. Green says someone took from the school—she suspended Harold over it." The whole incident still upset Frankie.

Netty looked confused, then shook her head. "It couldn't be hot. Schools are always selling off their old equipment." She turned to Lucie. "Right?"

Lucie nodded.

Netty and Lucie exchanged worried glances before Lucie trained an indignant gaze on Frankie. "That machine was donated."

Frankie held up her hands. "I believe you." She craned her neck. Good. Harold was still out on the field. "When it comes to my boy, I'm a mama grizzly."

Netty patted her arm. "'Course you are." She shrugged. "A lot of sewing machines look alike. And Singers are the most reliable, hands down."

Lucie said, "That's why I said, we need to hold out for another Singer. Model 99k, used or new."

Monny's face lit up. "Singer? That's the best one?"

Lucie smiled. "And for us, only the best!" She elbowed her cousin. "Right, Netty?"

Netty frowned. "Quality counts. But those machines don't come cheap."

Lucie said, "We'll hand-quilt everything if we have to."

Frankie looked up. "I could bring in my grandmother's treadle. Would that help?"

Lucie made eyes at Monny and then patted Frankie's arm. "Don't worry, Frankie. We'll get a machine somehow."

Monny smiled. "Somehow."

Frankie stared at the ground. A gust of chill wind added to her tension. She pulled her sweater tighter.

Nick downed his soda. "If I got half as lucky as you ladies, I'd be happy as a diamondback in the sun." He leaned in toward Netty and her cousin. "Don't say anything, but Martin Brown and the elders aren't exactly making this trip easy for me."

Lucie grimaced. "We heard. Navajo farmers? What a joke."

Netty picked up the orders and straightened them. "You can take the Indian from the land, but you can't take the land out of the Indian."

Frankie was about to add her two cents, when the public address system crackled and sang with feedback. "All contestants for Traditional and Modern Queen please report to the Big Hogan."

Lucie stood. "Keep your fingers crossed."

Several young Navajo women filed past. One especially beautiful girl, wearing a heavy squash blossom necklace, patted the small of Nick's back and winked as she floated by. Frankie pretended not to notice as her heart dropped to her feet.

Monny, a dreamy look on his face, squeezed Lucie's arm. He stood up straighter, until he almost matched Lucie's height. "I'm praying you win," he said.

Lucie's cheeks colored. "Thanks."

Netty clucked her tongue. "Let's go, Lucie." The three ambled off toward the Big Hogan.

When they were gone, Nick stood too. "Listen." He rubbed his chin. "Don't ask me how I know, but there's something eating you. I feel it. Whatever it is, I'm sorry." He walked away, shoulders hunched.

Frankie sat for a moment. She could forget what she'd seen, but she'd be lying to herself. And hadn't she taught Harold not to lie?

15

Frankie needed to round up Harold. The sun had dipped behind the mesas, casting long shadows against the exhibition tents and buildings. At the edge of the grounds, a cluster of tents stood pitched for travelers staying the night.

In Pine Ridge, winter's fingers penetrated the thin-as-paper walls of most Lakota homes. As a child, she'd often slept on the floor, and in the morning, her bones were so cold they'd ache all day, like a bad tooth. Was life here any better?

She found her son still on the field with his new friends. Harold didn't come without protesting, but this time she wasn't budging. Yes, they were among their people. But there were enough strangers to make a hen want to keep her chick close by. Not to mention the unidentified Navajo she'd caught staring.

Harold stomped along behind her, letting the whole world know how unfair his mother could be. "Ma!" He shouted. "I'm not a baby!" She shook her head until she was dizzy, but she didn't give in. Wouldn't Grandmother be proud?

At the doorway of the Big Hogan, the pair stood at the fringe of the crowd. Everyone's attention was on the Navajo

Queen contestants as each delivered a brief address. Harold stood beside Frankie, head down, pouting to beat the band. "All the other kids are still out there." He pointed to the field. "Please?"

"Sorry, kiddo," she said. "You're stuck with me."

Harold let loose an exaggerated groan, and then kicked at the ground with his sneaker toe. "I didn't even bring a book." He crossed his arms dramatically.

"Simmer down. They're about to start." Frankie wrapped her arms around herself. The air inside the Big Hogan was as chilly as the wind outside.

"Ma. It's a beauty contest. For girls." He peered through his bangs. "C'mon."

"And what happened the last time you sweet-talked me?" She couldn't let him get beat up a second time.

"I'm playing ball with the same guys." Harold put on a pleading look and pointed to the double doors at the back. "I won't run off. Cross my heart."

"On your honor?"

"Promise." His smile could melt a glacier.

Her will weakened, then evaporated. "If I look and don't find you . . ." In her mind, Grandmother sighed.

"Thanks, Ma." He raced off.

Frankie hoped she'd done right.

———

Nick caught himself gritting his teeth again. The fair was turning out to be a can of worms. First Wanda, then McCollum, and Martin—Nick itched to get back to Phoenix. "As soon as they crown the Queens," he told Monny and Abe, "we're out of here." Abe just nodded.

Monny grimaced. "Can't we stay until I work up the nerve to ask her out?" Any fool could see he was sweet on Lucie.

"Look, you've had all day to play Romeo." Nick hooked his thumbs into his jeans' pockets. "McCollum and Martin Brown are at each other's throats and they're putting the pressure on me. I need time to think." He paced a little. They'd skip both queen pageants, get back to the Valley. Even if it meant seeing less of Frankie.

Monny sighed. "C'mon Abe, I want to be in the front row where she can see me." They threaded their way close to the stage.

In the Big Hogan's shadows, Nick leaned against the outer wall where he hoped Wanda wouldn't spot him. What a joke—Monny was starved for Lucie's attention, and Nick couldn't shake Wanda. McCollum just gave him a headache. And Frankie? She was a mystery, pure and simple.

The emcee announced the first Modern Queen contestant, a girl whose voice was so soft it reminded him of a cat's purr. He couldn't understand a word, but she was lovely in a muted rose outfit and deerskin mocs. One after another, contestants paraded for the crowd and spoke of their qualifications. Although each had only three minutes to make her case, Nick could have drifted off—he was tired, mentally and physically.

The Big Hogan erupted with whistles and calls. Lucie, the final contestant for Modern Queen, stood at the microphone. "This is an exciting time to be a Navajo," she said. Her curves accentuated her trim figure as she stood straight and tall. "For the first time, women can make life better for our people."

She beamed as the people whooped and hollered—Monny, no doubt leading that charge. Lucie spoke about the "modern Navajo" and what it meant for the tribe.

But before Lucie's three minutes were up, Mama Brown paraded Wanda to the mic.

Lucie looked momentarily stunned, but wrapped up her presentation, said, "Thank you," and walked off stage. A few folks booed.

Nick shrank back as far as he could. Under the lights, Wanda's squash blossom necklace winked in the light as she talked about her weaving skills.

Cheering for Wanda would be easier if she didn't hound him. And kissing him in public—the nerve. Even now, she seemed to be staring straight at him. She crooned, "A Traditional Navajo Queen knows what it's like to stand in two worlds."

No matter she wasn't his type—her words cut too close to home for his liking. If only Martin and the elders saw things as clearly. His blood pressure had to be too high. He sifted through the gathering, hoping to spot Frankie in the audience.

Harold rushed past him and ran outside.

Nick yelled after him. "Hey! Where you off to?"

Harold called over his shoulder. "The team needs me!"

Nick scanned the crowd with more urgency. Did Frankie know Harold was running loose again? Nick made his way through rows of Navajo women in their long skirts and head scarves, men in blue jeans and straw cowboy hats. Where was Frankie? And why couldn't he stop thinking about her?

Aside from Lucie, Frankie knew none of the girls vying for Queen. Nick's girlfriend Wanda was at the microphone, going on and on. Go weave a rug, she wanted to yell. She fidgeted in her seat—wishing she could escape out into the fresh air, walk off the weariness behind her eyes. She checked behind her. Good. No trace of the guy who'd stared at her. She relaxed her shoulders and pulled in a few deep breaths. What a worrywart. She wasn't in Pine Ridge, fending off Hank's rowdy friends.

She wouldn't get too comfortable, though. No matter how grown-up Harold was, she should check on him for peace of mind.

Frankie slipped to the side of the audience and edged along the wall of the cavernous round room. Her breath caught.

In the deep shadows, a Navajo man stood with one boot propped against the wall, blocking her path. The same scar-faced man who'd ogled her earlier. He held a bottle and reeked of beer.

She couldn't show even a hint of fear. "Excuse me." She avoided eye contact.

"There you are, beautiful." The man grinned knowingly. "Been looking all over for you." He gestured with his bottle. "Now aren't you just the finest-looking squaw." His hooded, staring eyes gave Frankie goose bumps. "What's your name, honey?"

She glanced about for a way to escape. Before she could act, he grabbed her arm and pulled her close. His words slurred. "What's your hurry?" The man's breath brought back awful memories of Hank stumbling in drunk.

She twisted away, glared. "Let me be." If Grandmother had taught her anything, it was to stand up for herself.

But the man jumped in front of her, his outstretched arm blocking her exit. "What did you say your name was, honey?" Still gripping the bottle, he stroked her cheek with the backs of his fingers. "Mmm, mmm. My, my."

She pulled away. "I said, let me go." Her heart thumped against her ribs.

"Sure, let's go." Again he held her arm, squeezed too hard.

She tried flattery. "Your girlfriend won't like you flirting." She smiled, batted her eyelashes. "See you later, Chief." She tested his grip, but he only clamped down harder.

His bleary eyes turned predatory. "*I'll* tell you when you can go." For a drunk, he was surprisingly quick. Before Frankie could get out of his way, he took hold of her hair, pinned her against the wall, made it look as if they were a couple. His voice was a low raspy growl. "Now you just be nice, and we'll get along fine." The scar running across his cheek intersected with his sick grin.

Frankie froze inside. She opened her mouth. Why couldn't she scream? Her eyes pleaded but in the shadows, she was invisible. She finally found her voice. "Mister. I got a little boy to tend."

"Ain't that nice." His grip tightened as he pushed her toward the doors. "Just walk out nice and slow and nobody gets hurt." He tossed the empty bottle; it hit the ground with a thud.

In the background, the announcer was talking about the winner. A new Navajo Queen. Her ears began to roar. Her mouth was too dry. For once, she wished she believed in Grandmother's God.

16

Nick could hardly believe it. "Frankie?" He barely made out her form in the shadows where she stood next to Martin Brown. What could she possibly see in that bully? He raised his voice. "Frankie? You all right?" Was it his imagination, or was she shaking?

She turned toward Nick. She didn't say anything, just glanced at Martin and back at him. Her eyes said she was in trouble. Nick tensed, ready to rescue her.

Martin stopped short, wobbled, let go her arm. He trained a menacing look on Nick and was obviously tanked. "Mind your own business."

"Don't want any trouble, Martin." Nick waved Frankie away but she remained frozen in place. He stepped toward them with slow, calm movements. "Martin." Nick couldn't afford to aggravate the young man, who was known for his skills with a knife. "It's late. Let's all go home now."

Martin cursed. "Don't tell me nothing, bootlicker. The feds are selling us all down the river." Jabbing the air, he stepped toward Nick. "And you're helping them." He stood swaying. "Bootlicker."

Nick gestured again to Frankie. This time she heeded him and scooted out of range. He spoke in a controlled, reasonable tone. "Martin. You yourself said farming's never going to work. There's no water."

Martin brandished a knife. "You telling me as an Indian or as a white man?" The knife blade glinted in the moonlight.

Nick stood his ground. "I'm saying it as a man." A few steps away, Frankie hugged her middle. In the distance, Indian boys still played football. Nick kept his gaze on Martin's knife, ready to act.

But Martin Brown just stood there.

Nick took the opportunity. "I'm not looking for trouble. But you can't go around forcing yourself on the ladies."

Martin hung his head for a moment, then raised it and glowered at Nick.

"And even if it means quitting my job, I won't let Navajos turn into dirt farmers." Nick added, "I mean it."

Martin scowled. "I don't believe nothing you say, half-breed." He still held the knife.

Nick edged closer. "It's all right. We'll talk more tomorrow."

"Don't they see?" Martin's face contorted. "Navajos aren't farmers."

Nick took a chance. "Lakota have a saying. 'When a man moves from nature, his heart becomes hard.'"

Martin's arm dangled at his side. He dropped the knife.

Nick nodded. "Go on home now, get some sleep."

Martin Brown stood as straight as his unsteady feet would allow. After a moment, he nodded. "Thank you, brother."

Nick steadied Martin over to the Big Hogan. He found another Brown to hand him off to, saying, "He's had enough for one night." In the morning, there was no telling if he'd even remember what had happened, but at least Frankie was safe.

Frankie. Nick strode back to her. She sat huddled on a bench a few yards away from where he'd left her, her face softly lit by the moon. God never created a more beautiful woman. He stood in front of her. "You OK?"

She didn't look at him. "Yeah. I'm fine." She was still trembling. He longed to gather her into his arms but left his hands in his pockets. No sense in upsetting her more.

"Martin's not a nice drunk." He hoped she believed his own sobriety was solid.

Her teeth chattered as she glanced up at him. "Don't think I ever met one—a nice drunk, that is." She turned away.

He'd walked into that one. "Right." He moistened his parched lips. "Just wanted to make sure you and Harold were OK. I'll let you alone." He walked away as restless stars shot across the blackness.

"Nick."

He turned. "Yeah?"

"Sit down."

He glanced around. They were alone. He stepped closer.

In the dim light, he could barely make out Frankie's smile. She was still shaking. No sense in spooking her again. He sat down, leaving plenty of space between them. From inside the Big Hogan, a cheer went up as the emcee announced, "Let's give it up for the new Navajo Queen!"

He sat there, a whole universe away from Frankie Chasing Bear. What if he said the wrong thing again? His heart was mush.

She raised her head, finally, although she still shivered. "Thanks." She peered at him through her hair. "I mean it."

Nick feigned nonchalance. "Martin's a pain. More so, when he's blasted."

"You think he'd have, I mean, was he serious?"

He shrugged. "Who knows?" He swallowed hard at the thought.

She stared at the ground. "He scared the jibber-jabbers outta me." She drew in a long breath. "I won't lie—I have bad memories. They raise their ugly heads now and then."

"You and me both." Nick shook his head. "Eats at me every day."

Frankie looked lost for a moment, but straightened her shoulders. "I got something eating at me, too. I might as well just ask."

Nick wasn't sure where this was leading, but he had nothing to hide. "Shoot. Ask away."

She took a breath. "You said you're divorced. But are you involved with—I mean is there someone special?"

He put on a look of surprise even as his heart pounded. "What makes you think that?"

Frankie stood up. "No reason." She walked toward the open field.

Nick kept pace. "No reason?" A feeling of dread rose as he replayed the scene with Wanda. "Come on, tell me." She had to have seen them.

Frankie stopped. In distant fields, sheep bleated. She bit her lower lip and stared at the ground. "It's probably none of my business."

"I don't buy it." He crossed his arms, waited. "What?"

"I saw you with Wanda." Frankie took a breath. "You looked . . . busy." Her voice got smaller. "Are you . . . you and Wanda, you know?"

Sweat trickled down Nick's ribs. "Are we what?" He was right. Frankie'd seen him with Wanda. Guilt hammered at him.

Frankie paused. "Together." Her dark eyes seemed deeper than ever.

"Listen." His insides tensed. "It looks bad, but it's not what you think."

"And just what do I think?" Frankie's voice was tinged with hurt.

He may as well fess up. "I take it you got an eyeful—back by the hogan?"

"Yes." Her words sliced through him.

"I can explain."

She smirked. "Sure you can."

He held out his palms. "Wanda caught me off guard." He searched out her gaze. "Really. I'm not the least bit interested."

Frankie tilted her head. "Oh. I get it. Wanda the Navajo beauty queen tied you up and planted a juicy kiss on you." She clucked her tongue. "And you didn't enjoy it one bit." She glared.

"As a matter of fact . . ."

"Spare me." Frankie flipped her hair behind her shoulder—how could he convince her *she* was what he wanted? He fought the urge to fold her into his arms.

She stood up, eyes impatient. "I asked you a simple question." She walked away.

Nick grabbed her forearm. "Wait. Please, let me at least try."

Frankie sank back onto the bench. "This had better be good."

Nick's heart pounded double-time. He wiped his palms on the thighs of his jeans and swallowed hard.

17

Frankie wasn't about to let Nick make a fool out of her. "OK, hotshot." She stared at the field. She could make out Harold running with the ball, a gang of boys in hot pursuit. "Let's hear it."

He cleared his throat. "Like I said, I've never been drawn to Wanda."

"She makes up for that just fine." Harold's arms shot straight up. Must have scored. So far, Nick wasn't scoring any points with her.

He rubbed his palms together. "You ever have to kowtow to someone you didn't necessarily like? It's just how it is with Wanda." He couldn't look more nervous if he was about to be boiled in oil.

"Really?" Frankie crossed her arms. "I'm all ears."

Nick licked his lips. "I told you before. The Browns are a powerful clan. And Martin—the drunk I pulled off you—has the elders unhappy with me and the feds. All riled up about this farming scheme. And he's got a bunch of young warrior-types backing him."

"So he's a creep." She shrugged. "What's that got to do with you making out with Miss Navajo Queen?" Frankie looked past Nick. The sound of the yelling boys soothed her. "You looked a little too happy to be kissing *her*."

"Wanda."

She closed her eyes. "I don't care what her name is."

"Listen. Her name *matters*." Nick kicked at pebbles in front of the bench where they sat. "She's a *Brown*. Her Uncle Martin might be an irritating rabble-rouser, but he's a Brown, too. He likes to throw his weight around." Nick gestured with his hands as he spoke. "Browns are important around these parts. Since the day I got transferred to Arizona, Mama B's pushed her daughter Wanda on me." He shook his head as if to convince himself. "Only I'm not interested."

"Not interested?" Frankie looked sideways at him. "I walk around a corner and there you are, kissing a gorgeous woman—how could any red-blooded man not be interested?"

Nick held up his hands. "I'll admit it looked bad. But I swear, Wanda ambushed me—I didn't have a chance."

"To what? Breathe?" The more she relived the moment, the worse Frankie felt. "You make it sound like torture."

Nick's eyes brightened. "In a way, it is torture. Mama Brown's certain her daughter Wanda is the girl for me."

Frankie remembered the elder Brown woman, hustling Lucie off stage. "Mama Brown's sure about a lot of things."

Nick nodded. "I told them I wasn't interested." His shoulders slumped. "But so far, Wanda still hounds me and Mama Brown watches us like a hawk." He shook his head. "Today, Wanda caught me off guard."

"I'll say." Frankie relaxed a little—Nick seemed genuinely apologetic. But she wasn't about to put her heart out where he or anyone else could stomp on it.

Nick gripped the edge of the bench and looked out to where Harold and the boys still played. "Anyway, it's my job to sell this stupid farm scheme. If I tell Wanda to bug off, her mother might sway the elders' vote. Blame the fiasco with Wanda on simple politics." Nick held up his hand. "I swear."

"Politics?"

He looked serious. "C'mon. It's hard to stay out of Wanda's way and keep my job. Believe me."

"Maybe I do."

Nick wiped his palms on the thighs of his jeans. "Please." He kept his gaze trained on her, worry etching deeper into his face. "I have to know you believe me. It matters."

"The truth always matters." She feigned a breezy attitude. "Don't know why I got my dander up." She gestured. "I mean, shoot. You can kiss anybody you please. None of my business." She wouldn't give Nick eye contact.

He took off his hat and sat it beside him. "Look. Don't act all tough." He edged closer to her. "We've both known people who weren't exactly trustworthy."

"Tell me about it."

"*Will* you tell me about it? I mean, what was Pine Ridge like for you?" He radiated comfort more than danger, magnetism more than aversion. She thought briefly of scooting away, but stayed put. If nothing else, she welcomed the warmth. The wind had died down, but a chill lingered. She tugged down on the hem of her thin blue dress.

She tucked her hands inside her sweater's arms, held the frayed cuffs with her fingertips. "The winters were the worst." Frankie pictured the flimsy walls of the trailer in her girlhood home, the hole in the floor by the old wringer washer covered over with a thin bathroom rug. "Ma used to wait up for my father. Then the fireworks would start." She closed her eyes. Her mind echoed with the late-night accusations, arguments, and even physical fights that had kept Frankie and her siblings awake.

Nick's voice was low and tender. "Your dad was an alcoholic, too? I mean, besides Harold's dad."

Frankie nodded. "Pop drank anything he could get his hands on—beer, whiskey, aftershave." She drew in a breath. "He wasn't a mean drunk, though—at least not to us kids. But when he drank, Ma used to say his eye wandered. Pop called them his outside women." She hadn't meant to tell all to Nick or anybody else. But there was no taking it back.

Frankie stared into the sky. Cold air stung her eyes until they watered. She swiped at her cheeks with her sweater-covered hands. "Pop had one woman who used a lot of perfume. He'd come home smelling like roses." She forced a one-syllable laugh. "Ma complained he stunk up the house. He'd stagger in and she'd chase him with a cast-iron skillet."

His voice was reverent. "That would hurt."

Frankie's breath fogged in the air. "Not as much as it hurt when Ma found out the perfume belonged to one of my aunts."

Nick brushed away the tear snaking down Frankie's cheek. For an instant, she thought of taking his hand, but instead she leaned away.

"Oh man." Nick rubbed the back of his neck. "That's sad."

Finally she stood. "I should round up Harold." She tucked a strand of her hair behind one ear. When he didn't follow, she stopped, turned. "Aren't you coming?"

He grinned and broke into a slight jog.

For once, Harold was right where he said he'd be. Frankie's heart slowed a little, the weight of a long day slipping off her shoulders. She and Nick stood on the sidelines of the spirited game, cheering Harold on.

When he spotted them, he trotted over, out of breath and sweaty but happy. "Ma! Did you see that last play?"

Frankie wanted to smother him with kisses, but resisted. "You're a natural," she said. "Are you sure you're OK?" She held him at arm's length.

"Ma." Harold rolled his eyes. "Quarterbacks have to be tough."

Nick understood the game more than she did. "Those other guys don't have a chance against your passing arm."

Harold bent at the waist, rested his hands against the tops of his thighs. "This is the funnest thing ever, Ma. They like me." He flashed a grin. "I got a whole bunch of friends now."

Frankie made a visor with her hand and scanned the team. "Who are these friends?"

Nick peered into the dusky scene. "Blackfeet. From Montana."

Harold straightened up. "Montana's not that far from Pine Ridge, right?"

She tensed. On the field, the players hollered for Harold's return. "What makes you say that?"

Harold jogged away to where his teammates huddled. "I gotta get back!"

Frankie shouted after him. "Wait! We're leaving soon!" But Harold was already out of earshot. "My boy." She shook her head.

Nick chuckled. "You've got a live one on your hands."

"I'll say." Nick stood close enough that she caught his pleasant scent, somewhere between leather and pine.

He looked puzzled. "Not staying for the pageant tonight? What about the dancing?"

Frankie shook her head. "I thought we were only coming for the day."

Nick shrugged. "You'd better set off soon. Nighttime isn't the best time to travel in these parts. Especially by wagon." He folded his arms across his chest.

As the last sliver of sun slid out of sight, thousands of bats wheeled around in the darkened sky. Temperatures dipped as darkness overtook the field, but Frankie kept her worries about the overnight arrangements to herself. Had she misunderstood Netty? Frankie rubbed her arms to stave off the chill. Why hadn't she thought to pack any sort of bedding?

Nick frowned. "It's rugged terrain any time. You sure they said they were leaving tonight?"

Frankie glanced away. "No." A weary sigh escaped her. "I just assumed."

Nick chuckled. "Sorry, but you assumed wrong. Want me to find you a place to stay?"

Frankie couldn't believe it. Her head throbbed. How had she not made sure she and Harold would be safe and warm? "I feel like an idiot."

Nick stood there for a long moment. "Mama Brown could find someone for you to stay with."

She drew in a sharp breath. "*That* girl's mother?" Frankie didn't care if she did sound jealous.

"'Fraid so." Nick gave her a sheepish look.

Frankie hugged her sides. "A blind man can see Wanda's gorgeous. Sure you weren't enjoying her kiss?"

He shrugged. "Told you. She's just not my type."

Frankie blurted, "And what *is* your type?"

"Oh you know—intelligent, a decent sense of humor, good with her hands." He paused, and a flicker of a smile crossed his lips. "Wouldn't hurt if she trusted other people, either." Nick's hat shadowed his eyes.

She faced him. "How do you trust when every man you've ever known has been either drunk or trying to force himself on you?"

"I'm not every man."

She couldn't summon her voice louder than a whisper. "I want to believe you. Honest."

"And I want you to believe me."

They stood inches apart, watching and waiting as the earth quieted for the evening. Frankie listened for Grandmother's voice in the flutter of wings, in the crackle of campfires lit around the fairgrounds' perimeter.

Boys' voices rang out as they tumbled on the field. Frankie snapped to attention. She had to get lodging figured out. "Who else might be able to put us up tonight?" If nothing else, Harold had to have a safe place to sleep.

"Maybe Netty has it all arranged." He tilted his head to one side. "This really is your first Navajo fair, isn't it?"

She was tired. "Isn't it your first fair, too?"

Nick laughed, wide and easy. "That's true, but in just a few months I've had to drive up here more times than I can count. Didn't you ride overland from Holbrook?"

Frankie's backside still ached from all the jouncing. "Tell me about it."

Nick's voice took on a kindness. "You're not likely to get the driver to leave until tomorrow morning at the earliest. Netty didn't tell you?"

She bit her lip. "To tell you the truth, I didn't exactly ask." She glanced back at the exhibit buildings, where folks still milled around but the crowds had begun to thin out. "I don't know what we'll do."

Although Nick kept himself an honorable distance from her, she might've welcomed nestling against his muscular torso. But he seemed to respect her in a way no man ever had, a fact that warmed her almost as much as if she'd wrapped herself in his Lakota Star quilt.

Frankie marveled at her son's quick feet as he sprinted for another touchdown. She was proud of her son, but relieved when Netty came traipsing across the field, Reverend Abe's tall frame walking behind her.

Netty's round face reminded Frankie of a chipmunk with its cheeks jammed full of nuts. "Tallied up the new orders." Netty grinned. "We'll be busy until the first of the year—at least." Frankie had never seen her look so enthused.

In the semidarkness, Frankie smiled so as to seem cheerful. Later, when they were alone, she'd tell Netty about her close call with Martin Brown. "I thought we'd be going home tonight." She bit her lip. "I didn't exactly pack for an overnighter."

Netty laughed. "I was so busy, I never told you what to bring. My fault."

Frankie gestured at Harold out on the field. "It's just that . . ." She hated asking for anything.

Netty patted Frankie's shoulder "Don't worry. I've got you and your boy a place to bed down tonight."

Frankie hoped it wasn't with any of the Browns. She'd sleep in the bed of the wagon before she'd take hospitality from Wanda or her awful uncle.

18

Frankie thought Netty must have read her mind. "Lucie's got room at her sister's place. You may end up on her floor but she's got room."

Frankie let out her breath. "Thanks. It'll be fine." Just like old times in Pine Ridge.

Abe clapped Nick's back. "We'd best get over to the rodeo grounds. Don't want to miss out on the dancing."

Netty beamed. "Some of the finest anywhere." She touched Frankie's arm. "You feel like tagging along? We've got great seats in the stands."

Frankie didn't know if she could stay awake long enough to watch dancing or anything else, but she kept quiet and nodded. "Let me round up Harold first. It's too dark to see a ball now." She tried to find Nick's gaze, hidden in shadow. "You headed that way too?"

Nick touched his hat's brim. "Yes ma'am."

"Wait a sec." Frankie whistled through her fingers. The earsplitting sound always got through to her son, one of the few gifts she'd inherited from her father. "Harold! C'mon!" He began jogging toward her.

Abe's stride equaled three of Frankie's steps. He grinned at Nick. "Enjoying the fair?"

Nick nudged his hat off his forehead. "You bet. I've seen more beautiful stuff today than I've seen in my life."

Abe nodded. "God really outdid Himself when He made Navajo country."

Frankie cringed inside. More God talk.

Nick turned to Netty. "Where's Monny?"

Netty chuckled. "Cousin Lucie's the new queen—Monny's trying to fend off all the other guys."

Frankie turned. Harold trudged behind her as if his feet were made of lead. Letting him grow up was so hard. She massaged her temples, and looked sideways at Nick. "How do you stay so calm about things?"

Nick smiled. In the dark, he was even more handsome. "I finally surrendered. To God."

Frankie's blood chilled at the mention. "You gonna try to convert me like your friends?"

Nick spoke softly. "Wasn't trying to convert anybody." He shrugged. "You asked me a question and I answered. Simple as that."

She bit her lip, drew in a tired breath. "Guess you're right." She kept her head down as they walked, hoping that Nick couldn't see her frown; hoping Grandmother would help her sort it all out.

Nick wished he hadn't said a word about faith. For the rest of the evening, Frankie hadn't said much either, just sat holding onto Harold as if she feared he'd run off for the umpteenth time.

Tribal dancing, ceremonial bells, drumming, and singing had lasted into the wee hours. Nick liked a powwow as much as the next Indian, but by the end of the festivities he was dog-tired. And disappointed. Lucie and Netty had sat on either side of Frankie and Harold and he couldn't get a word in sideways.

He had to settle for a general goodnight. Monny and Abe claimed they were able to fend for themselves, so he tromped off to sleep in the truck.

Nick looked up. The night sky was ablaze with God's creation as shooting stars punctuated the Milky Way. Nick breathed in the clean high desert air, enjoying the fair's bounty, thankful to be alive. He could see his breath, proof the Navajo reservation's temperature plunged at night.

He walked with his hands in his jacket pockets and picked his way through the grounds to where he'd left the truck. He chuckled to himself. More than anything, he was enjoying Frankie's company.

The Lakota woman was a mystery. Her mood changed with little or no warning. But she was also magnetic, and he was pulled toward her, even when she got angry. Or maybe because she got angry. He turned as gravel crunched behind him.

He expected Monny or Abe, but Agent McCollum approached, wearing the same scowl he'd worn earlier in the day. "Parker," McCollum said.

He forced a smile, extended his hand. "Evening, sir. Did you enjoy the festivities?"

"Hmmph." McCollum looked impatient. "Listen. I don't have all night, Parker. I've got some news."

Nick groaned inwardly. "News?" He stifled a yawn. "Can't it wait 'til morning?"

McCollum's eyebrows arched. "Now see here, Parker. The young Navajo—what was his name?"

"You mean Martin Brown?"

A curt nod. "That's the one. I hear he's got a bunch of the young bucks in a lather—they're influencing the elders. And not in a way to help."

Nick knew better than to ask who needed helping. "With all due respect, sir, I'm not convinced farming is the right course for the Navajos."

McCollum's eyes narrowed to slits. "It's not your job to be convinced," he growled. "Your job is to make sure the government plan is implemented. Period."

Nick thought of every tribe's losses over the centuries: broken promises, forfeited homelands, grinding poverty. He hardened his resolve. "There's no water."

"Your point?"

He stared his boss straight in the eye. "There isn't enough irrigation water. The Navajos can't grow a decent crop up here without irrigating and you know it."

McCollum lit a cigarette, his lighter snapping shut with a metallic *chunk*. "Don't you get it?" He took a drag, blew the smoke into Nick's face. "The government can't afford to keep these jokers on the payroll. We've got to get these Navajos— and the rest of the tribes—to become self-supporting."

"With all due respect, sir." Nick cleared his throat. "How do you expect them to do so by farming, if there's no water?"

He cursed and waved dismissively. "I don't care if they'd have better luck farming on the moon." He returned Nick's stare and pointed. "You're one of them. You get them on board." He flicked the cigarette to the dirt and ground it out with his boot heel.

Nick squinted into the starlit sky.

"Gotta get going." McCollum blew smoke out his nostrils and checked his wristwatch. "I came out here to tell you the word from above is this: We need someone up here at Window

Rock to get things hammered out with the elders. You're the someone." He started walking away.

"Just like that?" He was stunned.

McCollum stopped, turned. "'Course not. I'll give you two weeks to get moved."

Nick's eyes stung as he watched McCollum walk away. The words *I quit* hovered on his tongue.

———

Frankie's bones ached. Sleeping on a floor could do that to a person. She was out of practice and she wasn't getting any younger, either. She patted Harold, asleep on the floor beside her. "C'mon, mister. Time to get moving."

Harold moaned, turned over. She let him be while she smoothed back her hair. She didn't even have a hairbrush with her.

Lucie was already up, humming some Native tune as she set a basket of fry bread on her cousin's table. "Penny Ann whipped us up some fresh bread and flapjacks. Come and get it."

Frankie yawned, used her palm to chase wrinkles from her dress. "How's it feel to be a queen?" She tried to imitate Lucie's bright outlook.

Lucie chuckled. "OK, I guess. Do I look different?"

Harold sat up and rubbed his eyes. "Ma. I'm so hungry I could eat a bear."

Lucie wore a less flashy outfit than yesterday, but Frankie admired her tasteful skirt and blouse, paired with sneakers and anklets folded down low. She smiled at Harold. "C'mon over then. More where that came from."

Frankie bit on her lip. She loved the fair, but something nagged at her. She couldn't think of anything urgent they'd left back in Phoenix, but she was anxious to get back there. Times like these she wished Grandmother was here to ask. Frankie would be polite, not sound too keen on making the cousins leave. "Say," she began, helping Lucie set plates around the wooden dinette. "Got any idea when we head back?" She smiled as she spoke, just casual conversation.

Netty appeared in the doorway. "Morning all." She finished tying a scarf over her hair, her eyes sparkling with mischief. "Chomping at the bit to get on the road, are you? What? You got a hot date back in the valley?" Her laugh made her belly jiggle.

Harold came to the table, plopped down into a chair and tucked into a large piece of the fry bread. Frankie didn't miss the fact his eyes widened at Netty's mention of dating. She tried to scoot his bangs out of his eyes, but he dodged her hand. "Ma!" He protested with his mouth full, but she wouldn't correct him. Not here.

Frankie carefully folded a cloth napkin. "Just wondering." She pictured the little house in Phoenix, dark and lonely. "The electric company's been breathing down my neck."

Lucie patted Frankie's shoulder. "Like Netty said, we did real well up here. We can lend you a hand with that stuff." Lucie turned to her cousin. "Can't we?"

Netty nodded. "Don't you worry, Frankie. You're one of the family now."

Frankie stared at a small hole in the toe of her canvas shoe. "I don't know what to say."

Netty waved her off. "We're a team, OK? Navajos take care of their own. Indians take care of their own."

Lucie chuckled. "And we just made you an honorary Navajo."

Harold stuffed bread into his mouth. "Guess what? The guys on the team made me honorary Blackfoot. It makes me

Lakota/Navajo/Blackfoot." He grabbed another piece of the bread, popped up out of his seat and made for the door to the outside.

"Stop right there, Mr. All-Indian." Frankie blocked his path. "We'll be leaving for home soon." She glanced at Netty, who nodded confirmation. "Anyway, don't be making me hunt all over for you. You stick close by. Hear?"

Harold made a face. "But I'm part of the team, Ma. I got to tell my buddies goodbye." He put on his most hangdog look. "Please?"

Netty and Lucie had quietly bowed out of the conversation, and busied themselves with cleaning up the kitchen. Frankie kissed the top of her son's head, and for once he endured it. She whispered, "When I call for you, come quick. OK?" A nod. Out loud she added, "And don't think you're going to get out of helping us load up the wagon."

Harold was a blur racing out the door. "My boy," Frankie said.

Netty grinned. "Is a good boy."

Lucie chimed in. "Is turning into a fine young man."

Frankie beamed.

Nick awoke with a crick in his neck and a burning in his belly. As dawn broke over the mesas, he unfolded himself from the truck's seat, where he'd spent the night trying to get comfortable. He hadn't slept much and when he did, dreams of McCollum's cockamamie plan had bedeviled him. He pulled on his boots and climbed out of the pickup.

Dew clung to the scrub and a chill fog still padded the fringes of the grounds. Still, the few high clouds meant sunshine was on its way. He stretched his arms over his head,

LINDA S. CLARE

moved his neck this way and that, tried to forget the meeting
with McCollum. No use. His boss's orders made no more sense
in the daylight than they had last night.

If he moved to the Navajo Rez, Frankie and her son might
well slip away. Not to mention that Mama B and Wanda would
stick to him like burrs on a dog. To keep his position, he could
go along and try to cajole the Navajo into farming. When the
federal plan failed—and it would—he'd probably be run off
the reservation. Or he could just quit now, tell McCollum and
the feds where they could go. Both options felt equally risky,
equally wrong.

He licked his lips, prayed for strength. Familiar cravings
nettled at him, mocked him as he stood with his back to
the world. He pictured Frankie's disappointment when she
thought he'd fallen off the wagon. Hang on. If he rode it out,
those cravings would subside.

He went off in search of Monny, Abe or anyone who had
brewed a pot of strong black coffee. A tinge of rosy pink still
colored the sky, and Nick stopped to admire the view, his
breath nearly stolen by the sunrise's delicate hues.

He had to believe a creator who could put on something
so beautiful could also help him stay sober. Had to, dear God.
Please. Nick held out his hands. A few jitters, even after all
these years. He'd better find that cup of joe.

As he neared the exhibition buildings, he ran into Harold,
literally. "Whoa, where you off to?" He held onto the boy's
shoulders.

Harold stopped, taking in long gasps of air. "Gotta go find
the team." Since he'd met the Blackfoot football players, he
seemed happier, more sure of himself.

Nick wanted to ask if Frankie knew where he was, but held
his tongue. No sense getting the kid riled. He pointed to a

160

clutch of cars and trucks parked at the edge of the grounds. "Thought the Blackfeet were camped over there."

"Thanks." Harold took off before Nick could say you're welcome. He smiled to himself. Kids.

He located Monny and Abe, thankful that Abe had brought a thermos along. And that it just happened to be full of strong black coffee.

Nick breathed in the warm aroma. "You two get all your goodbyes in real soon," he said. "McCollum laid a doozy on me last night. I want to get back to Phoenix by nightfall."

"What's up?" Monny asked. "McCollum a pain?"

"You're telling me." Nick ducked his chin. "I'm being transferred. Again." He took another slurp of the coffee, still too hot. "I've got two weeks." He shook his head, hardly believing it himself. "Whole thing stinks. To high heaven."

19

Nick told himself to stay calm. But he was a powder keg, ready for a lit fuse. He gulped down the rest of his coffee.

Abe looked sympathetic. "Where they sending you this time?" The reverend and Monny exchanged worried glances.

Nick forced out his breath and gestured. "Here. Window Rock. Right smack dab in the middle of Navajos. Who don't want what the BIA is selling." He worried his sandpapery tongue where coffee had scalded it.

Reverend Abe was his usual honest, spiritual self. "God's handing you a mighty big challenge." He paused, his long angular face thoughtful. "But I gotta say—He chose you for the job." A shrug as Abe gazed out toward the still foggy skyline. "He'll help you through it, too."

Nick felt like cursing. Instead, he tried to see the long view. "If it's the truth, then I'm as sorry as a sheepherder in a pack of coyotes." He eyed his pals. "And I'm gonna need all the help I can get."

Monny piped up. "What about the girl?"

Nick tried not to look irritated. "Girl?" Discussing his personal life was the last thing he wanted to do right now.

As usual, Monny didn't get the message. "You know. Frankie." He grinned wide, raised his eyebrows in a wolfish way. "A mighty fine specimen." He elbowed Abe.

Nick cut him a glare. "Knock it off." Monny could be such a lout.

Monny held up his hands. "Sorry."

Abe shook his head knowingly and handed the thermos back to Nick. "C'mon, Monny. Didn't you say you wanted to find Queen Lucie before we shove off?"

Monny's face lit up.

Nick said a silent thanks to Abe, always the practical one. Abe took Monny's arm, and they started to walk away.

Nick called after them. "We'll meet at the truck in a half hour." Abe waved behind his head to show he understood. Nick poured himself another cup, ignoring his shaking hands, which at the moment, would rather clutch a bottle. Before he could take another sip of coffee, he spotted Mama B and Wanda, headed his way. He groaned, stepped behind the truck. Maybe they hadn't seen him. No such luck.

Sunshine broke through high clouds as the two women approached. Wanda's silver squash blossom bounced against her chest with every step. She was still wearing her traditional Navajo Queen sash and tiara. Truth be told, she looked a bit silly in her getup, but Nick forced a smile. "Morning, ladies."

Mama's black hair knot glistened in the sun. "Morning. We heard the news!" The older Navajo woman returned his smile. "Agent McCollum told us you'll be moving up here. We'll have you around all the time!" She turned to her daughter. "We're so happy. Aren't we, Wanda?"

Wanda's cheeks colored as rosy as her sateen blouse. "*Yeth*."

Mama bubbled over with good cheer. "I should say *Traditional Queen* Wanda. What do you think of our girl?"

Nick wished he could disappear, sure. But he was cranky today, too—and sick of placating Mama B and her daughter. "I think it's too early to think." He touched his hat's brim and nodded at Wanda. "Congratulations on your win, Wanda." She smiled, her dimples deep pits on her cheeks.

Nick scanned the area, but no one was around to rescue him. Annoyance built to irritation as Mama Brown prattled on.

She linked her arm in his. "I've got several places in mind for you to stay, of course. Unless the government is putting you up in their housing." She swept her arm in a wide gesture. "Want to see a couple before you leave?" She pulled him forward, talking nonstop.

Wanda, her crown sitting lopsided on her head, practically jogged to keep up as Mama dragged Nick across the grounds.

He'd never get out of this unless he stood up for himself. He dug his heels into the dirt and came to a dead stop. The squash blossom necklace plunked against his back as Wanda walked straight into him. She smelled a little like wet wool. A confused Mama B shot a scolding glance at her daughter.

Mama put her hands on her hips. "Nick? What's wrong? If the elders aren't cooperating, just tell me. I can fix it."

Nick held out his hands but stood his ground. "Listen. It's not that." He shook his head.

Mama stared at Wanda as if her daughter was to blame for this development. After a moment, Mama's expression hardened. "What's this about?" She forced out a hard laugh. "It's Martin, isn't it?" She shook her head. "I've been hearing about his little escapades—all night, all morning. He's a trouble-maker, for sure." Mama's breath hung in the chilly air.

Nick stepped backward. "Sorry, ladies, but duty calls. I've got things I must attend to." He wanted to add at this very minute, he didn't give a hoot if he even had a job.

Mama looked disappointed. "Don't you at least want to look at places? I mean if you're going to live up here and all . . ."

Before he could say more, Wanda spoke up, her voice stronger and steadier than Nick remembered. "Mother! Nick said he's busy right now. Didn't you, Nick?" Wanda breathed heavily and stared at her mother.

Mama Brown's mouth hung open. She closed it and blinked.

Nick dragged out the diplomacy once more. "Thank you, Mama, Wanda for your hospitality. There's plenty of time to discuss my lodgings. Now if you'll excuse me . . ." He backed away from Mama B, who still looked as if she might tackle him on the spot.

Frankie couldn't stop shaking. No. Not again. "Harold! Harold Chasing Bear!" She'd called and called. He hadn't come. She broke into a run, not sure where to go. The Big Hogan? Lost & Found? Sun blinded her as she scoured the area for a thin boy with unkempt hair and an orange and brown plaid shirt. Her heart pounded out his name.

She stopped passersby, asking if they'd seen him. Most shrugged, some gave her pitying looks. All said no, they hadn't. One mentioned nigh on every young boy here had messy black hair. She raced on, looking for Nick.

She tried to remember what she'd heard. The Blackfoot team members Harold had spoken of were camped a short ways from the fairgrounds. She ran to where she thought their camp should be. Only a quenched campfire and a ring of rocks was left. A stray candy wrapper tumbled in the breeze.

She heard nothing save the wind, picking up speed the way it did in mesa country. Except for sheep bleating, the spare landscape had nothing to say, and even the birds were silent. Grandmother wasn't talking.

Frankie held down her dress's skirt, scanned the horizon once more in all directions. The vista went on for miles: flat pink-brown mesas, pastures dotted with scrub, a lone tree here and there. She broke into a jog toward the Big Hogan. Harold was her gift. She couldn't lose such a gift. She ran faster, calling out her son's name.

She ran until she cried, slowing to a fast walk when her shins ached. She was frantic now, willing to invoke Navajo or Lakota or even the Christian God if it would help. As she mumbled every prayer she'd even learned, she spotted Nick.

He caught her as she stumbled into him. "Frankie! What's going on?"

When she could see again, Frankie looked up into his face. He had hold of her shoulders, as if he knew she was falling apart. "Harold," she spilled out. "I can't find Harold." She wiped sandy grit from her eyes. "Where's Harold?"

Nick softly rubbed her back, held her for another moment. "Don't worry." He breathed into her hair. "We'll find him."

Behind Nick, Wanda stood with her mother. Frankie couldn't avoid their stares. Wanda's eyes narrowed and her mother set her hands on her hips in a way that said keep away. The older Navajo's lip curled slightly. "Need help keeping track of your kid?"

Frankie shot back a glare, but Nick had his back to the Navajos. Wanda added, "What kind of a mom loses her own kid so much?"

Frankie closed her eyes against the sting of truth. What kind of mom did lose her own son? Time after time? She wanted to crawl into a hole.

Nick stroked her hair. Mama B walked right up and ignored Frankie, addressing Nick. "Want me to get the tribal police on the horn?"

"No." Nick shook his head. "Not yet." He turned his back on Mama, eliciting a small gasp from the head of the Brown clan. Nick spoke to Frankie in a low voice. "You checked the Blackfoot camp?"

Frankie nodded. "Campfire's out." Her voice quavered. "Nobody's there." She clutched at Nick's denim jacket. "Please." She swallowed. The lump stuck in her throat only tightened. "We have to find him."

Awful seconds passed. She wanted to scream or cry or run off. No. Grandmother spoke to her heart. Stay strong for Harold. Stay strong.

20

Nick quickly rounded up Abe and Monny, filled them in. In minutes, word buzzed all around the fairgrounds Frankie's boy was missing. Netty and Lucie volunteered to help Nick's friends get back to Phoenix, and promised to stay on alert in case Harold was hiding around the grounds somewhere. The announcer from the rodeo and pageant called Harold's name over the loudspeaker every few minutes, and Mama B and Wanda were enlisted to organize a search.

Satisfied they'd covered the bases, Nick took charge. "The Blackfeet all came in a big old Studebaker. White." He pointed to the horizon. "My guess is that they're headed to Route 66, then up to Helena." He faced Frankie, her cheeks wet with tears. He couldn't stand for her to hurt anymore. "Think he's still trying to get back to Pine Ridge?"

She nodded. "Maybe." Her body shuddered as she took a breath. "Probably."

Nick frowned. "Harold came tearing by not a half hour ago." Guilt at not stopping the boy poked him. "There aren't many ways to Montana from here." He pulled Frankie along toward his truck. "C'mon. Maybe we can catch them."

Mama, Wanda, and most of the other Navajo women followed them with their eyes as they stood scowling. Mama could gossip with the best of them. No telling what she'd say to make Wanda look better.

He pulled Frankie along. She was a basket case, her nose running, eyes red and puffy. What mother wouldn't be? Still, she held her head up and glared right back at the women who taunted her. Nick liked that about her, the way she took no guff. Although, he had to admit, when Frankie turned her wrath on him she could be quite the she-bear.

Abe and Monny met him at the truck.

Monny's brows bunched and he rubbed the back of his leathery neck. "We can hitch a ride home with Lucie and Netty." He laid a hand on Nick's forearm. "We'll be praying up a storm, brother."

Nick nodded. "We'll need it." He was glad he'd told his friends about Harold's curious longing to be with his dead father in Pine Ridge.

Abe's gaze softened. "We'll be fine." He gestured to the old-fashioned wagon parked at the edge of the grounds. "You worry about finding the boy. Soon as I get back to the church I'll put out some feelers—see if anyone's heard anything at the Indian School."

Nick glanced at Frankie. "Check with Stu at the gas station, too. Wouldn't put it past Harold and Orval to start another fight."

Frankie's voice was small, so soft Nick barely caught the words. "Shouldn't we get going?"

Monny smiled at her. "Praying to the Almighty for you and your boy, Miss."

Frankie mumbled, "Thanks."

Nick held open the passenger door and Frankie climbed into the truck's cab. He ground the gears into reverse and then drove off the reservation as fast as the dirt tracks would allow.

He steered straight for any paved road, as the truck jounced across potholes and prairie. Frankie didn't complain, just sat gripping the armrest, her gaze scouring the vista.

A stray Navajo sheepherder's old truck was the only cloud of dust they came across. When Nick managed to flag him down, the old guy pointed to the highway in the distance. Nick's Navajo was rudimentary at best, but he gathered from the old man's gestures that a carload of Indians had passed him a short while ago. "Thanks," Nick had shouted over the truck's rumblings, and Frankie clutched the armrest as he gunned the BIA truck's engine. He hoped the old Navajo's idea of a "short while" wasn't too different from his own.

He liked the way Frankie had calmed herself, and now sat straight on the truck's bench seat. As she watched for a white sedan loaded with Indians, she reminded him of a mother eagle looking for her fledgling. A proud mother, who'd do anything to keep her eaglet safe.

Just outside of Flagstaff, Nick pulled into a station to gas up, to ask if any Blackfeet had passed through. The attendant wiped oil from the truck's dipstick and shook his head. Frankie's shoulders sagged. She rested her head against the seat back, said nothing.

Nick paid for the gas and got back into the cab. His heart ached for Frankie, who sat staring out the windshield. It dawned on him he cared for Harold as much as he cared for the boy's mother. He said a silent prayer for his safe return.

He stole a look. She'd wrapped her arms tightly around her middle and her bare arms were full of goose bumps. Before starting the truck, he removed his denim jacket, draped it around her shoulders. She smiled up at him.

He looked away. He'd failed her, failed himself. "I thought I could catch them." He stared at the steering wheel and his voice caught. "Guess I thought wrong." He should've grabbed Harold while he'd had the chance.

Frankie touched his shoulder. "It's not your fault. You tried."

He let another moment slip away, trying to think of a brilliant plan that didn't emerge. "What'll we do now?" He'd drive all the way to Montana if she asked him to.

She stretched her legs out in front of her, gazed at her hands. "Don't ask me why, but I have this feeling we should go on back down to Phoenix."

"Really?" He'd expected her to say she wanted him to take her to Blackfoot country. "Not sure I follow you." He wasn't sure about much these days.

"I know, huh?" She shrugged. "Makes no sense."

"Don't you want to stop in the sheriff's office? Coconino County offices are only a few streets over." They'd put in a missing child report. They could do that much.

Frankie laughed. "You really think the law's gonna care about an Indian kid who's with a bunch of other Indians?" She sniffed. "That'll be the day."

Nick ignored the burning in his stomach. "OK, then. The valley it is."

—∞—

Frankie couldn't shake the peculiar feeling. After a quick stop at a burger drive-in, they hit the road south. Common sense said Harold was likely headed to Montana, seeing as how that's where his new buddies lived. So why did she feel the need to get back to Phoenix? She didn't make sense to herself. But the feeling was strong, as if Grandmother were sitting right next to her in the truck's cab. And Grandmother had never let her down.

In spite of Nick's sheepskin lined jacket, she shivered as he raced down the highway. Hours marched on and her eyelids grew heavier. She was tired, sure, but sleeping would be like giving up. Instead, she watched out her window until her eyes stung from dryness. The view was boring, gradually shifting from high desert to plain old desert. As her lids drooped, the landscape of her heart kept trying to believe.

∞

She woke with a start. Gravel clattered in the truck's wheel wells as Nick steered onto the highway's shoulder.

He corrected the truck back onto his lane. "Sorry," he said. "Had to swerve to miss a jackrabbit."

"Must have drifted off," she murmured. "How far are we out of town?"

Nick answered without taking his eyes off the road. "Just over the hills now. We just passed Cave Creek."

Frankie nodded, hoped her feelings about getting to the valley hadn't been wrong. Grandmother had to be guiding her. Grandmother had never let her down.

Frankie's stomach dropped when they finally pulled up to the gate. The house was dark. She shot a worried look at Nick. "Well." She tried not to sound discouraged. "Looks like they didn't beat us here." The house's windows were a blank stare.

Frankie reached for the door handle, cracked open the cab. "I don't have a phone," she said. "I gave the cops your number. Hope you don't mind."

Nick exhaled. "It's fine." He reached out as if to take her hand but then withdrew. "Look." His gaze was deep, endless.

172

"I just wanted to say I'm sorry." His voice was soft as Navajo velvet. "It's my fault. I should've . . ."

Frankie shook her head. "No. I'm responsible for my boy." She made a fist; her nails bit into her palms. "Anyone's to blame, it's me. I shoulda kept better track of Harold." Her throat pitched her voice high. "You. You tried to help."

He reached for her again, brushed away a stray lock of her hair. "Frankie." He whispered. "Don't do this—don't beat yourself up."

She drew back. *Harold.* "We have to find him." It was the only thing she knew for sure.

21

At Frankie's doorstep, Nick wiped his palms on his pants. His heart ached for both her and her missing son. He kept his clammy hands at his sides. "I can't stand the thought of you sitting here all night worrying." He dipped his chin. He hadn't even told her about his transfer to Window Rock. "How will I know you're OK? You've got no phone."

Frankie unlocked the door and reached inside. "No lights either, apparently." She frowned.

"They turned off the electricity?"

"Looks that way."

Nick slipped his hands into his back pockets and shook his head. "When it rains, it pours." He had to keep her safe. He worked up his courage. "Look. It's a little awkward, I guess, but let me stay here tonight."

Frankie's eyebrows went up.

"I can sleep in my truck." Heat crept up his neck. "Don't worry. I'm not like Martin Brown."

She studied the floor.

Nick held up his hands, commanded them to stop shaking. "I'm serious here. I can't leave you alone with no phone, no lights, sick to death with worry. I can't and I won't." If he hadn't let Harold run off that morning, none of this would've happened.

She stared past him for a moment as if she'd heard his thoughts, her forehead furrowed into a delicate frown. Finally, she locked her gaze on him, her head tilted to the side. "You're something else, Nick Parker." She stepped aside, gratitude radiating from her face. "You don't need to stay." She glanced over her shoulder. "But I'll see if I can scare us up a little supper. Have to be cold, I'm afraid." She was still wearing his jacket, although the temperature here in the valley was too warm for a coat.

"I'm pretty handy at building a campfire." He grinned. "Boy Scouts." Maybe he could change her mind about letting him stay.

Frankie smiled back. "And I got a sack of potatoes—government issue."

"Roasted spuds. Mm-mm. Sounds delicious." He wanted to add he'd never met any woman—Indian or white—who got to him like Frankie Chasing Bear. Instead, he went out to his truck, found a couple of emergency candles, a flashlight, and a box of strike anywhere matches. He took the items back into the house, praying Harold was safe.

Nick built the campfire in the yard, fashioning a few stones and cement blocks into a ring. He gathered a pile of grayed, split grape-stake fencing and snapped pieces of the brittle wood across his knee. Dry grass was as good for tinder as any. He was glad the house's well still pumped water. He filled a pail and hauled it out to the ring of rocks, just in case the fire got out of control. He chuckled under his breath. Out of control. Lately, like just about everything.

He watched the fire dance until coals glowed, while in the west the sunset burned with vibrant reds and oranges. He prayed for Harold's safe return, throwing in an extra thanks for the dinner they were about to eat.

Moments later, Frankie came out with an armful of baker potatoes in a cast-iron dutch oven.

She set down the pot. "I found a stick of oleo, too." She made a face. "It's not butter, but at least the taters won't be dry."

Nick nestled the Dutch oven in the glowing coals. "Don't know what I was thinking." He hunched his shoulders up around his ears. "Shoulda just taken you over to my place for supper." He picked up a long, skinny stick and poked at the coals.

Frankie stood across the fire from him, hugging her sides, gazing into the embers. She shook her head. "I just keep feeling like I should be *here*. Harold could walk up any minute." She glanced up at Nick. "Crazy, I know."

Nick walked around the ring and stood beside her. "Not crazy." He twirled the stick in his fingers. "At least, not to me."

Frankie seemed puzzled. "What's that mean?"

"Oh, nothing."

"No. Really."

"You'll think I'm nuts."

"I will not."

"OK. Sometimes God tells me things."

Frankie's eyebrows raised. "What do you mean?"

He closed his eyes briefly. "I just mean sometimes I feel as if God is—telling me stuff." He swallowed. He should've kept his mouth shut.

"A great big God like yours knows everything, least that's what I heard." She wrinkled her nose. "The real God would tell you where my Harold is. Right?" Her lips squeezed together, pinched-looking.

Nick's stomach sank. His God was kind, loving. How could he explain that?

Frankie took the stick from him, her fingers brushing his. She hooked the Dutch oven's handle and lifted. The stick bent, then snapped.

"Here. Let me get something stronger." He looked around, wishing for a sturdy branch but only a row of dusty oleander grew in the yard. He left Frankie standing there while he got a crowbar out of his truck.

———

When the potatoes were soft, Frankie invited Nick inside to eat—the least she could do. He carried the dish of steaming spuds inside while she shone the flashlight in the bare cupboards. A lone can of peaches she didn't know she had lay in the corner of the empty larder. He hung up his hat and jacket on a nail by the door, the same nail Harold aimed for when he slung his coat after school.

He lit the candles. Then with their plates of hot potatoes oozing streams of margarine, Nick bowed his head briefly and closed his eyes. Grace.

A thorn poked her right in the conscience. Hypocrisy—it's what bugged her about Christianity. But what about Grandmother? She pushed aside bitterness and ducked her chin, out of respect. Maybe Nick wouldn't bring up religion again.

They ate without speaking, sitting on the sofa. Reminders of Harold permeated the room. A menagerie of borrowed books, pieces of the quilt she'd worked so hard to convince him he needed. Her appetite ebbed with every thought of her son, lost somewhere out there. Alone.

She couldn't look at the quilt, not now.

When she glanced his way, Nick was studying her face. He wiped his mouth politely. "You OK?"

"Why?" She made a fist to keep her hand from shielding her lips. A terrible habit, and hard to break.

"You seemed far away." His voice made her feel safe. "Thinking about Harold?"

She nodded, pushed her fork around the last few morsels on her plate.

He smiled. "Me too. Can't stop hoping." He stared past her. "Can't stop praying."

A hurricane swirled inside her. More religion. Was it mumbo-jumbo?

Nick touched her forearm. "Talking about faith makes you uncomfortable, doesn't it?"

A shrug. "I guess." She looked at him square, hooked a lock of hair around her ear. "Yeah."

"Maybe I'll keep my prayers to myself then."

She shook her head. "If prayers to your God bring Harold home safe, who am I to argue?" She shifted her knees to the side, bumped Nick's plate resting across his lap. He managed to catch it before it upended.

Her voice came out choked, faint. "Sorry."

He gave her a look, smiled in the way she'd come to fancy. "Don't be sorry."

But she was. Sorry for taking her eyes off Harold. Sorry for leaving Pine Ridge, the one thing he begged for. "Watch out—God might hit me with a lightning bolt." She swallowed. Inside her, Hoover Dam about to breach. Her lips trembled but she beat back the flood, drew a tattered breath. "I messed things up real good this time."

"We're all goofs." Nick tilted his head, met her gaze. "For what it's worth, God loves goofs. Rescues them. Even guys like me." He grinned.

She glanced away. "Sure." Maybe she shouldn't have ridden him so hard. But since her time at the Indian school, God talk only made Frankie think of Netty's chopped-off hair, the Klamath girl's deep hand gash. How could a good God allow such things?

She stood, abruptly, knocked Nick's fork to the floor. She bent, picked up the fork. "I'd say sorry but you just told me not to."

Nick's smile was generous. "Yes, ma'am. I did." He got up, carried away their dishes. "Stand by it, too. Can't go through life being sorry." He scraped the plates and stacked them next to the sink.

She sat crossing and uncrossing her ankles, picturing Harold out there all alone.

"Be right back." Nick slipped into his jacket and hat. "I should make sure the coals are dead out."

She nodded. "There's a bucket outside. In case, you need to pump a little water."

"Got the pail at the ready."

"Of course you do." He did have a kind of Boy Scout way about him, always loyal, always prepared. If he'd gone through a manhood ceremony, what had he been like? The pit in her stomach reminded her Harold had yet to finish the Lakota rites. Frankie appealed to Grandmother for wisdom.

Every cell in her body said to finish Harold's quilt. Harold must rise to meet the star. They had to find him first, she wanted to say. She wouldn't argue, though. Grandmother was usually right. Frankie's pleas for Harold's safety rose like smoke floating up to the stars.

Frankie waited until Nick was outside. The candles had burned low. She reached for the card table, where the quilt pieces waited. She picked up one of the star's points, finger-pressed along its edges. She set the piece beside the others to complete the picture. The war bonnet's array blazed as strongly as ever. Harold would rise to that. But what about the star of Bethlehem?

One of the candles flickered out. She set aside the Christian version of the star, along with Grandmother's beliefs. For Frankie, standing in two worlds seemed as impossible now as the day she'd left Pine Ridge. The only place she wanted to be was with her only son. She held onto the sail-shaped fabric, pressed it against her lips, whispered into it. Her baby. A hot tear followed the contour of her cheek.

22

The screen door creaking open made Frankie look up. She quickly mopped the tear with the back of her hand. Nick wiped off his boots. In the candlelight, she could barely make out his features. "Fire's out."

She put down the goldenrod piece of fabric as if she hadn't just been caught talking to it. "Wish the lights weren't out, too." Her smile felt as fake as those wax lips kids chewed on at Halloween.

"At your service." Nick pulled out more emergency candles, set them on teacup saucers and scratched a wooden match against his boot heel. The candles' glow softened his silhouette.

"Thanks." She thought of her boy, out there in the dark. Her stomach tightened. "When did Netty say they were heading back to the valley?" If she made small talk maybe he wouldn't see how close to the edge she really was. "Aren't your friends riding with them?"

Nick's eyes followed her shaky fingers as she slung her hair behind one shoulder.

She turned away and arranged and rearranged the loose pieces of Harold's quilt. "Wait'll they find out how bumpy the wagon is just going as far as Holbrook."

Nick wasn't fooled. "Frankie."

Even with the candles, shadows swallowed the room. She stubbornly fussed with the fabric pieces. "Showing off the quilts at the fair was my idea, you know. I've got a good feeling about the business. And with Lucie crowned Modern Queen . . ."

Nick moved next to her, close enough to hear his breathing. "Frankie." He touched her forearm. "Stop it."

She held her hand in midair. "Stop what?" Each time Nick touched her, her world lit up, but she held back on letting him know it. "I'm pretty happy about this quilt business—if I can make enough to get the truck going, we'll be on our way to Pine Ridge before you know it."

He scratched at his beard's stubble, as if he was tired of the game. "Aren't you forgetting something?"

Frankie thought for a moment. "Oh! Your quilt? Of course." She bent and pawed through a cardboard box full of quilt scraps and partially finished quilt tops. "Here it is." She pulled out the Lakota Star quilt Nick had entrusted to her to repair. She unfolded and shook it out. "I've got it nearly done—when I get finished you won't be able to tell where it was fixed up." She ran a hand across the once-tattered coverlet, its surface now smooth and unbroken. "What do you think?"

Nick fingered the quilt's edging. "Wow. Looks great." He nodded. "Thank you." His expression grew serious. "But that's not what I meant."

Frankie swallowed, braced herself. "What are you talking about?" She stared at the floor.

"Face it." Nick lifted her chin. "You won't be going to Pine Ridge or anywhere else until Harold comes home."

"Of course not." She glanced sideways, but he made her look at him. "But Harold might show up. Any minute."

"Maybe." Nick seemed patient. "In the meantime, why don't we call the Highway Patrol? Or at least the sheriff. Those Blackfeet are probably halfway to Montana by now."

She shuddered at the mention of the local law. "Oh yeah— I'm sure the sheriff will be helpful." She made a face.

"OK, maybe skip the sheriff. But if the highway patrol knows he's missing, they can be on the lookout."

Frankie stepped back and matched the edges of Nick's quilt to fold it in half. "And get the whole lot of Blackfeet tossed in jail for kidnapping? You're thinking like a white man." Frankie folded the quilt into quarters, eighths.

Nick was quiet a long moment, as if he'd deliberately ignored her comment. "I don't mind sleeping out in the truck tonight." His expression was open, expectant. "I'd feel much better if I was nearby."

She balanced Nick's folded quilt on the sofa's arm. "It won't be necessary."

"Sure you'll be OK?" She didn't need to look to know. His face had worry written all over it.

"Why wouldn't I be?" Using her finger, she traced the star on Nick's quilt.

He shrugged. "You're used to having your son here." His gaze was gentle but intent, as if he saw past her flimsy façade and liked her anyway. "C'mon." His voice velvet-smooth. "I'd feel better if you'd let me stick around." He stepped closer. Gathered her into his arms.

Frankie stood stock-still. For an instant, she waffled: pull away or melt into his embrace? She let out her breath, nestled her cheek against his shirt, its pearlescent snap buttons reflecting candlelight. She drank in the scent of earthy goodness mixed with charcoal from their cook fire.

Seconds rushed by. His hands light on her back, his face buried in her hair, adrenaline coursed through her and she shivered. She didn't want to move. Ever.

Finally, he whispered. "So what do you say?" A long exhale. "If I go home, I'll just worry about you."

Harold's face barged into her mind, as guilt and fretting overthrew excitement. She was a horrible parent—for an instant, she'd forgotten about her son. She tried to swallow the lump of shame choking off her voice.

He seemed to understand her agony. "I know—it's tough *not* to worry." Pulled her closer, his solid embrace saying what words could not say.

Again she relaxed, a stream carried along to the ocean. Nick Parker might be the puzzle piece that fit her lifetime of searching. She trembled, ached in ways she had all but forgotten. As powerful jolts rocketed through her, she pressed in closer, moistened her lips.

Nick pushed away, met her eyes.

She looked deeper. "What?"

"It's just." He seemed to search for words. "After what you went through up on the Rez, it's . . ." He glanced away. "It's just not right."

"What's not right?"

He pushed back further, stared at the floor. "I like you too much to . . ." A pause. "Take advantage." He looked up, his features tortured. "I'm supposed to be helping you find your boy."

"You are, and I'm grateful." Frankie was careful to keep her eyes on his face. "I like you, too. Really."

He drew in a sharp breath. "That's the problem. I." He stared over the crown of her head, his voice low. "Like you. A lot."

She laid a hand on his shoulder. "I'm a big girl. And neither one of us is married."

184

Nick's fists balled at his sides. "That's the point. We aren't married."

She calmed her breathing, doused the flame inside. "The white man's God made up those rules."

"And I made a promise to live by those rules." He was serious.

Her gut clenched. She was a pressure cooker of anger and attraction, ready to explode.

"I get it." She let her hands dangle at her sides. "Afraid I'll mess you up? Make you stray?" She regretted the sarcasm, but why couldn't Nick Parker leave his God out of all this?

He shook his head. "No. You don't understand. God loves me. I obey. Whether I want to or not." His eyes sad. Were they full of pity?

Frankie's spine stiffened. "I can take care of myself." Her heart squeezed itself into hard coal. She really could take care of herself.

"It's not what I meant." His eyes lost a little of their shine. "Not trying to be pushy—just wanted to know you're safe." His jaw worked enough so Frankie picked up on it. Ropy tendons in his neck stood out. "Does everything always have to be difficult?" It wasn't a question as much as an accusation.

"Don't know what you're talking about." She crossed her arms. "Difficult?" She leveled her gaze on him. "Life's difficult—even for those who can pass for white." She shouldn't have said the last bit. Too late to back down.

Nick narrowed his eyes, as though he'd just as soon wash his hands and be done with her. He returned her hard stare. "Look." He stepped closer to her, pointed at the quilt pieces. "You think I like being a half-breed?" He spoke through clenched teeth. "I'm doing my best to be a *man*. Not a Lakota man or a white man. A *man*."

She'd gouged a tender spot. Still, her temper chafed. "What do you mean, Nick? You're Lakota when it suits you, but white when it's to your advantage?"

He looked stunned for a moment. "Are you kidding?" His voice amplified with each word. "How can you stand there and tell *me* I'm not a real Lakota?"

"I never said that."

"Oh yeah? It's what you think."

Frankie blinked. Her mouth went dry. "How do you know what I think?"

"It's written all over your face."

Frankie narrowed her eyes, fought the lump in her throat. "I just want what's best for my son. For Harold to be proud. Proud of who he is."

Nick winced. "Hard to be a proud Lakota half-breed, that's for sure."

Her voice became a raspy whisper. "I like you. Honest. I just can't deal with the white man's God." Her breath ragged. "That's all."

"That's all?" Nick's chest rose and fell as seconds ticked away. "Let me tell you something. God cares about you. I care about you. I care about your boy." He yanked his jacket off the nail. "All I've ever tried to do is help the both of you." Nick jerked open the door, took a step, turned. "Sorry if that's too difficult." The door slammed behind him.

Frankie put her hand over her mouth, held it there.

———— ∞ ————

Nick drove too fast. Didn't care he squealed the tires and sprayed gravel when he turned into the apartment's lot. He thrust the gears into park, cut the engine. He slammed the cab door, marched into the apartment, threw off his hat, and plunked down on the sofa.

Curses rang through his head, curses no one would hear, along with the word *fool*. Fool. It's what he was, all he was. He raked a hand through his hair and eyed the wall phone. He'd given Frankie his number should something come up. Fool.

Women were his downfall, all right. And Frankie Chasing Bear was just another example of the female species' skill in ripping out a heart, stomping it in two. She tried to keep Harold on the straight and narrow, and yes, so far the kid had a good spirit. But he liked to wander, that much was plain. Like his dad and his grandad. Nick shook his head, but the Parker family ghosts blazed in his mind—ghosts he'd hidden from Frankie.

The wandering spirit was familiar to Nick, too—when he was a youngster, his own father had sometimes disappeared for months. Worry and not a little guilt had filled Nick's boyhood—what had Nick done to drive Papa away? Nick spent many a sleepless night watching for his dad's safe return.

But when his old man did come home, it was often only long enough to get drunk and keep Nick's mom having more babies. He'd sworn he would never be like that. And now look at him. He didn't need to check his hands to know they had the shakes.

He went to his wheezy old refrigerator, stood peering into it, one arm holding the door open. Inside was as barren as he was. A small jar of sweet pickles, an old ketchup bottle with a crusty cap and a plastic pitcher of lemonade was all that stared back at him. What he wouldn't give for a half-case of cheap beer right about now.

Nick paced. God had saved him from relapsing before. But this time. This time, it all just seemed too much. Again he eyed the black phone, its dial watching him like so many eyes. If he heard that Harold came home, fine. If not, well goodbye, and maybe he'd see her around. He felt like throwing something.

The craving swelled until it occupied him completely. He could think of nothing else. His head was ready to burst.

He tried to pray, but thirst mocked him. He remembered one night when his old man, a full Lakota, had dragged him out of bed in the wee hours, made him sit at the kitchen table while he drank beer and talked a blue streak. At the time, Nick hadn't known God—had his boyish pleas bounced off the ceiling while he'd sat there, half-dozing?

Now Nick sat and let his head fall into his hands. Please, please. Tonight, his prayers seemed to go nowhere, too. He balled his fists and called upon his will to shore him up. Maybe it was no longer possible.

He remembered his father's breath had been full of fire and his belly full of whiskey. The house in South Dakota was bone cold, especially at night. Nick's teeth had chattered uncontrollably.

When his eyes had closed, his father pounded the table with his fist. Papa smelled like booze and when his mother got up to see what the ruckus was, Nick had slipped back to bed. They'd argued. The very next week, Nick had been shipped off to Pine Ridge for the summer.

The wall phone rang. Nick jerked his head up. Had he dozed? He was still wearing his hat and held the truck's keys. The beast in him had subsided for the moment, but he was irritated as he barked a hello into the receiver.

Abe, calling from a pay phone outside Holbrook, asked if he was OK.

"Why wouldn't I be?" Nick tried to cull the gruffness from his voice.

Abe paused. "No reason. You sound a little bit upset."

"I'm fine."

Abe didn't push. "Called to say after you left a Navajo told us he saw the Blackfoot guys leave."

"Yeah?" Nick commanded his hands to be still.

"They were headed for the highway. Maybe we should call the highway patrol?"

"She doesn't want the cops involved. Has this cockamamie idea the boy is going to come back home." Nick pinched the bridge of his nose. "I don't know what else to do."

"Pray, brother." Abe exhaled into the receiver. "We can always pray."

Nick closed his eyes. "That's the problem, Abe." His heart was weighted with the sharp stones of lost hope. "That's the problem."

23

Frankie couldn't watch as Nick's truck peeled out and then roared down the road. She didn't need to see him leave to know she was a fool. Nick was the most considerate and responsible man she'd ever met. Now she'd insulted his identity and his manhood. And for what? She stared into the darkness. The remaining candles burned low, puddles of wax building in the saucers.

She squinted at an object on the floor. Nick's quilt—probably knocked off the sofa as he'd stormed out. She bent and picked up the folded fabric, brushed off dust. Frankie set the repaired quilt back into its box. She should've made him take it. Not much sense in crying over spilt bear grease, though. She'd let Nick Parker go. It was for the best.

The candles sputtered and died. She sat in the dark for a bit, just sat and listened for the sounds of Harold coming in through that creaky gate, for his barely audible footfalls. The edges of her mouth curved. A warrior who stepped silently through life would catch the world by surprise. She had high hopes for the boy.

Right now, if she was honest, she'd admit the stars in the heavens glowed far brighter than her hopes. She could almost hear Grandmother, saying she needed to trust the smoke and pray. With every thought of prayer, her heartbeat leapt out of rhythm and reminded her of Nick Parker. Frankie still wasn't sure about any of it.

She whispered. "C'mon, son. Come home." She felt around in the shadows for Harold's unfinished Lakota Star quilt, clutched the sewn-together coverlet to her chest. She pressed the cotton fabric to her face, and sobbed.

⸻

The next morning, Nick drained his third cup of strong coffee. Today, he'd make a point of being thankful—the more often he remembered gratitude, the easier sobriety seemed to be to maintain. The last two days had tested him by way of Frankie.

Nothing was easy about the woman, though. He fought the urge to go check on her. He hated the fact she had to sit there and worry about her son. She had no phone, no electricity, and no transportation.

Monny, Abe, and the Navajo cousins weren't likely to roll back into town until later in the day. As far as he knew, Frankie had no other friends to lean on, either. No wonder—she was such a spitfire. Or maybe it's what he loved about her. Didn't matter. He couldn't stop thinking about her or her son.

She was trouble. He knew it. But there was something about her that kept him intrigued. Maybe he'd drive by after work, just make sure she was OK. Put a little more pressure on her to get the law involved in Harold's disappearance.

He dragged a razor across his beard, splashed cold water on his cheeks, and dried his face and hands. He pulled on his

191

pants and threaded his belt through their loops. The bare bulb
hanging over the bathroom sink glinted off the agate buckle.

He started to fasten the buckle, stopped.

Was Frankie right? Did he toggle between Lakota and white
as it suited him? His father had worn the belt buckle before
him. When he handed it down, he'd made Nick promise to
honor all Lakota.

Frankie had accused him of passing for white whenever it
benefited him. Nick only cared about honoring himself. Her
words had dug a deep painful trench in him, gouged out most
of the Lakota pride he'd ever had.

He whipped off the belt, loops singing an angry hum as
leather chafed against denim. He hurled the belt into the
bathroom's tiled corner, the metal buckle clanking as it hit.
If people thought he was white, maybe he just wouldn't argue
anymore.

———

He *had* to get his head on straight. Besides the problem of
Frankie's missing son, Nick had McCollum breathing down
his neck about the Window Rock transfer. The tribe's resis-
tance to the farming idea was only getting started, that much
was clear. When it came to tribal matters, Martin Brown was a
real Gila Monster. Nick grabbed his hat and his keys.

When he arrived at the BIA office, McCollum was waiting.
"Don't sit down, Parker." His boss's expression seemed more
fearful than bothered. He exhaled sharply. "We got trouble."

Nick took off his hat and swallowed a sigh. What else was
new? He followed his boss into the honcho's office and shut the
door behind them. "What's going on?" If McCollum pressed
him to leave for the Navajo reservation, Nick would stand his
ground. He'd been promised two weeks, after all.

McCollum sank into his creaking wooden desk chair. "Have a seat." He shuffled through papers and made no attempt at small talk. He looked up, apparently surprised Nick was still standing, but didn't mention it.

Nick relished the thought of convincing McCollum Navajo farming was wrong. Dead wrong. Hadn't they already proved as much back in the late 1800s? He pressed his lips together. "So they rejected the forty-acre idea up at Window Rock?" He squelched the urge to smirk. *Told you so* rang in his ears.

Instead of acquiescing, McCollum's stare burned a hole straight through Nick's forehead. "I was young once, too, you know." He leaned back, the oak chair's thick iron springs creaking. "When I started working for the BIA, I was going to change the world. Navajos lived in squalor, like most reservation Indians."

Nick knew Southwest Indian history as well as anyone. Yes, Navajos tended to overgraze their sheep. Sure, many still lived without electricity or indoor plumbing. But he bit his tongue and stared at a series of framed photos of various Indian groups.

McCollum didn't seem to notice Nick's attitude. "But instead of bettering themselves, learning how to live as productive members of society, all the Navajos could think about was outfoxing the Hopi—any way they could." He nudged at his thinning hair, where a rogue piece fell over his shiny forehead.

"What's going on?" Nick hadn't meant to sound impatient.

McCollum eyed him like a headmaster about to wield a stick. "I'm getting to it." He paused. "Like I said, I was young and idealistic, too. Thought I had all the answers." He pointed at a photo on the wall across from him. "See these Indians?"

Nick inspected the picture. A class of Indian students standing in rows gazed out at him, a sad look on every face.

"Phoenix Indian School, class of 1935." McCollum stood and walked to the photo. "I was just starting out." He barked out a sharp laugh. "Thought I'd solve all their problems."

Nick peered closer, looked from the photo to McCollum and back again. He fingered one person's image. "This you?"

A curt nod. "Good eye. Yep, I was mighty green back then."

Nick frowned. "So what's the problem?"

McCollum waved him off. "Speaking of being green." He paused. "This morning I got a call from a *Mrs*. Green. You know her?"

"She's from the Indian school, right?" Why would *she* phone McCollum?

"The girls' headmistress. Seems they've had several burglaries over the last few weeks."

Nick shifted his weight. "Yeah. Something about a missing sewing machine, along with bolts of cloth." He scratched his head. "Mrs. Green came after one of the students—Harold Chasing Bear." Instantly he regretted bringing up Harold's name.

"Mm-hmm. The kid who belongs to that Indian woman you've been following around." He said this as if the newspaper plastered Nick's affairs on the front page. "He's run off. Right?"

Nick ignored McCollum. "I was there when Mrs. Green claimed she'd caught him red-handed." He stuffed his hands into his pockets. "She dislikes both the boy and his mother—I have no idea why. Before Mrs. Green left in a huff, she accused me too." Nick narrowed his eyes. "What would I want with a sewing machine and some cloth?" He shook his head. "Makes no sense at all."

"You're right about that." McCollum massaged the back of his neck. "But the thing is, she called this morning about *another* robbery."

Nick blinked. "Another one? What now?"

"Cleaned out the school safe."

Nick whistled low.

⸺◦⸺

Bright sun forced Frankie awake. When her eyes stung from too much peering into the dark, she'd drifted off. She sat up, catching Harold's partially finished quilt before it slipped to the floor. Her heart pounded as she flew down the hall, in case this was all a dream and Harold was asleep in his bed.

Had she really expected him to be there? The bed sat empty, the blanket wrinkled, his bookmobile books stacked at the foot. She bit back a cry. No. She had to keep hoping.

Frankie stuffed Harold's quilt and remaining pieces into a grocery sack to take with her. She ran a brush through her hair, which crackled and floated up with static electricity until she twisted it into a low knot. Her chapped lips and raw cheeks stung as she washed up and dressed. She put on her brightest red blouse, in her boy's honor. She touched the doorknob, static nipping her fingers. Winter air was dry and brittle. Just like her.

Frankie pressed the sack against her and walked through a headwind that pushed her back. Dust, empty food wrappers, and dry leaves skittered along the sidewalk, and she paused only at stoplights. She held her scarf like a veil as she passed the Indian School. Frankie ran the rest of the way to the quilt shop.

Netty and Lucie looked tired and worried. Had they even slept?

Netty glanced up from her place at the quilting frame. "Any news?"

Frankie shook her head.

Netty shut her eyes briefly before resuming a running ditch stitch on a quilt.

Lucie's eyes filled with tears. "Anything we can do to help?"

Again, Frankie shook her head, adding a smile of appreciation. She set down her bag, pulled out Harold's Lakota Star quilt. "Mind if I work on this today?"

Lucie patted Frankie's shoulder. "Go right ahead, honey."

"Thanks. Gotta keep busy." Frankie sat and scooted up to the sewing machine, clicked on the light. She arranged the loose pieces of Harold's quilt, pinning together matching sections, finger-pressing wrinkled seams. Her fingers were shaky, but just touching the points of the star made her feel stronger. Not strong enough to sing, but maybe enough to hum.

Netty was chewing gum, and popped it like any teenager. "Did you call the law? In the movies they put out an APB and set up roadblocks."

Lucie added, "So they can't leave the state without the highway patrol knowing."

Netty chided her cousin. "It's not up to us you know."

Frankie wouldn't choke up. "I want Harold back as much as you do." She swallowed. "But everyone's asked me about the cops, about why I wanted to come here instead of trying to catch up with the Blackfeet." Frankie's hand ached to park itself in front of her mouth like generations of Lakota women before her, but she resisted. "Yes, it's crazy. But I have this feeling Harold will show up. Here."

Lucie stepped closer. "Whatever you need, just say the word."

Netty blew a bubble with her gum. "You're smart, Frankie." When the bubble popped, it stuck to her face. "You'll figure it out." She peeled the popped bubble from her cheeks.

"Like Aunt Grace did the time little Bart hid in an empty barrel? The boy had the whole tribe thinking he'd joined the

Hopi." Lucie stared at her needle. "Shoot! My thread's knotted up."

Frankie's neck got a crick as the two Navajos prattled on. She thought about Harold's vow to return to Pine Ridge. In her mind, a light glowed to life. Of course. Her son needed to get to Pine Ridge to become a man. A Lakota man.

Frankie's fingers trembled as she threaded extra duty quilting thread through the sewing machine, the Singer electric portable she'd used since joining the Navajo girls. She raised the presser foot, but the wheel refused to turn. The needle wouldn't move up or down, and when she forced it, the thread popped in two. Great. She checked the tension. It seemed all right.

She removed the plate and peered into the machine's dark innards. The problem jumped out at her right away— in the bobbin case, a mess of goldenrod-colored thread lay tangled in an angry scribble. She wished she was working on her old treadle Singer—just as prone to thread snarls but much simpler overall than this new-fangled electric version.

She turned to the others. "Machine's tied up tighter than heifers at a rodeo." She pointed to the bobbin case but was careful not to pin the deed on either of her coworkers. "There's a whole wad of thread wedged under here."

Netty stood and came to inspect. "Boy howdy."

Lucie hovered over Frankie's shoulder. "You're not kidding." She offered her small embroidery scissors.

"Thanks." Frankie gripped the scissors point, pried out the bobbin case. "Nobody besides us uses this machine, right?"

Netty and Lucie looked at each other. Shrugged. Netty said, "Nobody."

Frankie picked at the tangled thread, cutting at it until the bobbin was freed. "There." Frankie shook her head. "Maybe I'll oil it too."

Netty nodded her approval and went back to the quilting frame. Lucie sat back down, but warned, "Better check the base, too—make sure lint and thread aren't still gumming up the works."

"Good idea." Frankie went to the supply box and pulled out a slim can of sewing machine oil. She used a small paintbrush to coax dust and lint out of crevices, and carefully oiled the moving parts. She lifted the machine's top, exposing its undercarriage. She blew hard to dislodge any remaining dust and then stopped as she was about to set the top back down again. A shaky engraving, etched in a tall script, had been scratched in the metal: Property of Phoenix Indian School. Her breath caught.

24

So." Nick planted his palms on McCollum's desk and leaned in. "Did Mrs. Green mention any suspects?"

McCollum shrank back against his chair. "Come to think of it, she didn't."

Nick stood tall. "This time I've got an alibi. So does the boy."

McCollum's eyebrows lifted.

Nick set his jaw. "We were all up at the fair. You'd vouch for us? Wouldn't you?"

"I'd vouch for *you*. If it came to that. Beyond that, no way would I stick my neck out. Can't let the agency be dragged through the mud."

He didn't miss McCollum's hedge. "What about Harold?"

McCollum shrugged, "Far as I heard, he's disappeared. Gone off with a bunch of visiting Blackfeet."

"What does that mean? You think the boy's behind these thefts?" Heat climbed his neck, but he tried to wrangle his temper. "Well? Do you?"

McCollum held up a hand. The oak chair's springs groaned when he stood. "All I'm saying is we can't account for his whereabouts for the past two days." He came around the desk and faced Nick. "I've worked with Indians for years, Parker. Poor wretches, alcoholics most of them. I know how desperate they get."

"They?" Nick's fists balled at his sides. "Who do you think I am?" His breath pushed out quick and hard.

"Sorry, if I stepped on a nerve." A sour look. "I'm just keeping an open mind."

He couldn't hold back one more second. "Maybe I'm a half-breed, but I know one thing. Indians deserve better than this. A lot better." He started to turn, then spun back to face his supervisor. "And another thing: Harold Chasing Bear is no thief. But maybe you know who is?"

McCollum looked away, but when he stared back, his eyes had lost their light. "Let's be clear, Parker." He growled through his teeth. "You're on *my* turf here." He jabbed his forefinger. "Get yourself moved up to Window Rock and get those Navajos on board." He held the door open. "*If* you want to keep your job."

"Maybe I don't give a plug nickel about this job." Nick put on his hat and strode out, the heels of his boots echoing sharp down the long hall.

—∞—

Nick pulled into the gas station. The truck's tires rolled over the black driveway hose, setting off the bell. Moments later, Stu, wiping his hands on a rag, came out of one of the service bays. His hat, with the star on the front, was slightly askew, but as usual, his white uniform was spotless.

Nick rolled down the driver's side window, rested his arm on the ledge. "Fill 'er up?"

Stu took his time answering. His tone could've frozen over the desert spread out behind him. "You want regular or Sky, chief?" He emphasized the *chief.*

Nick eyed him. "Regular's fine."

"Hmmph." While the gas pumped, Stu checked the oil but didn't bother with Nick's windshield. Typical. But Stu surprised Nick with conversation. "So you're back from the Navajo Fair?" For once Stu didn't sound as if he were talking to a subhuman.

No sense giving him any ammo. "Right." Nick watched Stu's expression closely, in case he sprang another "Chief" joke.

But Stu seemed open, with more than a tinge of admiration. "Heard that Navajo girl, Lucie, took Modern Queen this year."

"You heard right."

Stu's cap teetered on the side of his head and a silly grin spread over his face. "I got to say, Lucie's one red-hot babe, even for an Indian. Almost as cute as your little squaw."

"Frankie's no squaw." Nick gritted his teeth—now Stu was pushing it.

The station attendant wiped off the dipstick, slammed down the truck's hood. His smirk was back. "Heard your girl-friend's kid ran off. He come up for air yet?"

Nick shook his head, nudged his hat back. So everybody in town knew about Harold.

Stu pulled the nozzle out of the truck's gas tank and hung the hose back on the pump. He screwed on the gas cap and sauntered back to Nick's open window. "What a shame—about the boy I mean. That'll be five even."

Nick handed him a bill.

"I'll get your change. I tell you—the Indian kid's on the road to ruin, he keeps it up. A juvenile delinquent."

While Stu went to the cashbox, Nick tossed that last remark around in his mind. Delinquent? Why did everyone think the kid was a criminal? Nick squinted into the west, where the late day sun had dipped low enough to glare directly into his eyes.

Every Lakota he remembered from his boyhood had all been honest, hardworking. Sure a lot of them battled with the bottle, but Indians didn't own the market on alcoholism. He'd known plenty of alkies in his day, all different. All the same.

The thirst didn't care who it destroyed. Not really. Nick's hands squeezed into fists. Just thinking about booze made him feel vulnerable, like a hungry child in a candy store. When Stu wasn't looking, Nick bowed his head and shot up a simple prayer. Help.

"Well." Stu handed Nick his money through the open cab window. "I hope they find him." Stu laughed, a kind of hollow sound. "If my Orval's ten minutes late to supper I just about call out the militia—these days you just never know what's around the corner." He seemed to be sincere, but like most snakes, it was hard to tell if Stu was harmless. "I can't begin to picture what it's like to lose your kid. I'll keep my eyes open."

"Thanks."

Stu's eyes got that dreamy look again. "And if you see Lucie—Queen Lucie I should say—tell her congrats." He winked at Nick as if he was in on a joke. "I'd like her number. If the opportunity presents itself, that is." Stu licked his lips.

"If the opportunity presents itself." Nick's stomach turned as he cranked up the window and started the truck's engine. What a nut. A sick nut. He drove back over the black hose, setting the bells off again.

Frankie stifled a gasp as she stared at the Singer's engraving. For a moment longer, she sat frozen. What if her coworkers already knew? What if they'd stolen the machine? No.

Couldn't be. Lightheaded, she inhaled slowly, eased the sewing machine back into place.

Best to act as if nothing was wrong. Frankie rethreaded the machine, guided a pair of Harold's quilt pieces into place over the feed dog. She got a straight stitch going, but this time, over her heart's pounding, she couldn't hear its song.

She sewed together the remaining quilt shapes, tacking the ends with a couple of backstitches. What about the bolts of cloth that had appeared in the shop one day? And hadn't Mrs. Green said something about a side of pork? Frankie could almost smell the bacon Netty and Lucie had cooked up, the rashers Harold had gobbled.

She glanced back to where Netty and Lucie sat chatting quietly while they quilted. Both Navajo girls had shown themselves to be loyal and kind—they'd even adopted her and Harold into their extended family. But when Mrs. Green had accused Harold, the cousins hadn't exactly rushed to his defense.

Her insides twisted at the mere thought of the school's headmistress. Frankie lifted the Singer's presser foot and clipped the thread on the final seam. There. Harold's Lakota Star quilt top was finished. Now the real quilting could begin.

Frankie glanced at the girls, still murmuring in what Frankie decided must be Navajo. She fought off anger, but another wave rolled in behind it. When Mrs. Green came down on Netty, Frankie had risked her neck. How could she just sit by while an innocent boy like Harold got suspended from the school? Frankie stood abruptly, sending her chair clattering to the floor.

Netty and Lucie started and exchanged puzzled looks. Still holding her needle and thread, Netty stood, ambled over to where Frankie stood as if in shock. Netty lightly touched her arm. "You all right?"

Frankie did her best to corral her roiling emotions. "Yes. No." She pressed her fingertips to her temples. "I mean it's just a headache."

Netty tsked. "You'd feel a lot better if you'd get the highway patrol on it." The bridge of her nose was beaded with sweat. "They'd set up roadblocks, search all the Indians who come by."

Frankie narrowed her eyes. "Really?"

Lucie broke in. "Netty. For all we know, Harold could have stowed away in the car's trunk. The Blackfeet may not even know he's in there."

Frankie massaged her temples, a new wave of pain stabbing at her head. The idea of her son in a dark airless car trunk terrified her even more.

Netty made a face. "If the Blackfeet don't know he's in there, how can they bring him back?"

Lucie put her hands on her hips. "Well they'd have to open the trunk. Of course."

Frankie's trust in Grandmother's prediction was dwindling. Maybe it had been her imagination, and she'd needed to believe it.

She chewed on her lower lip—trusting the white man's law was hard. But stubbornness gave way to practicality. "OK. I give in. But where do you call?" She couldn't bring herself to say she had neither phone nor electricity.

Netty tore off a scrap of the paper they used for quilt patterns, scribbled on it. "Arizona Highway Patrol." She handed it to Frankie. "If you can't find the number, call the sheriff's office."

Frankie shuddered. "I was hoping to never talk to the sheriff again." She pocketed the paper. "But you're right—I have to do something."

Lucie snipped several loose threads from her work. "We just want your son home safe."

Netty added, "Stay strong, sister."

Frankie started to smile, but the engraved sewing machine again loomed in her mind. She swallowed the tightness in her throat. She had to ask—for Harold's sake. A deep breath. "Netty. Remember how Mrs. Green was so sure Harold was stealing stuff?"

Netty's cheeks jiggled as she nodded. "Goodness, yes. What on earth would a ten year-old want with a sewing machine?"

Lucie forced a sarcastic groan. "Right. If he could even pick the thing up."

Netty sidled around to the quilting frame, plopped into her chair and resumed her stitch-in-the-ditch technique. She shook her head as if she'd never understand someone like the Indian school headmistress. "She's about as mean as they come. Why she thought Harold took the goods never added up." Netty flashed a mischievous smile. "I tell you—sometimes I dream about pinning her down and whacking off all her hair."

Lucie held up a large pair of scissors and snipped the air. "Oh. Give me a chance and I'd have Mrs. Green looking like a shaved poodle dog."

Frankie let a hint of smile tug her mouth's corners. Netty's idea was appealing, if only to get revenge. But she had to dig deeper. "What about all the bolts of calico?"

Lucie rolled her eyes. "We came in one morning and the fabric was all neat and stacked. Sitting next to a big paper sack full of frozen meat—chops, roasts, bacon."

"But who left it here?" So far, Frankie didn't know any more than before.

Netty shrugged. "We never knew. No note, nothing." She pulled up on a stitch with thread as long as her arm.

Frankie wanted to mention to Netty her thread would snarl if she didn't keep it cut shorter. Instead, she said, "How'd they get in? You locked the door. Right?"

"Of course, the door was locked." Lucie shot Netty a wide-eyed look. "I guess we figured our landlord either let them in or delivered the stuff himself."

Frankie was almost afraid to ask. "Landlord? Who's that?"

25

Nick's heart thudded as he drove away from the gas station. What a jerk. Stu's attitude toward Indians was bad enough. The way he treated women disgusted Nick. His throat burned. He'd love to punch out the man's lights and then go get stupid drunk. No. *Help.* Today, he knew no other prayer.

Help arrived in the form of a plan. He'd run through a drive-in restaurant, pick up some burgers and head for the First Americans church. Of course. Nick whispered a raspy, "Thanks."

The route took him past the Phoenix Indian School. Inside the red brick building, Indian students were getting the Indian drummed out of them daily—literally, at times. And for what? So the kids could go home to their reservations and take up the tribal pastime of leaning against buildings, drinking their lives away?

He'd witnessed one such tragedy himself. On a Christmas visit to Pine Ridge, an old Indian called Two Legs had staggered out of a bar one freezing night. He'd leaned against a light pole, to rest some said, and in the morning, they found him dead— frozen, still leaning against the pole. Nick shuddered.

Once, he'd planned to start a vocational school for Indian children. Now he had a choice: convert Navajos from sheep-herders to farmers or join the ranks of the unemployed. Every minute a move to Window Rock sounded more impossible.

He pulled into the burger joint, ordered through the loud-speaker set on a post next to his truck. If he'd wanted to sit there and eat, a girl in a short skirt would deliver his meal. Then later, he was sure he'd end up with a bottle in his hand. The urge to relapse was that close. He could almost feel its sour breath on his neck. Nick ordered enough burgers for himself and his buddies and drove to the church. His friends would give him strength.

Honest Abe greeted him with a clap on the back, but then his expression turned serious. "Any news about the boy?"

Nick shook his head. "Nope." The pounding urge to drink died down. He set the food on Abe's desk, stepped back. He'd keep his hands hidden in his pockets until the shakes left.

Abe eyed Nick. "You OK, brother? You look a little piqued."

Nick laughed. "Me and old devil drink been going a few rounds. I like to think I won."

Abe gazed at him, nodded. "Extra prayers and a medicine pipe. That's what you need."

"Amen to that." Nick took off his hat, set it on the book-case's top shelf. "I've been laced up tighter than a hog on a stick—knowing Frankie's boy is out there someplace."

Abe sat thoughtful. "We're all worried about Harold. You're taking it pretty personal aren't you? After all, he's not your son." Why did Abe always know what made a guy squirm?

"It's partly my fault the kid's gone." Nick shifted from one foot to the other.

Monny, who sat cleaning his fingernails with his pocket-knife's blade, had tied on a red armband that read, "Navajo

208

Queen." "I told the boy not to wander off but he wouldn't listen to me." He looked up. "Just like everybody else."

Reverend Honest Abe shot a look to his pal. "Can it, Monny."

Monny shrugged.

Abe leaned toward Nick. "So tell me again. Why is the boy's disappearance *your* fault?"

Nick stared out the high windows, where a weak autumn sun filtered in. "Harold ran right past me. I could've stopped him."

Abe came out from behind the desk, laid a hand on Nick's shoulder. "You know as well as I do that you couldn't have kept Harold there. That kid's been running off since the day you met him."

Nick hung his head. "That's the point—I knew Harold liked to run off, yet I didn't try to stop him."

Abe's gaze hardened into a cold, brown stare. "You just keep telling yourself that. In no time, you'll have enough guilt and misery to push you right over the edge. And into the bottle."

Nick's eyes widened.

Abe shook his head. "I mean it, brother. You gonna let the demon win? Or are you willing to let go and let God for a change?"

Nick waved him off. "I know the AA slogans. Spare me, OK?"

Abe went back to his desk. "I call 'em as I see 'em."

"Yes, you do." With any luck, he didn't look as hopeless as he felt. He let the subject drop, but not before it burned a hole in him.

Monny held up the sack of food. "You bring these burgers for us?"

Nick jumped at a chance to get off Abe's hot seat. "Yes sir, I did." He set the burgers on Abe's desk, and Monny opened a couple of metal folding chairs.

After they'd polished off the food, Abe passed around paper cups of coffee. "At first, I got why Frankie didn't want to call the cops." The reverend shook four packets of sugar into his cup. "But it's been what? Going on three days?" Abe stirred his coffee with the wrong end of a plastic fork.

Nick nodded; drained his cup in three gulps. "Too long, you ask me." Good strong coffee quieted the beast, at least for a time. He took a deep breath, stretched his legs out in front of him. "If it were my kid, I'd be out combing the highway myself, if I had to."

Monny propped up his boots on the desk. "Didn't you say she's had some bad run-ins with the sheriff?" He shifted in his chair, one boot barely missing Abe's cup.

Abe put the cup out of reach. "A lot of Indians have had, shall we say, less than pleasant dealings with the white man's officers."

"True. But it's more than that." Nick rubbed the back of his neck. "Frankie's stubborn. She's got this crazy idea her boy's just going to show up at her house, poof, like magic."

Monny raised his eyebrows. "She oughta try praying instead of magic."

Nick shot him a look. "Like I haven't tried. She's accused me of trying to convert her. More than once." If only it were as easy as Monny made it sound.

"Too late to argue about it." Abe leaned on one elbow. "The important thing is to get Harold home safe, right?"

Nick and Monny exchanged glances. Nick said, "Sure. But what do we do?"

"For starters, contact the Blackfoot tribe." Abe pulled over his desk file, flipped through the cards.

Nick leaned closer. "And the Navajos, too—in case they drop him off at the fairgrounds."

"Got it." Abe picked up the telephone's receiver, his fingers twisting around the cord. He dialed the number on the black rotary phone.

———

Frankie didn't know why she needed to find Nick. She only knew that she did. Netty donated bus fare—the BIA was half-way across town. After finding Nick out of the office, she was tempted to give up. She'd die before she'd beg for more change to ride the bus home. She walked toward First Americans as fast as her sore shins allowed.

The September day was sunny and mild—not a cloud in sight, the sky the color of a robin's egg, only bluer. Old-timers claimed the weather never cooled off this much until mid-October. Frankie trotted, broke a sweat even though she wore her thin blue dress. With every heartbeat, Harold's name spoke to her. Why hadn't she reported him missing or at least called the police right away? What a fool.

Her canvas shoes slapped the sidewalk as she picked up her pace. She'd flat-out run past the school if she had to. Her troubles had started here, and all because she'd tried to help her and her son be something. Somebody. Education had been their ticket out. The only way to escape. Now nothing mattered beyond hugging her boy. She put her head down as she walked, her vision blurred. No one should see her tears.

Frankie bounced off something. Someone. "Excuse me," she mumbled. "Sorry."

By the time she figured out she'd run into Mrs. Green, it was too late to take back her apology.

"Hmmph. Watch where you're going." In her pencil skirt and drawn-on eyebrows, Mrs. Green's pompous stare turned Frankie's stomach as much as ever. The woman brushed off her clothes as if Frankie had soiled them. She forced a pitying look. "I heard about your boy. I'm sorry."

Frankie blinked away tears. "Sorry?" Her voice choked. "As sorry as when you chop off an Indian kid's hair?" She could feel eyes watching as students poured out of the building.

Mrs. Green scowled and jabbed her index finger. "Now see here, Frankie Chasing Bear. We're trying to help young Indians assimilate. Become productive members of society."

Frankie forced out a hard laugh. "Really? By forbidding us to speak in our own languages? Forcing us to abandon our customs?"

Mrs. Green's eyes flashed, but she suddenly regained her composure. "Shall we continue this discussion in private, like civilized people?"

Frankie stood there, arms crossed, mouth pressed tight. She wouldn't waste her breath.

Mrs. Green seemed flustered at Frankie's refusal to obey. The headmistress turned to the small knot of students and flapped her arms. "Move along now. Nothing to see."

The main doors opened again. The aged headmaster teetered as he came down the stairs of the front entrance. "What's going on out here?" He stood on the bottom step and leaned on his cane.

Mrs. Green's cheeks flushed. "Nothing I can't handle, sir." She addressed Frankie. "What is it you want from me, anyway? I can't snap my fingers and make your delinquent son appear."

"Delinquent?" Frankie stood tall, remembering Grandmother's words. *Sheep to be slaughtered.*

Mrs. Green narrowed her eyes. "Yes, delinquent." She got her finger in Frankie's face. "You and your boy are nothing but trouble. Have been from Day One. I've a good mind to make the suspension permanent."

"Go ahead, then. Kick me out. But leave Harold alone."

Mrs. Green took a step. "Fine. Frankie Chasing Bear, you are expelled from this school. Now leave the premises before I call the sheriff."

"No need." Frankie held her head high as any Lakota woman. The students had to keep their Native ways alive, needed to see an Indian making her own way. The headmaster seemed troubled as she went past the main staircase. Frankie paused, looked directly at him. "Let me know if you hear anything about Harold. Anything at all." She strode down the sidewalk, the late September sun in her eyes.

⁂

Frankie stood outside the door of the church. The place made her palms sweat. She hugged her middle, turned to walk away.

"Frankie." Nick leaned in the doorway.

"Nick." Her hand started to go in front of her mouth. No. She was a modern Lakota and she had no more use for this tradition. She held her arms at her sides.

They went inside.

Reverend Abe looked up from his desk. Monny sat on a long utility table, his cowboy boots dangling. Bright sunshine flooded in from the high windows.

Frankie clasped her hands behind her back and avoided Nick's gaze. She peered through her hair, loose and probably full of tangles. "I came." She eked out her plea as though the words were made of barbed wire. "To ask for help."

Reverend Abe nodded, squinting into the light. "I see."

Monny called out. "What kind of help?"

Frankie swallowed. "Help." She glanced at Nick. "To find my son." Her voice was barely audible.

213

Abe smiled. "We're way ahead of you. We got through to the Blackfoot tribal council—they're on the lookout. Put in a call to Window Rock, too."

Frankie added, "What about Pine Ridge?" Her body had started to tremble. "Harold always talked about getting back to Pine Ridge. To become a man."

"We thought of that. But they wouldn't get there until today and that's if their jalopy didn't break down." Nick stepped next to her, draped his arm around her shoulder.

She stiffened, and Nick backed off. "I suppose you're right." Frankie drew in a breath, steeled herself. "There's something else." Goosebumps prickled her skin. "Earlier I was sewing at the shop with the girls. The thread tangled on the machine I was using."

By now the men looked at her as if she had three heads. She sped up her explanation. "I lifted up the machine—Property of Phoenix Indian School."

Abe's eyebrows went up. "In Lucie's shop?"

Frankie nodded. "One day they came in and there it was." Monny got up and used a long hooked pole to pull the curtains shut. He stood the pole in the corner. The table creaked as he sat on it once again.

Nick crossed his arms. "And just today, Mrs. Green called my boss and reported another theft. This time they robbed the safe. The old bat's sure an Indian did it." He set his mouth into a straight line. "But this time both Harold and I have an alibi."

Abe's forehead creased. "What does a ten-year-old want with a sewing machine?"

Nick propped his boot on a folding chair and leaned his elbow on his raised knee. "Sounds like a bad joke."

Frankie pushed her hair behind her ears. "Or a bad dream. I can't believe Netty or Lucie would steal anything."

Monny hopped down from his perch on the tabletop. "Indians get blamed for a lot of things."

Too many things, Frankie wanted to add. "Netty mentioned the landlord is the only other person with a key to the shop. I ran off so fast I didn't hear who it is."

Nick shook his head. "Stu owns the shop space."

Frankie blinked. "Gas station Stu?"

Nick nodded.

Abe gazed up at the ceiling. "Lord, we need a miracle."

"Come on, Nick." She took his hand. "There's someone we need to visit."

Nick put on his hat. As Frankie dragged him out the door, she caught the faint aroma of leather and pine.

26

Nick played along until they got to his truck. "Frankie. We can't just go accuse the guy of robbing the school." A sudden wind kicked up. Pieces of trash skittered along the side of the road. The whole business seemed ridiculous, but maybe he'd best take Frankie seriously. "Why would Stu want a sewing machine?" Or anybody else, although he kept that thought to himself.

But a fiery brown sparked in Frankie's eyes. "Look. Stu's had it out for me and Harold since the first day our old rattle-trap truck overheated." She set her hands on her slender hips. "His kid beat the tar outta my boy. And he hasn't been all that friendly to you either." Her hair danced in the stiff breeze. She had a point.

Nick got into the cab and started up the engine. Frankie slid in on the passenger side. He squared his jaw. "On one condition—things get nasty, we call the cops."

"Deal." Frankie smoothed her dress over her knees. "Let's go."

Ahead on the right, the red star sign loomed. As he drove, Nick stole glances at Frankie. Was she still upset? She sat against the door, clinging to the hand rest, not saying a word.

He gripped the steering wheel. The truck bumped toward the station, Frankie saying nothing.

He was relieved when she finally spoke. "Listen." She stared out the windshield. "I'm sorry." Her voice soft, gentle. "About the other night."

Nick held back his emotions. "No sweat." For a split second, he allowed himself full eye contact. "You're under a lot of pressure." The signal changed from green to yellow.

"I didn't have to bite your head off."

Nick shrugged. "We all do stuff we don't mean." He downshifted, braked as the light turned red. "Especially under pressure."

Frankie scooted across the bench seat until her knee rested next to the gear shift. She laid a hand on his arm. "What about you? What kind of pressure are you under?"

He hadn't seen that one coming. "Me?" He listened to the truck's idle, telling him not to hide anymore. "As a matter of fact, I just got the word that I'm being transferred." He paused. "To Window Rock."

Frankie seemed disappointed. "When?" Or was it what he wanted to see?

Nick inhaled. "McCollum gave me two weeks. And the clock's ticking." He could only hope Frankie wasn't imagining him with Wanda.

But all she said was, "Oh." She fixed her gaze on the floorboards. "One more thing," she said.

The light turned green. Nick let off the clutch and got going. "What?" He couldn't ignore the sparks shooting up his arm as his knuckles grazed Frankie's knee. He felt another jolt—she didn't bother to move away from his touch.

She pointed to his waist. "Your belt buckle. The agate one. It's gone." This time Frankie searched out his gaze. "Why?"

His heart pounded with every gear shift. "Long story." Nick signaled a right turn and coasted into the gas station.

———∞———

Frankie tensed as Nick pulled up to the gas pumps. She could hardly contain the brew of feelings sloshing around inside her. As he shifted the gears, every contact with Nick's fingers made her heart miss and her skin tingle.

Yet her stomach churned too. Why did Nick cling to the white man's faith? So far, it hadn't brought Harold back. Besides, her own father used to pray to that God too, but only to save his sorry self from the punishment he deserved. She couldn't forgive Pop or Hank for the drunken messes they'd made of life. Pity, maybe. Forgiveness? It only made things worse. Frankie studied her hands, only snapping to attention as Nick drove across the hose, sounding the bell.

The instant Stu walked out of the gas station's office, Frankie added rage to the stew of emotions. She'd love to wring his puny neck. And another thing about Christians—always forgiving people who didn't deserve it.

Stu eyed the pair as he stepped up to Nick's window. He stood there saying nothing for a long moment. He pushed back his cap. "What'll it be?" Stu's voice was flat.

Nick propped his elbow in the window. "We just dropped by to have a little chat."

"I got a gas station to run here." Stu's gaze darted from the other gas pumps to Nick and back again. "And no, I haven't seen hide nor hair of your kid." Stu looked like he'd smelled a skunk.

Frankie leaned across the bench seat. "Look. I might be interested in renting a work space—I heard you might have something available." If Stu took the bait maybe he'd let something slip.

Stu crossed his arms. "Who told you that?"

"Some Navajo friends of mine said you own property around here. You're their landlord."

He backed away from the window. "Don't have nothing to let. And if I did, I wouldn't rent to a squaw like you."

"You'd best watch yourself." Nick growled.

"What was that, Chief?" Stu curled his lip, crossed his arms.

"I said, back off."

"Get off my lot." Stu stepped closer to the open window. "Now."

"Coward!" Frankie shouted. "My son got kicked out of school on account of your thieving."

"Now that's just crazy talk. Besides, who's gonna believe a . . ." He looked her up and down. "Squaw?"

Frankie was nearly in Nick's lap now. "You call me a squaw?"

Nick laid his hand over hers. "Frankie. Let me handle this."

She shot Nick a horrified look and wrenched away. "I'm not afraid of this scorpion. He only wants . . ." A sudden idea popped into her head. A sewing machine would make an impressive gift for a fledgling businesswoman. Especially a gorgeous one like Lucie.

Frankie pulled back, smiled at Stu. "I get it. You only rent to beautiful squaws. Squaws like Lucie."

Frankie could've sworn Stu turned white as chalk. "You're nothing but a . . ." He let out a string of curses, lunged at Nick's throat, throttling him.

Nick abruptly swung open the truck's door, hitting Stu square in gut. The gas station owner doubled over, then rose up with hate in his eyes.

Nick started for Stu. Frankie clambered out of the truck too, ready to help Nick. She'd climb on Stu's miserable back if she had to, and box his ears.

"Dad!" The action stopped. Stu's son Orval stood in front of them, tears streaming down his pudgy cheeks. "Stop hurting my dad!"

Nick had Stu by the collar, and he kept his hold. As much as she wanted to avenge Harold, Frankie felt bad for beating on the kid's father, no matter how awful he was.

Stu choked out, "Orval! Go on home, son."

Someone had called the sheriff, who rolled up with his lights flashing. Frankie felt like a player in a cops and robbers movie—but this was real.

<hr />

Fury Nick didn't know he had spilled out as he tightened his grip on Stu. The sheriff crouched behind his patrol car's open door and shouted orders. "I already done called for backup. Hands up, all of you!"

Nick obeyed. His lungs burned and he gasped for breath. He hadn't been in a fistfight since that bully named Moose had bested him in grade school. He glanced at Frankie, standing with her hands in the air. Images of Bonnie and Clyde flashed through his mind. But this was no laughing matter.

The sheriff was blunt. "I got a good mind to take all of you off to the hoosegow." He shook his head. "Now, let's hear it. What in the world is going on?" He motioned for them all to put their hands down, which Nick appreciated. Nothing like standing in public looking like a criminal. Stu picked up his hat and brushed it off.

Stu's son, tears still trickling down his cheeks, stepped forward. "I saw the whole thing." His voice quavered as he spoke and he pointed at Frankie. "She says my dad stole something." He narrowed his eyes. "But my dad's not a crook." Orval used his shirt's sleeve to wipe his nose.

The sheriff eyed Frankie. "Uh-huh." He took out a notepad and pen, poised to jot down notes.

"Let me tell you, sheriff." Stu jabbed his finger at her. "She's a troublemaker and she's trespassing on my property. I asked the both of these, uh, Indians, to move on, nice and friendly-like."

Frankie's eyes blazed. "Not before you'd called us names."

The sheriff held up his free hand. "Enough." He tilted his head. "What's this about stolen property?" He scribbled on the notepad.

Frankie pointed at Stu. "The Indian School claims somebody stole a sewing machine—and somehow it ended up in our quilting shop."

Stu smirked. "Proving nothing." He shook his head. "See what I mean? She's a pain in the you-know-what."

The sheriff scratched the back of his neck. "I'd say you're all pains." He turned to Nick and spoke in a low voice. "You and your girlfriend run along now, lay low a few days."

Nick was amazed. "*We* should lay low? But he threw the first punch!" Anger sizzled again, until his eye twitched.

Frankie looked as if she'd swallowed a rattlesnake whole. "What about the missing sewing machine? Stu's as mean as a wolverine—nothing you can do about that. But he's a thief, and he let my Harold get blamed for it!" She lunged in Stu's direction.

Nick held her shoulders. "Don't make things worse."

Frankie shook off his hold. "Worse? How much worse could things get?" Tears shone in her eyes and she trembled in a beautiful, yet sad way. "My son disappears, I'm kicked out of school, and they shut off my lights. This guy wants my son to take the fall for something he did to win over a beautiful *squaw*?"

"What in the world would I want with a sewing machine? Darn my own socks?" Stu's mocking laugh punched the air and he stared at Frankie. "It's none of your business who I'm interested in." His tone was calculated as he turned to the sheriff. "I'd say that this woman is jealous." He stood taller. "You know what they say about a woman scorned." He shrugged, as if he could rid himself of such lower creatures.

"I don't have time for this." The sheriff looked out of patience. "I've got real cases to investigate." He pocketed his pen and pad, started to walk away, stopped. "In fact, I just got a new report saying the school's been hit again. And this time, Frankie Chasing Bear, it's about more than a sewing machine." He thought a moment. "Thief could be anyone. For all we know, it's you." He headed back to his patrol car.

Orval blurted, "Wait!"

"What is it, son?" The sheriff took out his notepad again, tapped his pen on a page. "Make it quick, will you?"

All eyes were on Orval, whose dirty shirt had ridden up, exposing his doughy midsection. "I just wanted to say," he began, staring down at the station's asphalt, "even though I fought her son, she was still nice to me." Stu's eyes widened as Orval met his gaze. "She even invited me in for dinner."

Stu gestured, his arms in the air. "So what?" He growled, "The Indian kid deserved to get the snot pounded out of him."

Nick stood incredulous as Orval calmly shook his head. "That's the crazy part," the pudgy boy said. "I picked the fight with Harold—he didn't deserve it." Orval hesitated, then added, "And I sure didn't deserve dinner. But Harold's mom was nice to me anyway."

With her mouth agape, it was all Frankie could do not to bump her chin on the asphalt. Orval, the kid who'd bullied Harold since school started, was now standing up for them. Was this some sort of trap? Maybe Stu had coached his son to say stuff that would trick her into letting down her guard. What other reason could there be?

Neither Nick nor the sheriff seemed to understand what had just happened either. The sheriff finally snapped shut his notepad and went to his car, shaking his head. Stu yelled after him, claiming she and Nick were still trespassing, but the sheriff just kept on going.

She turned to Nick. "Take me home."

27

Frankie climbed into Nick's truck. She couldn't stop trembling, just as she couldn't stop thinking about Orval's words. *Deserving.* Wasn't this world all about getting what you deserved? She glanced up at Nick, who stared out the windshield as if he couldn't think of anything to say. She leaned against the seat back—it would be easy to become caught up in disgust for guys like Stu.

Blame was a trap, like the steel-jawed contraptions she remembered from Pine Ridge. Varmints were known to chew off their own legs trying to escape. She knew the feeling now—while the gaping wound of losing Harold oozed, anger ate away at her and refused to let go.

She jumped when the truck roared to life, the engine's growl busting through her resolve not to cry. Grandmother stood at the back of her thoughts, silently gazing at Frankie, as if to remind her she knew the right thing to do. No matter who the real thief was, she could return the sewing machine to the school.

Harold had nothing to do with it, she was sure. But if Mrs. Green wanted to think of them both as thieves, at least her hands would be clean. She drew in a breath and turned to Nick. "Could we stop by the shop first? I need to pick up some things."

Nick raised his eyebrows. "Really?"

Frankie nodded, hid her hands in her sweater's sleeves. "Stu's a bully and I don't like him. But I guess pigeonholing folks runs both ways." She smiled. "He calls me squaw and you Chief. But I'm the same way—I can't see anything but white eyes out to get us."

Nick shifted into gear. "Hadn't thought of it that way— leastways not 'til now. What's come over you?" He seemed to be treading carefully.

Frankie shrugged. "Indian, white, black, and everything in-between—we like to keep each other in the box we think they should be in." She paused, bit her lip. "But you. You don't belong in any box."

"A half-breed spends his whole life trying to find where he fits."

"So why aren't you wearing the belt buckle?"

Nick wouldn't look at her. He put on the truck's blinker and eased out onto the road.

Frankie watched Nick from the corner of her eye as they bumped toward the shop. He sat as tall as any Lakota she'd ever known. He'd been a gentleman since the moment they'd met and yet she'd served him nothing but grief. The kiss with the Navajo queen still rattled her, but maybe he'd told the truth about it, too.

The truck slowed to a stop. Nick wasn't smiling. "What are you staring at?"

Frankie ducked her chin. "Staring? Oh. Nothing."

Nick frowned. "You're not about to pick another fight with me, are you?" He shoved the gears into first. "Cuz if you are, I'll just be on my way."

Heat climbed Frankie's neck. "No." She heard the sadness in her voice. "I'm about all fought out." Tears edged into the corners of her eyes. She stared down. "I was just going to say I'm sorry. For climbing your back about being a half-breed." She pulled in a breath for courage. "You're the finest Lakota I've ever met."

"Frankie."

She raised her head. He was gazing at her with a softness she'd never seen.

"Know how your grandmother gives you wisdom?"

She nodded, unable to swallow the lump in her throat.

"Keep listening for that wisdom." Nick reached for her hand, squeezed it. "For me. For Harold."

She didn't pull away, just let his touch's warmth bubble all the way to her toes. The steady pulse in his fingers soothed Frankie's fears and for an instant, she was no longer alone. As the sun reached its place overhead, she took another breath. This was no moonlit evening—it was just past lunchtime. She dared another sideways look at the half-breed who was such a mix of Indian and modern ways.

Nick turned to face her and there was that winning smile, that coppery hair. She would've liked nothing better than to fall into his arms, never come up for air. But there was business to attend to. She reached for the door handle. "We should go in."

The bells on the shop's door announced their arrival. Frankie was surprised—not only Netty and Lucie were there, but Monny and Reverend Abe leaned against the long work table. Monny's usual buoyant expression was absent—hangdog even. He must be as worried about Harold as she was. A cheap composition book sat next to him on the table.

Lucie looked up from where she sat next to the quilting frame. "Heard any more on Harold?"

Harold. Frankie's heart squeezed even tighter. She'd already cried his name until hearing it felt like salting a gaping wound. She shook her head.

Netty sat on the stretched quilt's far side, a worried look on her face. She pulled her thread up through the quilt layers. "We're all so worried—if there's anything else we can do . . ."

Monny interrupted. "We're all praying like thunder."

Reverend Abe cut his friend a sharp glance.

Monny looked wounded. "Least I am." His expression turned somber and he fingered the theme book's edges.

Frankie smiled at Monny, shook her head. She'd never seen Monny read anything but the Bible. What a crazy world this was, where Indians worshipped the white man's God and white men stole sewing machines. "Thanks," she told him. "We need all the help we can get." She gestured to Nick. "Come over here." Frankie led him to the table where the Singer machine sat. She had to prove she wasn't imagining things. "Lift it up," she said, pointing at the machine's undercarriage. "What does it say?"

Monny leaned against the table, looking as if he'd just seen something terrible.

<hr/>

Nick followed Frankie. He'd gladly go with her to watch paint dry, but he was afraid he knew why she was so adamant on showing him this thing.

Before Nick could so much as lay a finger on the machine, Monny stood and blocked his path. Nick stopped—his Navajo friend looked as if his dog had just died. "What?" Nick turned to Frankie, who shook her head.

Monny stared at the ground.

Reverend Abe came over, and Netty and Lucie followed. Reverend Abe laid a hand on Monny's shoulder. "You OK, Gila? What's wrong?"

Monny shook his head, wouldn't look at anybody. He brought the notebook to his chest, hugged it. Seconds ticked by.

Nick took off his hat and then stepped toward Monny. "We love you, brother. We're your friends."

Monny nodded vigorously, still pressing the notebook to his chest, his gaze still cast down. When he finally looked up, tears shone in his black eyes. He swallowed. Nick got the feeling he was about to see the grace of God at work.

Monny cleared his throat. "I'm not proud of a lot of things," he began. "In fact, I became a Christian cuz I couldn't face myself anymore."

Abe nodded. "God forgives you, Monny. You know that."

"Hear me out, Reverend." He swallowed hard. "Then we'll see what kind of forgiveness we're talking about." Monny went to the sewing machine Frankie had pointed out. He yanked off the machine's dust cover.

Netty and Lucie exchanged puzzled glances. Nick tried to pay attention to Monny without taking his eyes off Frankie. Would she turn and walk out in a huff, saying she couldn't stand to hear one more religious word? But she stood with her head tilted to one side, her hair cascading over one shoulder.

Monny lifted the machine up so that the undercarriage was exposed. He invited the others to come closer. "See what this says?" He pointed.

Nick leaned in. "Property of . . ." He whistled softly. "Oh man."

Netty stood with her hand over her mouth, as Lucie's eyes widened. Frankie finished the sentence. "Property of Phoenix Indian School."

Nick scratched at his head. "What in the world?"

Monny held up the theme book. "I've got it all written down, see? I'm going to pay it all back."

Lucie looked stunned. "Pay what back? *You* left the machine here?"

Frankie suddenly paled.

Monny's voice was as gravelly and uneven as a wagon track. "I wanted to help you get the business going." He choked out the words. "After what the school did to Netty and the rest of the Indian kids, I had to do something."

Lucie's forehead creased and she shook her head. "But why would you take something that wasn't yours? You're Navajo—this is not the Blessing Way." Nick's head felt about to explode—he couldn't wrap his mind around the idea that Monny, usually pious to a fault, would resort to thievery.

Monny's face screwed into a tortured look. "Don't you see? Jesus said we should help the poor. Anyway, I'm paying it all back." He opened the theme book to a page filled with rows of numbers recorded neatly in pencil. "See?" Monny's hands shook. He squeezed his eyes shut. "Every single penny, so help me." He choked out a sob. "No matter how long it takes."

Frankie's head throbbed in time to her heart's every broken beat.

———

Frankie's legs wouldn't hold her up a moment longer. She found a chair and sat down, her heart bursting with indignation. She'd never felt betrayal like this, and it nearly took her breath away. Finally, she managed a raspy whisper. "How could you stand by and let Harold take the blame for all this?" Tears and apologies couldn't make up for the damage done. She itched to wring Monny's miserable neck.

Reverend Abe massaged his temples. "Lord, have mercy."

Nick came to her side, his fingers light on the back of her neck. She flinched—if he thought he could calm her down, he'd better think again. But he just stood there. She tried to control her shaking, but it was bigger than she was. "All right, Monny." She narrowed her eyes and spoke through clenched teeth. "Let's hear your story. It had better be good."

28

Frankie pinned her gaze on the floor as Monny spilled out his story. Rage built up behind her eyes. She and her son might never get an education, thanks to Mrs. Green and her accusations. And Monny, the Scripture-spouting Navajo, had done exactly nothing to clear them—except rob the school twice more.

Netty hugged Lucie as the cousins stood quietly, tears running down their cheeks. Reverend Honest Abe wore a disappointed look and Nick didn't seem to know what to do.

Monny repeatedly claimed to be keeping track of every penny. "I aim to pay it back—every cent." Monny searched everyone's faces, as if looking for an ally. "You've got to believe me. Growing up, I can remember a lot of cold nights, cold winters," he was saying. "My brothers and I, we'd sleep all huddled up like spoons, just to keep warm."

Frankie whipped around in the chair. "Cold winters? Ha. You ever been to South Dakota? Some real winter out there." She had her own tales to tell of cold winter nights, of lying half-frozen while the wind howled through the trailer's walls, the cheap wood-grained paneling shivering right along with her and her siblings. Monny would need to do better.

"I know I did wrong," Monny said. "But Navajo country gets a lot colder than you might think. And every time I thought about my kin up on the Rez, freezing off their hind ends, I got so mad. I had to do something." He got up, began to pace in the small shop. "The school treats Indian kids like cattle. They wouldn't miss one measly sewing machine."

Lucie wiped her eyes. "What about the pork and all the bolts of cloth?"

Monny stopped pacing. "Kind of an accident." His lower lip trembled slightly. "I didn't set out to take any more stuff." Monny leveled his gaze on Frankie. "Until one day I heard your boy say he was hungry. When I was a kid, I looked that hungry, too—your boy's way too skinny, you ask me. I only wanted him to get a decent meal or two." Monny stuffed his hands into the pockets of his jeans.

Frankie briefly closed her eyes, remembering Harold's appetite for bacon. "I appreciate the gesture, but then you let Harold get suspended for the missing stuff *you* took." She shook her head. "Doesn't wash."

"You're a hundred percent right." Monny took a step toward Frankie, held out his hands. "I got no right to call myself a Christian. Fact is, when Stu found out, I got scared."

Frankie stood. "Found out what?" Stu's pale face at the gas station came to mind.

Monny glanced up at the ceiling. "Lord, help me." He paused. "I brought the cloth and the side of pork to the shop real early one day. And who's already here?

Lucie murmured, "Stu."

Monny nodded. "You got it. He's got a thing for you, Lucie."

Lucie groaned. "I've tried to discourage him."

Monny glanced at Reverend Abe. "So Stu and me we kind of get into it, you know? I say I'm gonna tell Lucie she's got a not-so-secret admirer. Stu threatens to call the cops on me for breaking in. I tell him he best keep his mitts off you and Netty." He tossed his notebook back onto the table. "Next thing I know, Stu's squeezing me for every cent I got and then some. Hush money."

"That why you had to camp out at my place?" Nick asked.

Reverend Abe added, "I was sure surprised when we couldn't make rent."

"Sorry. Stu had me." Monny started to pace again. "I prayed like there was no tomorrow. But I didn't know what to do."

Nick stepped closer to Frankie, until she picked up his comforting scent. She craved comfort, if only to help her stop trembling. She no longer knew what was right and what was wrong. Monny wanted to help poor Indians in the name of the white man's God, so he stole stuff from the white man and gave it to the poor Indians? Her mind swirled—and what about Harold?

Nick eyed Monny. "Just today my boss said he got a call from the Indian school. Seems they got robbed again—this time for a pile of cash." Nick tilted his head. "Know anything about that?"

"Guilty. I'm guilty." Monny's voice cracked and he plunked into a chair next to the quilting frame. "Stu kept leaning on me," he said in a near-whisper. "The devil told me I'd never win over Lucie if I was just another poor Navajo." His eyes sparked. "But then old Stu hits me up again. I'm a coward, I admit it. I just handed over the dough." His expression turned wistful as he gazed at Lucie. "I'm not good enough for you, I know it now. I'll face what I've got coming to me."

Frankie couldn't shake the image of Stu's pasty face. "When did you give Stu the loot?"

Monny's eyebrows arched. "Before the sun was up—the trickster was waiting for me."

"Banks are closed on Saturday." Nick seemed to understand what she was getting at. "So maybe Stu might still have the dough on him?" He turned to her, brushing aside a wisp of her hair across her eyes. "Don't tell me you want to go back over there?" He made it sound like the worst plan on earth.

"I'm a little crazy, but not that crazy." She smiled up at him. "Maybe for once I'll let someone else take care of it." She went to the shelf, pulled Nick's now-repaired quilt and Harold's quilt from the cardboard box. With her back still turned, she hugged the quilts and closed her eyes for a moment, listening for Grandmother. What did a good Lakota do when another Indian deserved punishment?

29

Grandmother's words tumbled into Frankie's mind, clear as a summer's dawn and wrapped in love. Finally she inhaled deeply, buried her face in the quilts she held tight. The old Lakota woman's advice settled over her until it covered her like a cloak of wisdom. Wisdom that Frankie gratefully accepted.

"Nick's going to take me to the school." Frankie patted his shoulder. "Aren't you?" She went to the sewing machine and unplugged it, winding the cord, carefully brushing away the film of dust on the flywheel and tucking the foot pedal under the cover. She turned to Nick. "I'm personally going to hand this machine over to Mrs. Green. And then you can drop me off at home. Sound OK?"

"Sure thing." Nick put on his hat. His *are you nuts?* look wasn't lost on Frankie. "I just *happened* to be headed that way." Nick hefted the machine and they started toward the shop door.

Netty rushed to Frankie's side and squeezed her hand. "Frankie! You're not going home now are you?"

"Well, after we get rid of this." Frankie pointed to the Singer.

LINDA S. CLARE

"What about Harold?" Netty's forehead creased and she frowned. "Just say the word and we'll go with you—all the way to Montana." The Navajo's eyes shone with tears. "Whatever it takes, we'll do it." Lucie nodded and came to stand next to her cousin.

Frankie briefly closed her eyes before embracing both women. So this was how it felt to have family. Real family. She blinked back her own tears. "I love you both. And I'll let you know if we need to head north."

Monny scratched his head. "Don't you want us to help you find your boy?"

Frankie ran her thumb along the edge of Harold's quilt. "Thanks—all of you. I'm grateful for all the help." Frankie managed a reassuring smile and breathed in the fabric's fresh cotton scent. "But right after we return the machine, I need to get back to the house. Harold's going to make it back there." She smiled as genuinely as she could. "It's kind of crazy, but I know it."

Netty still wore a concerned look. "But how . . ."

"I just know."

Monny stepped forward. "Let me come with you."

Nick held up a hand. "C'mon, Gila. Mrs. Green's just going to have you thrown in the clink. Shouldn't you . . ."

Monny blurted, "I ruined everything for Frankie and her kid." His lips pressed into a thin, hard line. "Whatever Mrs. Green does to me couldn't be any worse than trying to live with myself. Whatever the punishment, I figure I deserve it."

Nick cut Abe a look. "Can't you talk some sense into him?"

Frankie interrupted. "No." She forced herself to face Monny, who now wouldn't look *her* in the eye. As Grandmother's wisdom threaded its way into Frankie's heart, she understood. No matter the reason behind his actions, Monny needed to be willing to face his mistake. Frankie stared at Monny. "Let him come along."

Monny spoke low and quiet. "I'll do whatever I can to make it right."

"I believe you." She tucked the quilts under one arm and extended her free hand. "And I don't know why—you really don't deserve it—but I forgive you."

Monny teared up again, but took her hand. "Thank you," was all he would say, his lower lip trembling. "Thank you."

Netty put her hands on her hips. "Will someone please get this hot sewing machine out of our shop?"

"Amen to that." Lucie wiped her eyes on a tissue.

Frankie smiled. For once, the prayer didn't bother her.

———

Nick's shoulders tensed as he drove Frankie and Monny toward the school. Even with Frankie's arm pressed against him Nick felt like he'd spent the night on a bed of cacti. Mrs. Green wasn't exactly known for tolerance.

Nick parked at the curb. Should he cut the engine or leave it running? He turned to Frankie. "You want company?"

She glanced at Monny, who shrugged. He still couldn't look Nick in the eye. Frankie let out a sigh. "Suit yourself." She elbowed Monny. "Let's get this over with."

They clambered out of the truck. Nick reached into the pickup's bed to grab the sewing machine, but Frankie clamped a hand around his wrist. "I'm not giving Mrs. Green any more ammo." She gestured at Monny with her chin. "Let him carry the thing back where he got it."

Still holding his notebook, Monny scooped up the machine. Nick led the way up the school's front steps, stopping to hold the door open for Monny and Frankie.

Frankie managed to brush against Nick as he held the door. She smiled sending jolts rocketing around him. He had to admit it—he'd never met a woman who made him feel this honest, this good. As Monny walked in behind her, Nick reminded himself they were all entering a lion's den. And as the only half-breed among them, he might be the only one to walk out again.

As they made their way through the main hallway, Indian students stopped to stare. Older children knotted themselves into clutches and buzzed with whispers. "It's Frankie," one hissed, while another announced, "She's the one who got kicked out for stealing."

"Her and her kid both got canned," the first student said. Nick shot them all a look and the groups hushed. Frankie walked with her head held high, while Monny carried the machine under one arm as if it were a football. Football. Nick pictured Harold out there with the Blackfoot boys, the happiest Nick had ever seen the boy. As they neared the girls' Home Economics Room, the sewing machine's cord trailed behind Monny.

Frankie broke the silence. "Home Ec's just past the kitchen." Nick could hear pots banging and knives chopping, and female voices. She stopped at the open kitchen door, held up her forefinger. "Listen."

Nick inclined his head. The Indian girls in the kitchen were singing as they worked. He recognized the traditional Navajo song—a beautiful tune about the Blessing Way. Nick looked back at Monny. Tears shone in the Navajo man's eyes.

Frankie began to walk again. "At least they're still singing." She tried the Home Ec room's door. "It's locked." She looked surprised.

Nick tried the door himself and then laid a hand on her arm. "Makes sense."

Monny shifted the sewing machine to his other arm. "Can't we just leave it here?" He licked his lips and glanced around. The notebook slid out of his grasp and hit the floor.

Nick bent and picked up the booklet. "Let's think this through, Gila." He peered down the dimly lit hallway. "You've asked for God's mercy and Frankie's offered her forgiveness. But Mrs. Green and the school need to know the truth, too."

"We'll have to see if she's in her office." Frankie spoke softly, the school's weak amber lights creating a halo around her. "Come on. Monny. We'll do this together."

Monny nodded, as if he might change his mind if they waited a moment longer. They made for the upstairs. Nick stepped lightly to keep his boots from echoing, but he winced with each new crack of his heels against the stairs. Maybe he'd done right to remove the agate buckle—he was nothing but a half-breed Lakota after all.

30

Frankie ignored her churning insides as they climbed the stairs to Mrs. Green's office. Their last meeting still tasted sour in her mouth. Monny's breathing reminded her of a bear's chuffing, and she momentarily wished she hadn't forgiven him quite so easily.

Lakota society might banish a thief from the tribe, but here in the white man's world, Monny might spend time in jail. Wouldn't be the first Indian they ever locked up, but maybe the first Scripture-quoting Indian. They rounded the corner just as Mrs. Green was locking her office door.

The woman's drawn-on eyebrows shot up. "I have nothing to say to you, Frankie Chasing Bear." She wore a sanctimonious look. Then she caught sight of Monny and the sewing machine tucked under his arm. "Oh." She stuck the key back in the lock and opened the office door. "I mean, come in."

They filed inside. Mrs. Green sat behind her desk and motioned to the chairs in front of it.

Frankie wasn't about to sit down and neither would her friends. Nick leaned against a wall crowded with black and

white photos of Indian students standing in rows, class pic-
tures of sad-eyed Native people from different tribes.

Frankie skimmed through the photos. Any one of those
students could be her or Harold, or Netty, her black hair axed
almost at the roots. Frankie looked up. Monny stood on those
bowed legs of his, still cradling the sewing machine.

Mrs. Green let out a long sigh, stared at Nick. "Mr. Parker.
Surely you're not directly involved—I can send a report to Mr.
McCollum."

Nick took off his hat but shook his head. "I'll stay—if it's all
the same to you."

Mrs. Greene leaned back in her chair. "Hmmph."

Monny stepped forward. "I guess you've been missing this."
He hefted the machine onto the desk. "I'm here to turn myself
in."

Mrs. Green seemed confused. "What?" She riveted her gaze
on Frankie. "What kind of scheme have you cooked up now?"

"Don't listen to him." Frankie tilted up her chin and smiled.
"It was me. I'm guilty."

Mrs. Green sank back against her chair. Her expression
transformed from disdain to something else. Pity? Frankie
wasn't sure. The headmistress spoke carefully. "I've been here
for twenty years—thought I'd seen it all. But you and that boy
of yours." Mrs. Green shook her head. "I've never seen the
likes." Her hand looked poised to pick up the phone.

Nick's warmth radiated as he stepped closer and slipped his
arm around Frankie's waist. The heat strengthened her. She'd
never be able to explain it, but Nick had somehow changed
her too.

"Mrs. Green," Frankie began, careful to strain the resent-
ment out of her voice. "I came here to get an education for
Harold and me." She swallowed. "Is schooling important to
you too?"

Mrs. Green seemed surprised. "Well, yes. I want to see Indian students become productive members of society. It's all any of us wants." She fiddled with a stack of papers on the desk.

Monny interrupted. "Can't we just get this over with?" He put his hands on the sewing machine. "I did it, ma'am. I took the sewing machine, the cloth, all of it."

Mrs. Green looked confused. "What? You're not a student here."

Monny dropped his gaze. "No. But my friend Netty is. Or used to be."

Frankie scooted out of Nick's embrace and elbowed her way in front of Monny. "My friend's trying to protect me." She glanced at Monny. "Don't listen to him. I'll return the cloth bolts too. I can't give back the pork, but . . ."

Mrs. Green narrowed her eyes. "What about the money? There was more than three hundred dollars in that safe—money used to teach your fellow students, I might add." Mrs. Green's lips pressed into a thin line. "Without it, we won't be able to . . ."

Monny cut in. "Look. I can prove I did it!" He produced the notebook and flipped through its pages. "It was wrong—I know it now. I'll repay every cent, though." He trained his gaze on Mrs. Green. "I swear it—on the Bible."

Mrs. Green stood and threw her hands up. "This is ridiculous! Why would you take from your own kind?" Her voice rasped. "I should have you all arrested."

"I deserve it." Monny's cheekbones glistened as he stepped forward. "St. Paul didn't fight being thrown into jail and neither will I." He held out his arms, wrists together.

Nick turned to Mrs. Green. "Before you go calling the sheriff, you should know that Monny's being blackmailed." The word sent chills shooting down Frankie's spine.

"It's true." Monny looked sheepish now. "He threatened me, and I just panicked. Turned over the school money to keep him quiet."

"Who?" Mrs. Green sank back into her chair. "Keep who quiet?"

Nick spoke. "You know that gas station down the road?"

The headmistress nodded blankly.

Frankie smiled. "You might want to ask the station's owner, a guy named Stu."

Nick followed Frankie back downstairs. Every time he thought he had her figured out, she lobbed another zinger. Monny insisted on staying to negotiate with Mrs. Green. Gila was stubborn, but he was no monster.

Mrs. Green had actually sympathized about Harold—even pledged to help find him. Nick treasured the look on Frankie's face when the headmistress offered to reinstate them both as students at the school. Frankie said she'd think it over. He loved that about her, the way she held her head up no matter what happened.

Nick held open the main door for Frankie. She said, "I don't get it."

"Get what?"

"Why Monny wouldn't let me take the blame—Mrs. Green already couldn't stand me or my kid."

Nick smiled. "Because you didn't do those things?" Frankie's try at self-sacrifice only made her even more beautiful in Nick's eyes.

She shrugged out of her sweater and laid it across her arm. "I'd disappear to Pine Ridge. End of story."

"Nonsense." Nick chuckled, the door of the school swinging shut behind him. "You'd never leave without Harold. Would you?"

"No." Frankie ducked her chin. "What about you? Moving to Window Rock?"

He had no answer.

They strode toward his truck, the BIA agency letters emblazoned on the cab's door. Nick couldn't steal enough glances at Frankie. He'd fallen for her, hard. What was the right answer?

She was beauty and wits and guts, all packaged in a blue dress. But if he turned down the transfer, he'd be just another unemployed fellow.

"What'll it be?" She was smiling. "Phoenix or Window Rock?"

Nick returned her smile. "What do *you* think?" Maybe a little dose of attitude would buy time.

But Frankie looked serious. "C'mon. I need to know."

He opened the passenger door and she climbed in. He slid in the driver's side. Frankie had scooted to the center of the seat. His heart sped up.

Nick leaned in close, so close that her breath puffed softly against his face. He didn't know what to do with his hands or his hat. "I don't care where I live—as long as you're there."

"But do you want to leave?" Frankie pushed his hat back. "If you do, say so."

"You want the truth?"

She nodded.

"Until Harold's home safe, none of that matters." He touched Frankie's cheek.

She pulled back. "I'm such a dull knife—Mrs. Green could've sent me to jail and thrown away the key." Her voice caught. "But I didn't think about Harold."

He'd ask her gently. "Why'd you try to take the fall for Monny?"

She glanced down at her hands. "Your God says to forgive— even when people don't deserve it. It was my way of forgiving."

Nick leaned against the truck's window. "God forgives us when we don't deserve it, sure. But in real life, we have to pay the price." He softened his gaze. "If you were locked up, how would you take care of Harold?"

A tear snaked down her cheek. "Like I said, I'm a dull knife."

Nick wiped away the tear. "Dull, you are *not*, Frankie Chasing Bear." His fingers slid idly down her bare arm. The smooth coolness of her skin set off fireworks he'd kept suppressed for what seemed like forever. "You're cold." He sloughed off his jean jacket and hung it around her shoulders. When she leaned into him, he nuzzled the curve of her neck. Her hair smelled like flowers.

The world shrank to a distant hum. God was quiet, and even the ancient ones, Lakota whose spirits watched over them, were mum. Or maybe he simply didn't hear them.

Every bit of him ached for her. She was a jewel, gorgeous, powerful, and solid. He closed his eyes to savor the smooth of her skin, the delicate small of her back.

Energy surged through him. Even if she rejected him again, the urge to kiss her burned in him. He reached for her, certain she tasted sweet.

—∞∞∞—

Frankie pushed Nick away. "Harold. We've got to find him."

Nick nodded. "We will."

"We shouldn't think about anything else." She leaned in closer and closed her eyes.

"OK." He cupped her chin in his hands. "We won't."

245

LINDA S. CLARE

"Good." She looked deeper into those smoky, brown eyes.
"Well?"

"Well what?"

"Aren't you going to kiss me?"

She melted into the richest kiss she'd ever known.

Her fingers lost in Nick's hair, she pressed against him, his
scent the perfect meld of strength and character. She didn't
have to close her eyes to know Nick Parker may have been
only half Lakota, but he was all man.

When they finally looked at each other again, the truck's
windows had started to fog.

Frankie smoothed her hair and straightened her dress.
She grabbed the rearview mirror, and peered at her face to be
sure she wasn't too disheveled. His denim coat slipped off her
shoulders. He quickly draped it around her and she laid her
hands over his, to savor his touch one more moment. His eyes
twinkled and he chuckled.

"What's so funny?"

"Nothing." His lips belied his words. "Coat's a little big on
you, though."

"You think so? Well, I like it." She wrapped the denim
jacket tighter around her middle and held one sleeve to her
nose. "Smells good. Like you." Maybe she'd just take it home,
never give it back.

Home. The word swelled in her mouth. Frankie couldn't
stop the flood of worry rushing back. Could she really have
lost her son? "Home," she whispered, folding her hands in her
lap. "I need to get home."

Nick started the engine.

Even as she sat nestled next to Nick, Frankie's heart ached and pounded and hoped, all at once. When they neared the gas station, she couldn't look. Stu was probably standing at the roadside shaking his fist in her direction.

Nick whistled low. "Well I'll be a wooly woodpecker. Look."

Frankie opened one eye. "Mrs. Green?"

Nick shook his head and slowed the truck. "The one and only. And she looks none too happy."

Frankie gawked. Next to the gas pumps, Mrs. Green stood shouting, waving her arms at Stu. Poor Stu backed away as she spoke, but it was clear he'd met his match.

"Should I stop?" Nick downshifted.

Frankie considered what Grandmother would have her do. "No. Keep going." She removed Nick's jacket from around her shoulders and pulled on her sweater.

31

Nick did as Frankie asked, just rolled right on by the gas station. Maybe they'd read about it in tomorrow's paper. At any rate, he had a feeling Mrs. Green wasn't the ogre everyone had made her out to be—although the headmistress wouldn't win the Miss Popularity contest. Not by a long shot.

Nick still shook his head at the whole shebang. He hadn't seen Frankie's actions coming. If Monny was a Robin Hood of sorts, Frankie was a mystery. A mystery he'd fallen in love with.

He pulled up behind Frankie's old Chevy truck. Weeds had sprung up around the chassis, and the left front tire was flat. Even with the checked yellow curtains in the windows, the place looked forlorn, sitting abandoned in the middle of a brown lawn, the remains of their camp fire ring a black eye. He cut the engine. "House looks like it missed you."

He didn't want to let on he doubted Frankie. But her insistence Harold would show up here? Far-fetched. She believed it, but it was one of the craziest ideas he'd heard. He rested his wrists on the steering wheel and turned to Frankie. "What now?"

"Come on in." She picked up the quilts she'd brought from Netty's shop and let herself out of the truck. She leaned in the open door. "Aren't you coming?"

Nick shook his head and got out, putting on his hat as he shut the cab door behind him. Frankie unhooked the rickety gate, went to the house's front door, and let herself in. "Place smells stale, don't you think?"

Nick ducked inside. "Smells like you." He smiled. "Perfect." He removed his hat and jacket, hung them on the nail.

"It'll smell more perfect once we smudge some sage." She felt around in a drawer and pulled out a bundle of sage twigs tied together. "Got a match?" She looked around the room. "Can't see a thing."

Nick felt his pockets. "Sorry." He went to the lamp and flipped the switch. The room lit up.

Frankie looked stunned. "They cut off the lights. And I haven't paid the bill." She raced around, turning on every light. "Do you know anything about this?"

Nick held up his hands. "I'm innocent."

She crossed her arms. "Netty and Lucie."

He went to the window, kept an eye out for Harold. Just in case.

Frankie found a match and lit the sage bundle. She waved it throughout the house, singing in the Lakota tongue.

The thick smoke and the tune transported Nick back to those boyhood summers in Pine Ridge. Cousin Aggie had fed him hush puppies and great helpings of love. He'd shot his first arrow, danced his first Lakota dance at Pine Ridge.

At night, they'd all listened to stories told by elders. He learned Lakota ways. At least until summer was over and he'd been shipped back to his own family, where fighting and drinking seemed the only things to learn.

"Nick?"

He licked his lips—the craziest things brought on the cravings for a drink. He squinted through the sage smoke. She held something out to him, an offering laid across her forearms. He raised his eyebrows but didn't reach for it.

"Your Lakota Star quilt." She gestured for him to take it. "I repaired it best I could."

He opened his mouth to thank her. No sound emerged. He searched out her gaze and let his eyes do the talking. The cravings vanished. When he could make his arms work, he lifted the quilt from her and held it against his chest. He uttered a feeble, "Thank you." Her face softened into a blur.

Frankie brushed the tear from his cheek. "It's not perfect. But it's better than it was."

She was still talking about the quilt. He pulled her close. Lakota boys needed things like star quilts and agate buckles. From now on, he'd wear his belt buckle with pride.

She held out a corner of Nick's quilt. "Grandmother taught me the bright yellow Lakota star stands for the circles of eagle feathers, the rays of the sun."

He laid his fingers over hers. "Frankie." He wanted to blurt out the truth. He was her prisoner now.

Before he could coax out a word, she went on. "Grandmother was a lot like you, Nick. She stood in two worlds, too."

He tried to think of something poetic, something original. He couldn't. "Frankie."

"The star is also the star of Bethlehem." Frankie held up the quilt and ran her fingers over it. "The star the three magi followed to Christ's birthplace." She draped the covering around her shoulders.

Nick's bottom lip quivered.

Frankie frowned. "You OK?"

He nodded. He was entirely too warm, but he didn't move. If he keeled over right here, at least he'd die happy.

"Sure you're all right?" When he nodded again, she still looked puzzled. "See, I never understood how Grandmother could be Lakota *and* a Christian."

The words *Lakota* and *Christian* splashed into his mind like cold water. He found his voice. "Do you understand now?" He couldn't be pushy or self-righteous. Not with Frankie.

She stared at the floor for what felt like forever, then gazed at him, a smile in her eyes. "Don't know exactly. But if Harold gets home safe, who knows?" She tilted her head. "Now. Was there something you wanted to say?"

Frankie could've lost herself in Nick's embrace. She rested her head on his chest and let his pulse speak to her. Her own heart—her whole world, really—was expanding, exploding out in all directions. Common sense told her miracles didn't happen anymore. Still, hadn't Grandmother assured her Harold would come home? Frankie had to believe it.

Dread seized her. She started to clamp her hand over her mouth, but forced herself not to give in to the old habit.

Nick asked, "What's wrong?"

"Grandmother saw something terrible in the smoke," Frankie choked out. Why hadn't she put two and two together? Her knees went soft.

Nick helped her to the sofa. "Sit down." He put his arm around her shoulders. "Tell me."

She covered her face. "Since Harold went missing, Grandmother's told me he'll come back here."

She drew in a ragged breath. "But I forgot. How could I forget?"

"Forget what?"

"Grandmother saw something in the smoke. Something terrible." Frankie couldn't hold back tears. "Oh, no. Please. Let Harold be OK."

As she wept, Nick prayed as he embraced her. Frankie remembered Lakota infants comforted in cradle boards. Maybe Nick didn't see why she was distraught, but maybe it didn't matter. His strong arms comforted her.

Gravel crunching outside made Frankie sit up straight. Maybe she was wrong, maybe the smoke was wrong—Harold would be here any minute. She went to the window, her heart about to burst.

She sucked in a breath. Nick stood behind her, stroking her hair. "I'm sorry," he mumbled.

She spun around, too disappointed for words. Outside, Reverend Abe, Monny, Netty, and Lucie marched through the gate and up the path. Frankie swiped away her tears and opened the door. "Come on in."

Reverend Abe wiped his feet. Monny stood just inside the door, wearing a half-smile.

Nick asked, "What's happening?"

Frankie managed, "I'll get some cups—anybody up for tea?"

Abe held up a thermos. "I brought coffee."

Netty and Lucie each hugged Frankie. Everyone talked at once until Frankie said, "Wait a minute. What about Mrs. Green?"

Monny wore a contrite look. Frankie knew the feeling—she wished she could undo some things, too.

He sat for a moment, his cheekbones craggier than usual, and then eyed Frankie. "God does miracles, you know?" His voice grew thick with regret. "Every other time, Mrs. Green's mean as can be. No mercy for you and Harold." He shrugged. "So I said go ahead, call the law." He exhaled loudly. "But she didn't. Wouldn't." Monny fiddled with a loose sofa thread.

Lucie patted Monny's shoulder. "Gila got lucky."

Frankie glanced at Abe, who wore a knowing smile.

Monny laid his hand over Lucie's. "Not lucky. I got the grace of God."

Frankie wouldn't roll her eyes. Not when Harold was a huge empty place in her. She picked up her son's Lakota Star quilt.

Netty rested her elbows on the sofa back, but Lucie sat down beside Monny. "Then what happened?"

Monny could barely believe it himself. Mrs. Green was holding off pressing charges. Monny swore to replace whatever he could through payments or volunteer service. And Mrs. Green and the sheriff had gone directly to the gas station to chat with Stu.

Monny faced Lucie. "I'm a Navajo. I gotta live the Blessing Way."

Lucie smiled. "You sure?"

Monny nodded. "God gave me a second chance."

Second chance. Frankie's ears roared. She felt Nick watching, waiting for . . . what? She turned away and her hair fell forward like a shroud. No one should see her pain.

In her mind, Frankie begged Grandmother for help. The old woman stood on a hill, her arms outstretched toward heaven. The Lakota star, Grandmother reminded, was God's star, too.

Guilt and the sound of her heart breaking filled Frankie to bursting. Could the God of the Bethlehem star bring back Harold? Or was it too late? She buried her face in Harold's quilt.

Frankie felt Grandmother nearby, a cool breeze against her cheek. *Ask for help, and whenever you receive more than you deserve, give thanks.* Frankie silently offered a simple prayer.

Nick said, "Frankie? You OK?"

She opened her eyes, tasted the salt of her tears. Her friends—no, her family—stood around her, concerned. She forced a smile. "I might as well admit it." She shook her head, mentally blowing on her last embers of hope. "I thought Harold would show up here." Her voice hitched. "Guess I was wrong." She stifled a sob.

Reverend Abe stood behind her. "You did the best you could."

Netty added, "Nobody's blaming you."

Frankie stared at the ceiling. "I shouldn't have let him go off with those boys." Her voice held a sharp edge. "I'm his mom. I'm responsible. Period."

Nick seemed to know better than to contradict her. "If you're guilty, then I'm guilty. Harold ran past me that morning. I could've stopped him. But I didn't."

Frankie glanced at Nick, standing with his hands in his pockets, shoulders hunched around his ears. Tears glittered in the man's eyes. She whispered. "Harold isn't your son."

Nick took his hands out of his jeans' pocket and gestured. "But he could be." He eyed the group, then gazed at Frankie. "I mean, I'd love for Harold to be my son."

The others exchanged surprised looks.

Frankie was too stunned to speak. Outside, a vehicle's loud muffler broke the silence. She bristled and went to the window—she wasn't looking forward to another scene with Mrs. Green or the sheriff. Nick joined her and lightly kissed the top of her head. "I love you, Frankie Chasing Bear."

Frankie's voice disappeared. She mouthed she loved him, too, and peered through the yellow curtains, her shaking fingers still clutching Harold's quilt. With Nick's hand at the small of her back, she felt a peace she couldn't name.

Her mouth dropped open. Maybe she was seeing things. But no.

Monny, Lucie, Netty, and Abe all crowded around them. Netty exclaimed, "Look!"

Harold unhinged the gate and bounded up the path.

"Ma!" Harold made a beeline for Frankie, hugged her long and hard. She didn't care who saw her cry. With the Lakota Star quilt sandwiched between them, she murmured, "Thank God, thank God."

Nick joined them.

When they couldn't hug anymore, Frankie held her son at arm's length. She wanted to smother him in kisses and then wallop him good for running off. "You know you're in big trouble, don't you?"

"But I made it back, didn't I?"

"How?" Nick frowned. "You hitchhike?" He shot Frankie a look.

"Sort of." Harold peeked through his bangs. "The Blackfeet said they'd take me to Pine Ridge." He looked up. "But I changed my mind. Some old Navajo gave me a lift."

Frankie shuddered. "Hitchhiking! You could've died!"

"Ma!" Harold rolled his eyes.

She did her best to look stern. "All right, mister. You're on house arrest until you're at least twenty-one." And he'd get a haircut if she had to use pinking shears.

Harold groaned.

A general chaos ensued as everyone peppered Harold with questions. Netty, Lucie, Monny, and Abe took turns hugging and reprimanding her boy. This was family.

After a while, the four announced they had to go to the quilting shop and piled into Lucie's Rambler. It was a thin excuse, but Frankie didn't hold them back.

When there was just the three of them, Frankie led them inside, Harold already complaining about everything. His protests were music to her ears.

Nick unfolded Harold's quilt, and held it out to him. "Your mom spent a lot of time making this for you." Nick wore a stern look. "Still planning on running away to Pine Ridge?"

"No." Harold shook his head. "I wanted to be with my dad, but now I know he's not there. He'll always be with me, though." Harold tapped his chest. "In here."

"Good." Nick held out the quilt. "Think you've earned this?" Harold nodded.

"I think so too." He draped the Lakota Star quilt around the boy's shoulders.

Harold pulled the quilt closer.

Frankie ducked between Nick and Harold and linked her arms with theirs. She stood in two worlds now. The secret lay in the forgiving, she'd learned, not in the deserving. "Lakota Star, star of Bethlehem," she whispered. "Both full of love." Frankie squeezed Harold's warm hand and they stared up into heaven. Somewhere, Grandmother was smiling.

Discussion Questions

1. Frankie and her son, Harold, are stranded in a world they view as hostile. Have you ever had to relocate or otherwise enter a new situation where you initially felt threatened or left out? How did you handle it?

2. In the early 1950s, Native Americans were still being forced to "assimilate" into white society by attending schools where their cultural heritage was stripped from them. How do you think you would react if your ethnic, cultural, or religious heritage was suddenly forbidden? Has this happened to you or your loved ones or some of your ancestors? If so, what activities are/were being carried out in spite of being shunned or worse?

3. Sometimes racial or religious prejudice is generational, but other times it is learned. In what ways does Frankie start out as blind to her own prejudices as Stu the gas station owner is? What about Mrs. Green, the Indian school headmistress? Monny and his Christian zeal?

4. In American society, uncontrolled anger is a problem for many. Why do you think Harold is such an angry boy? Is righteous indignation an acceptable form of anger? Where do you draw the line between acceptable anger and out-of-control anger?

5. Grandmother's wisdom acts as a guiding force in Frankie's life. In your own life, do you have a loved one whom you count on for wisdom? Who is this person? What are some examples of how that person's wisdom has helped you in tough times?

6. Several times in the story, Frankie's son, Harold, is accused of stealing. Have you ever been accused of something you did not do or felt justified in doing something viewed as wrong? Are there circumstances in which people might be forgiven for breaking laws and/or rules? Why or why not?

7. Nick hasn't had a drink in years, but stress causes familiar cravings to resurface. What kinds of habits do you struggle to control when you are under a lot of stress? How do you

handle the situations? How difficult or easy is it for you to give your problems to God?

8. Lucie and Netty introduce Frankie to Navajo ways, and the Navajo women informally "adopt" Frankie and Harold. Have you made someone an honorary family member, or been made an honorary family member by someone else? What are some ways that exclusive behavior tends to isolate people? How does inclusive behavior unite people who otherwise wouldn't be together?

9. For much of the story, Frankie rejects a relationship with God on the basis that too many awful things have happened in her life—things that God somehow didn't prevent. She acts this rejection out on a smaller scale with Nick, believing she can't trust him not to hurt her or her son. Have you ever kept people or even God at arm's length for fear they might not live up to your expectations? Why do you think we tend to blame others or even God when things don't turn out the way we wish?

10. How does Nick finally prove himself trustworthy to Frankie? How easy or difficult is it for you to forgive when others disappoint you?

11. At what point do you think Frankie realizes God has been there for her all along? Why do you think grace and mercy are so difficult for people to embrace?

12. Monny is forgiven by Frankie but still must pay the consequences of his actions. How far do you think mercy should be applied after someone confesses? If you sincerely forgave someone like Monny, would you be able to trust that person in the future? Why or why not?

13. Frankie sews the Lakota Star quilt to keep Harold wrapped in Lakota tradition and heritage. Nick wears the agate belt buckle, and Wanda weaves a Navajo rug—all symbols that not only identify them to others but also remind them of significant traditions and heritage. What visual symbols are important to you? What does each represent, and why are they important?

Want to learn more about author
Linda S. Clare and check out other great
fiction by Abingdon Press?

Sign up for our fiction newsletter at
www.AbingdonPress.com
to read interviews with your favorite authors, find tips
for starting a reading group, and stay posted on
what's new on the horizon. It's a place to connect
with other fiction readers or post a
comment about this book.

Be sure to visit Linda online!

www.lindasclare.com

We hope you enjoyed *A Sky Without Stars* and that you will continue to read the Quilt of Love series of books from Abingdon Press. Here's an excerpt from Joyce Magnin's *Maybelle in Stitches*.

—∞∞∞—

1

October 1943
Chester, Pennsylvania

My dearest Maybelle,

Another long day has finally come to an end. We just finished dinner. Paxton is already snoring. He can sleep anywhere. I don't have to tell you how sleep eludes me here. But, supper was good, lamb stew with potatoes and carrots. I had three helpings. I can't tell you how or where, but we actually ate supper at a real house, not a foxhole. But now, I am in our tent, shivering because it is so cold and it makes me wish even more you were in my arms. I love you, darling, and miss you more than anything. I know you are worried, but don't be. I'll be home soon, I promise. I can hear artillery off in the distance, but if I listen real hard, I can hear your voice, singing the silly song you always sang. Oh, sorry, sweetheart, I have to go now. My sergeant is waiting for me. Some sort of (censored) duty. Good night, darling.

Your Ever-Loving Husband,

Holden

Maybelle slipped the V-Mail letter into her pocket and headed off down Ninth Street toward the Sun shipyard. The main reason she had taken the job was because she thought it would help take her mind off of missing Holden. And because most of the men had been sent off to war, they needed her. As it turned out, learning to be a welder repairing huge war ships did accomplish some of her goal, but it also accomplished something else. Maybelle had become a part of a small group of army wives whose husbands were fighting in Europe. A group that worked together, laughed together, ate together, and far too often cried together. Try as they might, the wives had a difficult time refraining from long talks of their husbands and the war. There was no use trying to hide their true feelings, although each and every woman was proud as punch her husband was doing his part. It seemed to be the motto on the home front. Do Your Part. Well, Maybelle certainly believed she was doing hers.

She lived only five blocks from the massive shipyard on the Delaware River in Chester—a small but bustling suburb of Philadelphia, Pennsylvania. After Holden enlisted, Maybelle moved in with her mother. Maybelle and Holden had plans to move into one of the blossoming communities a little farther west. But for now, home with Mom and Bingo, her black mutt of a dog, was the best of all places for Maybelle. Still, she missed Holden more than anything. They had gotten married only two weeks before he shipped out for Europe. His orders came early. Six whole months early and so Maybelle and her mother scrambled to get the wedding organized in time. Pastor Mendenhall was more than accommodating. As a matter of fact, Maybelle was delighted the way the entire congregation, what was left of it, pitched in.

Maybelle could hear the shipyard whistle blow all day long from the house. The yard operated twenty-four hours a day, seven days a week. The whistle announced the numerous shift changes, lunch, starting and stopping times. She felt fortunate for having the day shift.

———∞∞∞———

Ninth Street was a nice tree-lined street with large row homes, mostly stone and wood but a few clapboard singles with small yards. Although the houses might have been identical in architecture, each one had its own personality, the mark of the owner. Just like her house, many of the homes had red-and-white service banners with blue stars indicating the number of men from that house who were fighting. Many of the houses around town displayed a black banner in honor of a fallen soldier. Patriotism was something Chester was not short of.

Maybelle stopped in front of her friend's house. She was a friend who had been her matron of honor and did more than any friend should to keep Maybelle cool, calm, and collected. Maybelle and Doris had been friends since they were babies. It was the end house on her row—her parents' house. Doris's house displayed a banner with one blue star in honor of Doris's husband, Michael. Everyone called him Mickey. They inherited the house after Doris's father passed away some five years ago. Her mother succumbed to influenza years before. Doris never really knew her and was pretty much the woman of the house since she could remember.

"Hey, Maybelle," Doris called from the door. "I'll be down in a second."

"Okay." Maybelle said with a wave.

Maybelle waited. She always waited for Doris. Doris would be late for her own funeral. But Maybelle was used to it and always arrived a few minutes early. Then they would not be late for their shift, something foreman Logan T. Frawley did not tolerate.

Maybelle watched Doris pull the front door closed. She wore a straight, no-frills dress with pretty pink flowers against a yellow background. Her hair was short, like Maybelle's. A decision they both made after hiring on at the shipyard. Long hair was not the best when working around machinery and welding torches. Doris's cut made her appear cute and flirtatious, while Maybelle often had to remind people she was a girl. Even wearing a dress to work was risky. There were posters all over the yard reminding women not to wear skirts and to keep hair tied up or short. Doris always changed into overalls once she got there.

"What?" Doris said as if she read Maybelle's mind. "I like dresses."

"Suit yourself," Maybelle said. "But one of these days you're gonna get caught in a fan or something."

"Never happen," Doris said. "We better scooch. Don't want Logan breathing down our necks." She said it every morning. Maybelle had come to look forward to it.

"Right," Maybelle said. "What did you pack for lunch?"

"Leftover meatloaf."

"I got ham—again. It's one thing about this war that's annoying. Food rationing."

"Yeah, I'll say. Everything is so hard to get. Hazel was completely out of Off-Duty Red nail polish. I had to settle for this." She wiggled her fingers at Maybelle. "Dark burgundy. Yuck."

"It's not so bad."

―――

The two picked up the pace a bit as they crossed Front Street to the shipyard. It was a wide street with a lot of traffic and a traffic cop who directed folks in and out of the yard. His name was Wiley. Officer Wiley.

"Morning, ladies," he said as Doris and Maybelle crossed. "Have a good shift."

"Yeah, yeah," Maybelle said with a backwards wave. "Build those ships."

To Maybelle, the entrance to the shipyard, at least Department 59, where they worked always looked so disproportionate to the rest of the yard. A little, well, normal-sized steel door against a building large enough to house a battleship.

Doris located her card first. Maybelle had to wait for Big Murray Johns, one of the only men on the line. Murray wanted to go to war, but a heart murmur kept him home. He was not happy about it. "I woulda made a great soldier."

And standing over six and half feet tall and broad as an oak testified to that fact.

"Morning, Big Murray," Maybelle said.

Murray only grunted as usual and headed toward Slipway number seven.

"Always a cheerful guy," Maybelle said.

"Yeah," Doris said. "He is just way too happy."

They giggled and headed for the women's locker room. Inside they found the locker each shared with three other women. Maybelle pulled on her overalls and snagged her goggles from the many on hooks near the entrance to the actual dock where they worked welding seams.

It was a good job, a job Maybelle felt, in some strange way, rather suited for. She always was a tomboy, more eager to play baseball and climb trees than fuss over clothes and baby dolls. Doris, on the other hand, was practically absorbed with her concerns about how she looked and dressed. Even under her heavy, oily overalls and welder's shield, you could tell Doris was pretty, slight, and trim with a figure to pretty much turn any head.

Logan met them just before they took their station. "Boss said we have to get a step on. We're under quota," he said.

"Yeah, yeah," Maybelle said. "Get a step on."

Doris just let a *phttt* noise leave her mouth. "He says it all the time, doesn't he? I swear the boss just likes to get under our skin. And besides, what will happen if we don't make quota? Will the Jerries win?"

"Just get to work," Logan said from behind. "This is serious business."

"Ohhh, I'm scared," Doris said. "Look, just do your job and we'll do ours and we'll all get to Scotland before ye."

Maybelle gave Doris a punch on the shoulder. "Don't get him angry, Doris."

"Ahh, he's just a sourpuss. Never met anyone so grumpy. Besides, the ships always get launched, don't they?"

The shift went as usual. Maybelle and Doris usually worked from seven in the morning until three or sometimes four in the afternoon before the next shift came on. Sometimes they worked later depending on demand and on exactly what task they had been given. And lately, it seemed President Roosevelt was adding more and more ships to their already bulging demand.

Maybelle worked steadily, while every so often feeling for the letter in her pocket and dodging welding splatter—the sparks flew everywhere making the yard look like a perpetual Fourth of July celebration. Somehow, just knowing the letter was there helped pass the day and keep Holden close, almost home. Even though she would often remind herself anything could happen, and she really had no idea when Holden would be coming home. Or, as with the hundreds of other military wives in the yard, *if* he would be coming home.

"Doesn't it bother you?" Maybelle asked on the walk home. "How can you be so cool and so collected all the time?"

"Doesn't what bother me?" Doris asked.

"The war. All the death and destruction. We build ships so our guys can kill their guys. What sense does that make? I mean, if you stop to think about it. It's kind of crazy."

"Hitler has to be stopped, Maybelle. We're making it possible. So no, it doesn't bother me." Doris stopped and snagged a tiny rosebud still hanging on to one of Ruth Bradshaw's bushes.

"What about Mickey, then?" Maybelle asked. "Aren't you worried about Mickey?"

Doris stopped walking and looked in Maybelle's eyes. "Sure I miss him. I worry every single day, but I also pray every single day. God is watching over him and won't let any harm come. I figure as long as I keep getting letters, I ain't gonna worry. I just ain't." Maybelle could feel Doris's determination to stay brave.

"Yeah, yeah, I suppose that's best." Maybelle didn't know for sure. She didn't know much for certain except her feelings about the war, and the restrictions on gas and food and electricity. She desperately wanted the war to end. And as for God? Well, things of that nature had started to elude her. She went to church every Sunday, and if push came to shove, she would admit God was in control, but lately she had started to wonder.

"It's like this rosebud," Doris said as she picked up her pace. "I got no real guarantee it will bloom. But . . . but I believe it will. All I have to do is put it in some water and wait."

Maybelle chuckled. She wished she had Doris's optimism. But she didn't. She reached her hand into her pocket and felt the letter. Still there. Still close. She still worried.

They reached Doris's house. "All I can tell you is to try not to worry too much. Don't ask so many questions and, like the president keeps reminding us, do your part to help. I think it makes me feel like I'm fighting with Mickey, not just waiting for him to come home or for victory—which by the way is more sure than ever if you listen to the news reports."

"I do. I guess I'll try harder."

Doris kissed her friend's cheek. "Look, I'll see ya tomorrow."

"Hey," Maybelle said, "why don't you stop down for supper in a bit? Mom's making chicken and dumplings."

"Oh, boy, chicken and dumplings. I love your mom's chicken and dumplings. It's a deal."

"Great. Get changed and come by. About an hour."

Maybelle picked up her steps a little as she walked; the air had turned chilly as late October settled into the Delaware Valley. Maybelle thought living so close to such a huge river might be part of the reason for the cool winds in winter and the steamy zephyrs in summer. She wanted there to be a spring in her step like Doris's. Like some of the other women in the yard. They were all in the same boat, so to speak. But she couldn't shake the terrible feeling haunting her for three solid days. Every time she read Holden's letter she felt it. Every time she touched the letter, she felt it. Every time she mentioned his name, she had to hold back tears. Something was not right.

Maybelle stood a moment outside her house. She loved it. It was one of the biggest ones on the block and set off on a large lot now gone to mostly dirt and weeds. A huge oak tree grew on the side. Maybelle's father had told her it was there when William Penn first walked the streets of Chester, the oldest town in Pennsylvania. She liked knowing this. It made her feel a part of history, the way the war was making others feel, perhaps.

"Mom, I'm home," Maybelle called as she pushed open the front door. "Mom?"

Maybelle slipped off her boots as she did every day. The boots were heavy and made her feet hurt. Then she put her handbag on the couch. "Mom?"

Bingo came bounding into the living room to greet Maybelle. "Hello, puppy," Maybelle said. She kneeled and rubbed the dog's ears and head. "I missed you, too, boy."

"What is it?" her mother called from the kitchen.

"Nothing, just letting you know I'm home."

Maybelle played with Bingo another minute before heading up the stairs. "I'll be down in a minute," she called. "Just want to wash my face and change."

Blue jeans and flannel shirts were pretty much all Maybelle wore lately. She was comfortable and happy and saved her dresses for important things like church and the occasional party at the Canteen. She quickly washed the oil and smudges from her face and then joined her mother in the kitchen. The wonderful, enticing aroma of chicken simmering in the pot permeated the room. A smell like spring, with celery and roasted pepper, carrots, and peas. Truly one of Maybelle's favorite meals, especially on a chilly evening.

"How was work today?" Francine asked.

Maybelle lifted the lid of the simmering stew and let the steam encircle her. She inhaled. "Mom, you make the best chicken and dumplings. I invited Doris."

"I thought you would. I'm making plenty."

Maybelle sat at the kitchen table. "I had a good day. You know, same old stuff. Logan was a bear, though."

"Ahh, don't let him bother you. He's just sore 'cause he can't be fighting in Europe."

"I know, but he doesn't have to take it out on us. But yeah, it was a good day."

"Good, good." Francine dumped a bunch of confectioner's sugar into a bowl. A small white cloud drifted up.

"Whatcha making?" Maybelle asked.

"Frosting. I baked a chocolate cake this morning."

"Really, Ma? That sounds good. Where'd you get chocolate?"

Just then, Roger walked into the kitchen, yawning. Roger was a boarder that Maybelle and her mother had living in the house. Since things had gotten so busy at the shipyard and there were so many rooms left vacant as men and women went to war, many folks rented out their beds. Some houses had two and three people sharing one bed in different shifts leading some folks to remark there was never a cold bed in Chester.

"Hey, Roger," Maybelle said. "Graveyard again?"

Roger lifted the lid on the stew. "You make the best chicken, Francine." He replaced the lid and joined Maybelle at the table. "Yeah. Graveyard. It's killing me. Except well, I probably shouldn't be saying this, but I understand we're starting some top secret job tonight."

"Now, now," Francine said. "Loose lips sink ships."

Roger snorted air from his nose. "Yeah, yeah. I ain't sayin' nothin'."

"Hey," Maybelle said. "Doris is coming by in a bit."

A grin the size of Francine's soup pot stretched across Roger's face. "That's nice, real nice. But I ain't hangin' around tonight. I'm meeting a couple of the boys down the taproom before work."

"Ahh, you and the taproom. How can you go there before putting in a full shift?" Francine asked as she tapped a large spoon against the pot.

"I can't sleep, once you hens start yakking, so I might as well." Then he smiled and kissed Francine's cheek. "See you tomorrow."

"No, no, hold on. Sit. Let me give you a bowl of stew before you go. No dumplings yet but you can eat the best part."

"Fine and dandy," Roger said. "But Francine, we all know the dumplings are the best."

Francine ladled a heaping helping of the chicken stew with carrots and peas into a bowl and set it in front of Roger. Then she tore off a chunk of bread from a freshly baked loaf. "Here you go. Eat up."

Roger was definitely charming. Maybelle had always thought so. Even in high school he could always get the girls. He moved in with her and Francine after Pearl Harbor, once the war was in high gear. Roger intended to become a soldier, but unfortunately, a small hearing loss in his left ear kept him from duty. But he stayed on at the house becoming for all intents and purposes the man of the house.

Francine pulled two cakes from the refrigerator. "Want to frost the layers, May?" she asked.

"Ah, Ma, you know I can't bake or cook to save my life. I'll just ruin it."

"I know you are not exactly a great housewife, but give it a try. You'll learn as you go. Use this wide spatula."

Roger laughed. "Maybelle is too much a tomboy."

Maybelle stuck her tongue out at Roger. "Gimme that spatula," she said. "I'll show you."

Bingo barked twice. Francine slipped him a piece of the chicken cooling on the counter. Bingo ate pretty well, considering. Table scraps, leftovers, the occasional fried egg.

But try as she might, Maybelle just couldn't get the frosting to spread evenly, and in one swipe, she took a large chunk off the top. "I'm sorry, Ma. I told you."

Francine took the spatula from Maybelle. "Sometimes I think you do this stuff on purpose."

Francine expertly reassembled the top of the cake. "Why you can't do the easiest domestic chores is beyond me," Francine said with a chuckle. "Did I ever tell you about the time she tried to make a dress?"

"Mom." Maybelle said. "Don't."

"No, come on, Francine, tell me. I can use a laugh."

Francine continued frosting as she spoke. "I can't believe you never heard this story. Anyway, it was in high school, so just a couple of years ago. She was supposed to be making a dress. A simple, no-frills dress."

Maybelle sneaked a spoonful of frosting. She then sat at the table and cringed as her mother continued speaking.

"She was going along okay, sort of, the sleeves were crooked, her seams were not straight, but at least it sort of resembled a dress. But then came the hard part. The zipper."

"It wasn't all my fault. No one really explained it very well." Francine shook her head and spread more frosting.

"Yeah?" Roger said. "What happened?"

"She sewed it into the neck hole." Francine drew her index finger across her neck. "No foolin', my little girl zippered up her own neck hole."

Roger laughed and laughed. He smacked the table. "Hysterical! Wait till I tell the guys."

"I ain't a monkey, Ma. I'm just not suited for it. I'm better at more . . . whatcha call brainy stuff." She stood and made a hoity-toity motion with her head. "I can't help it if I got the brains in the family."

Francine elbowed Roger. "My genius daughter."

"Ha, ha, make jokes," Maybelle said. "Frost your own cake. I'm gonna go take a bath before supper."

"Can't do that," Roger said. "No hot water left. I used it all."

Maybelle heaved a sigh, "Fine. Then I'll go . . . read a letter."

"Haven't you read that letter enough?" Francine asked.

"No, it's never enough." Maybelle felt tears rush to eyes. It was hard to know if the tears were from missing Holden or from embarrassment. Probably both.

Francine set the spatula down. She pulled Maybelle close. "I'm sorry, dear. I know you miss him."

"I do, Mom. I miss him so much."

"Ahh, don't cry," Roger said. "I can't stand when girls cry. Holden is tough. He'll be home, you'll see."